SUITORS AND SABOTAGE

CINDY ANSTEY

𝒮woon READS

Swoon Reads | New York

A Swoon Reads Book

An imprint of Feiwel and Friends and Macmillan Publishing Group, LLC
175 Fifth Avenue, New York, NY 10010

Our books may be purchased in bulk for promotional, educational, or business use. Please
contact your local bookseller or the Macmillan Corporate and Premium Sales Department at
(800) 221-7945 ext. 5442 or by e-mail at MacmillanSpecialMarkets@macmillan.com.

Library of Congress Cataloging-in-Publication Data is available.

ISBN 978-1-250-14565-9 (hardcover) / ISBN 978-1-250-14566-6 (ebook)

Book design by Eileen Savage

First edition, 2018

1 3 5 7 9 10 8 6 4 2

www.swoonreads.com

For my cheering committee, aka my family

chapter 1

In which Miss Imogene Chively prays for a
sudden rainstorm or a stampede of goats

GRACEBRIDGE MANOR, FOTHERINGHAM, KENT—
EARLY JULY 1817

"Jasper!" Imogene Chively shouted as she jumped to her feet, flinging her sketch into the grass. "Don't move! Stay. Stay exactly where you are!" Grabbing her skirts ankle-height with one hand and desperately waving the other, she raced across the courtyard of the old castle. "Emily, help!" she shouted over her shoulder without a backward glance.

She couldn't look away; Imogene's eyes were glued to those of Jasper. If she looked away, he might try to leap off the crumbling wall. And he couldn't. . . . Shouldn't. It was too high. There was no doubt of an injury—a broken leg or, worse yet, a snapped neck or a blow to the head. "Stay," she said again but in a softer, crooning tone, almost a prayer.

Having reached the wall, Imogene found Jasper two feet

above her reach—even on tip-tip toes. He stared down at her, pleased with all the attention, tail wagging, tongue lolling.

"Oh, Jasper," Emily Beeswanger said behind her. "You silly dog, what have you done now?" Emily, Imogene's fast friend for all their eighteen years, was well versed in Jasper's antics.

The St. John's water dog continued to wag.

"Can you keep him from jumping, Emily? Yes, hold your hands up like a barrier. Exactly. I will go around behind him."

"You can't climb the wall, Imogene. It's too fragile. It will fall down, taking you with it."

"Yes, I know. But I need to get higher. I have to encourage him to back up—he doesn't have room to turn," she said, looking up at the narrow ledge of the ruins. Frowning, she glanced across the courtyard to where they had lain a coverlet on the grass beside the moat. "Or," she said, her eyes settling on the basket atop the blanket. "I have a better idea; I know what always encourages obedience."

"Food," Emily said knowingly.

"Indeed." Imogene turned and sauntered back across the cobblestone. She would have preferred to run, but doing so would have fueled Jasper's excitable nature and encouraged him to leap over Emily's outstretched arms to join her. She had just reached into the basket when a nearby voice startled her. Spinning around, Imogene locked eyes with a young gentleman standing on the arch of the moat bridge.

Imogene gasped in dismay. Ernest Steeple? Surely not. Her suitor was not due until the next day.

"Can I help?" he asked again when Imogene did not answer.

Gulping, Imogene tried to calm her panicked thoughts. She could feel the burn of embarrassment flaring up her cheeks as soon as she realized that the stranger was not Ernest but Benjamin Steeple, her suitor's younger brother.

Suddenly the air was filled with a cacophony of barking, whining, and yipping. Imogene turned to see Jasper's body undulating in serpentine waves as his excitement grew to a fevered pitch. He was staring at the new arrival.

"No!" Imogene shouted as the dog crouched. "Stay!"

Even as she called out, Mr. Steeple moved. In a flash, he was across the courtyard and almost to the wall when Jasper launched himself into the air. Emily jumped up to catch him, but Jasper sailed over her head with ease.

Imogene screamed as time slowed to a crawl. Jasper seemed to fall forever, but in those seconds, Mr. Steeple must have known he would not reach the dog. He flung himself under the dog's path in a spectacular sprawl, sliding across the ground on his back. The dog landed with a heavy thump on the poor gentleman's gut, eliciting a sharp gasp as they tumbled together. The tangled mess of dog and man finally came to a rest at the base of the wall.

Naturally, Jasper was the first on his feet. Bouncing with excitement, showing no injury or awareness of his peril, the dog licked Mr. Steeple's face with abandon. The poor gentleman tried to fend off the affection to no avail; he finally succumbed to the wash and laughed as he struggled to his feet.

Imogene wanted to ask if he was hurt, but her tongue would not cooperate.

"Are you all right?" Emily asked in an easy manner that Imogene wished she could emulate.

"Oh yes, indeed. Just a little dirt here and there," he said as he swiped pointlessly at the ingrained dirt on the elbows of his well-cut coat. "Nothing that can't be fixed."

"That was quite impressive. I'm certain Jasper would have done himself an injury had you not caught him."

Mr. Steeple laughed again. "I'm not certain I would call that a catch."

"It was impressive nonetheless." Emily smiled up at him as he smiled down.

It was a charming tableau: Emily, with her pretty, round face framed by cascades of brown curls peeking out from her bonnet, staring up at the handsome visage of Benjamin Steeple, with the old castle ruins behind them. The smell of flora wafted through the air while cattle lowed in the nearby fields. Yes, indeed, a lovely tableau.

Imogene huffed a sigh. This was dreadful.

Mr. Benjamin's presence had only one possible meaning—disaster was about to befall them. Mr. Ernest Steeple had arrived early. There would be no meandering through the estate, sketching and chatting with Emily about their London Season. No relaxing at the old castle, chasing butterflies or picking wildflowers today. Guests were about to descend upon Grace-bridge Manor *en masse*.

Imogene sighed again. It was a long-suffering sigh, not that of eager anticipation.

Benjamin Steeple bent to accept Jasper's continued attention.

It was the respite Imogene needed, and it gave her time to take a few deep breaths, release the tension in her shoulders, and lift her cheeks into the semblance of a smile. As the mutual enthusiasm continued for some minutes, Imogene had an opportunity to observe Mr. Benjamin without reserve.

They had met once before, at a soiree in Mayfair. Though her glance of Ernest's younger brother had been for a short duration—and she had spent the entire length of the conversation staring at his shoes—she had seen the likeness immediately.

There was no doubting that Ernest and Benjamin were brothers, and being so close in age, at twenty and nineteen, it would be difficult for anyone without the knowledge to say who was the elder.

Similar in build, the Steeple boys were tall, loose-limbed, and broad-shouldered. They both had dark brown hair, but Ernest wore his longer, brushed back from a widow's peak. Ernest's face was slightly broader; Benjamin's chin was slightly sharper. And while Ernest had an open smile, Benjamin's smile was wider, getting wider and wider—as Imogene continued to examine his face without speaking.

Oh Lud! She was *staring*.

Imogene gulped in discomfort and prayed for some sort of distraction—anything: a sudden rainstorm, a stampede of goats . . . or a fast friend coming to the rescue.

"It is a pleasure to see you again, Mr. Steeple, and a lovely surprise."

Imogene's eyes grew wide—horror of horrors, was Emily going to tell him that they had not been expected until the next day? While true, it might cause him embarrassment. Imogene cringed with the thought of mortifying poor Mr. Benjamin. What should she say? How could she prevent this travesty?

However, instead of flushing and looking uncomfortable, Benjamin Steeple executed a well-practiced bow. "Yes, we are a day early, aren't we? Ernest would not be stopped; he could think of nothing else but to see this part of the country." He did not turn to look at Imogene, but his eyes flicked in her direction and then quickly back to Emily. "I apologize for the interruption. I did not know that you were here."

"That is disappointing, Mr. Steeple. I thought it was *our* company that brought you to the ruin—that you sought us out."

"Had I known, had Ernest known, we would have been here an hour ago, but alas it was indeed the call of these old stones that sent me down the hill." He gestured toward Gracebridge, the large sandstone manor visible behind Imogene, and then turned, making a show of looking at the ruin's tower and south wing, where the sun glinted off the many panes of the mullioned windows. It was the only part of the castle still intact. The adjacent great hall and the floor that had been over it were gone; three arched doorways, and above them six glassless windows, led into the roofless shell, where all but the staircase had suffered from the ravages of time.

"And what do you think, Mr. Steeple? Does the castle live up to your expectations?" Emily turned toward the old hall. Imogene knew her interest to be a pretense. The building had lost its allure to her friend when Emily had learned that there were no ghosts or ghouls within its crumbling walls.

Mr. Benjamin took a deep breath, almost a sigh. "Indeed, yes, indeed. Wasn't really a castle, though, was it? Not any longer. More of a fortified manor. Elizabethan?" Still staring up at the tower, he turned his body, stepped forward, and almost collided with Imogene. "Oh, I do beg your pardon."

He glanced down, arms outstretched, preparing to catch her should she take a tumble. With effort and relief, Imogene retained her balance. She nodded her appreciation.

Mr. Benjamin shrugged with well-executed nonchalance, then offered Emily one arm, Imogene the other. "Shall I escort you back to your piazza?" he asked, using his head to indicate the blanket by the moat.

Emily grinned, accepting with alacrity. Imogene, however, was loath to put her arm in the crook of his elbow. . . . But it would be the height of bad manners to ignore the gentlemanly gesture. She timidly lifted her arm.

The young gentleman hooked her hand and with little fuss tucked it in place as if he took the arm of young ladies every day—which she supposed he did, being that he had been in London for the Season. Oh dear, and now he was walking. Imogene tried to match his pace, saw him look over with a friendly smile, and then, suddenly, their gait was in harmony. The awkwardness of their promenade disappeared, and Imogene sighed in relief—and then worried that he had heard it.

But if he had, Benjamin Steeple showed no sign and merely led them to the blanket by the moat. Jasper trotted happily in their wake. He assisted Emily as she gracefully reclined beside the basket.

"Yes, I believe the old Norman castle was rebuilt in the Elizabethan era." Emily returned to the question at hand, glancing toward Imogene for a sign.

Imogene nodded, and Emily smiled. "Yes, Elizabethan." It was a brilliant smile, well executed: spontaneous, friendly, and slightly sassy.

Imogene thought Emily had pulled it off with great aplomb, but when she looked to see how it was received, she noted that Mr. Benjamin was not looking in Emily's direction. He was still studying the ruin.

With a shake of his head, Mr. Benjamin turned to face them. Silence reigned for eons—perhaps a moment or two— and then Emily and Benjamin Steeple began to speak at the same time.

Laughing at their folly, Emily indicated that Mr. Benjamin should go ahead.

"I apologize again for disturbing you. I will leave you to your . . ." He glanced at the basket. "To your alfresco meal."

"Oh no, Mr. Steeple, don't go. There is no need." Emily sounded amused. "It is just a spot of tea . . . without the tea, to see us through until dinner. We have plenty to spare if you would care to join us."

Mr. Benjamin's brow folded for the merest second, and then he nodded. "Thank you. So very kind; however, before I do, I might take a wander around this fine building." He looked over his shoulder almost wistfully.

"Of course." Imogene surprised Emily by answering before her. Imogene wanted to say more, though—warn him about the decay and less-than-sturdy walls. And it would seem that Emily had forgotten about the danger, for her friend silently gestured toward the castle with a bright smile.

Taking full advantage of the offer, Benjamin Steeple swiveled and quickly crossed the old cobbled courtyard to the crumbling great hall.

"Emily," Imogene whispered, "warn him—about the hazards."

With a jerk of realization, Emily called, "Stop, Mr. Steeple, please. The floor is weak in the center and the wall rickety. Best go round the other way. Yes, there is a path that goes around the back. . . ." Emily snorted a laugh and dropped her voice. "Well, I guess he found it." Benjamin Steeple had disappeared around the corner of the south wing with a casual wave, Jasper scurrying after him. "Methinks the gentleman likes your . . . ruins."

"Not everyone can say that." Imogene grinned as they turned back to the coverlet. She sat on her side with proper decorum and then pulled the basket close. "Help me spread this out, Emily. We can make a pretty display of it. As usual, Cook has been generous."

Spreading out the savory tarts, fruit, and sweet squares, Imogene sighed at the loss of their solitude. While it was clear that Mr. Benjamin had not intended to intrude, he had done just that. Manners dictated their behavior from here; he would stay long enough to nibble on the light repast, discuss the weather or the beauty of the countryside, and then he would be off.

With another deep sigh, Imogene realized that her sense of disappointment was not for her lost sketching time, but the loss of a suitor-free day. Ernest Steeple was now waiting up at the house, and she would have to be *enchanting* and *engaging*, as dictated by her mother. How was she meant to achieve such lofty traits without . . . the proper disposition?

"It will be fine," Emily said as if understanding the source of Imogene's discomfort.

Imogene shrugged, but it didn't look as nonchalant as she had wished.

"You'll have to practice that," Emily offered.

"I'll have to practice a great many things." Imogene sighed, yet again, wishing that her feeling of dread would go away.

"Try not to think on it overly. You'll only end up tying yourself in knots. Just remember, Ernest Steeple would not be visiting if you had not made an impression. Your most awkward moments are over."

"I wish that were true. Just as I wish Father had not invited him to spend a seven-night with us. We don't really know each other—a mere three or four conversations does not indicate a lifelong attachment—Pardon?"

"I think that's the point, Imogene. Your father invited Mr. Ernest so that you could get to know each other. I wish the idea didn't make you so uncomfortable."

"I'll be tongue-tied or say all the wrong things."

"Well, then focus on art—a topic so close to your heart you'll forget to be shy."

"Yes, but that was how I survived our first four encounters. I can hardly continue in the same vein."

"Bat your bright blue eyes, then talk of the weather."

Imogene smiled and shook her head. "Yes, that will win his heart for certain."

"Do you want his heart?" Emily suddenly looked serious.

Imogene didn't answer immediately. She mulled over the effects of Ernest's proximity, and though she quite liked him, she thought that her quickening heart might not indicate attraction, but fear. But was it fear of losing Ernest's good opinion or fear of disappointing her parents?

"I don't know," Imogene said finally.

"Well, whatever you decide, your dearest mama cannot complain. Mr. Ernest Steeple is an excellent prospect. Your Season was not a failure as was mine; I did not *take* as you have so clearly done."

Imogene laughed at the absurdity. "You were the belle of many a ball and were not looking for *any* offer, but the *right* offer. Mrs. Beeswanger seems quite enamored with the idea of giving you a second Season. My mother . . . well, she wants me settled and away with no more wasted expense." She uttered the hurtful words as if they were of no consequence, but Emily knew better.

"They are so very different. Really, I don't know how our mothers have remained fast friends all these years; they rarely agree."

"Cousin Clara," Imogene said, nodding without looking up

from her paper. Clara Tabard was not only a cousin of Imogene's mother but also a great friend of Diane Beeswanger, Emily's mother. At least, she used to be. A disease of the lungs had carried Cousin Clara away the previous autumn. "She kept the peace. It will be a strange summer without her."

"Yes, indeed."

By the time the tealess tea was spread out, the strawberries moved closer to the peaches and then shifted nearer the apricot squares . . . and then back again, the tarts moved in line with the fruit . . . and then back again, Imogene began to wonder why Mr. Benjamin was taking so long to return. She looked over her shoulder. "Where do you think he has gone? The old castle is not that big."

"Do you want me to go look?" Emily appeared eager.

"Yes, absolutely. After all, he might be lost on this tiny spit of land that has only one way on or off."

Ignoring the teasing in Imogene's voice, Emily shifted as if about to rise, and then her face fell. "Oh, there he is. I missed my opportunity." Emily straightened. "We were despairing of you, Mr. Steeple. Thought you had fallen down the well."

The young gentleman stopped partway across the court-yard, the warm breeze fluttering his hair. "There's a well? I didn't see that. Where?"

"It was a jest, Mr. Steeple. The well was filled in years ago, for safety's sake."

"Oh, that is most unfortunate. I find studying the foundations, the base structure of a building of this age, fascinating. It is nothing short of amazing that the Normans had such advanced knowledge of weight-bearing and distribution principles. The Elizabethans used it to great advantage when they built on top."

Upon reaching the blanket, he joined them on one of the unoccupied corners and continued to extol the virtues of the castle's architecture. "The tower would be an excellent vantage point to see the great hall in its entirety. There appears to be a door at the top of the stairs leading into the tower. Is it still function—" He stopped midsentence, staring at the sketch Imogene had rescued from the grass. It was propped up on the basket, out of the way.

Imogene felt the flush of heat rise up her cheeks and spread across her face. She hadn't bothered to hide her drawing of the old castle; she thought it of no interest to anyone—and yet Mr. Benjamin continued to study it with deep interest.

"This is quite . . . accurate."

Imogene rolled her shoulders forward and dropped her gaze to the blanket, wishing she could disappear into the ground.

"Impressively accurate," he continued.

Suddenly it would seem that the Fates had answered Imogene's call. The earth began to rumble as if it were thinking about splitting open. However, the noise was not coming from beneath her feet; it was coming from the ruin. Startled, Imogene jerked her head to look over her shoulder. As she watched in alarm, the floor to the great hall collapsed into the cellar below in a cascade of stone and dust.

Jumping up, they backed away from the huge cloud of debris until they could go no farther. The moat was at their backs.

And then the rumbling stopped—except for the occasional skitter and plop of an errant rock dropping into the newly formed hole visible through the arched doorways.

Imogene waved the dust out of her eyes, coughing in the thick air.

"Oh dear, that is most unfortunate," Mr. Benjamin said with more tragedy in his tone than his words implied.

Even Emily looked upset.

Imogene shook her head in dismay. As the dust and dirt began to settle, it became apparent that the floor was not all that had been damaged in the collapse. The front wall of the great hall was leaning in at a worrisome angle. "We might lose the entire face as well," Imogene said in a whisper of melancholy. The castle was her favorite sketching subject. More than half of her artwork featured the castle in some capacity. . . . And now it . . . "Well, it's not gone," she said with conviction. "The tower still stands, and with bracing, I imagine we can secure the wall." She looked over to Mr. Benjamin. He seemed to know about these things. "Would you agree?"

"Most certainly. It is still a beautiful structure—worthy of praise and study."

Imogene nodded and turned back to stare at the mess. "The lower floor will have to be dug out."

"Yes, but as you can see, the stairs are still intact. Once the debris around is cleared out—Miss Chively? Is something wrong? Why—Miss Chively, stop! The wall might give way. Where are you go—?"

Imogene ran toward the ruined ruins, her heart hammering. She couldn't breathe, so acute was her fear. "Jasper!" she screamed. "Jasper! Come, Jasper!"

She listened.

And in the silence, she heard a terrible sound. A whimper. Coming from under the collapsed floor.

chapter 2

In which rubble and a peeved father confound
Miss Chively and Mr. Benjamin

"No!" Imogene shouted as she tried to race forward, tried to get closer to the hole—tried and tried . . . to no avail. Something prevented her from moving. Looking down, Imogene saw a hand on her arm, clamped and holding tight. She looked up at Mr. Benjamin, confused. "Why . . . ? Let go, Mr. Steeple. Jasper is in there. He is hurt."

Mr. Benjamin immediately released his grip, placing his hand in front of her instead. While not truly barring her way, his stance gave Imogene pause.

"I hear Jasper whining—" she said in a shaky voice. "He is hurt," she repeated, for, really, what else was there to know?

"I beg your pardon, Miss Chively, but could you wait—just for a moment? I really should check the wall first. It could come down on top of you, and then you will be of no use to Jasper whatsoever." His voice was calm and matter-of-fact.

"Yes, of course." Imogene nodded, ignoring the blur in her eyes and the trickles of moisture down her cheeks.

She watched as Mr. Benjamin strode to the central arch. Leaning across the threshold, he shifted back and forth, looking up. "I think there is little danger for now," he eventually called over his shoulder. "But we will have to be very careful not to jar it any farther. And it will have to be braced sometime in the very near future."

With a nod, Imogene stepped through the nearest doorway, stopping at the brink of the collapsed floor, listening for Jasper. Other than a few feet of stone edging the walls and central fireplace, the floor was completely gone. It was now a *tremendous* pile of rubble, filling what had once been the storeroom below the hall. Dust had painted every inch of the clumped and crumbling debris in the same hue of gray. Contours were near impossible to discern—certainly nothing dog-shaped.

Was Jasper under the rubble? Imogene caught her breath and swallowed with difficulty.

Squinting in concentration, she stepped gingerly down onto the top of the nearest collection of rocks. She listened for any change in Jasper's tone. The stones shifted under her feet, and Imogene landed on her knees. It was jarring. Rocks cut into her palms and through the thin material of her gown, but Jasper's whimper remained the same. She had not fallen on him or the rocks on top of him. And now his whine was louder, but it echoed. Cocking her head, she listened, but it was near impossible to understand the direction from which the high-pitched whine was coming.

"Imogene, are you all right?" It sounded as if Emily were standing directly behind Imogene.

"Yes, I'm fine. But I need to hear. Shhh."

"He's whining, Imogene. Jasper is whining. That is not a good sign."

"No, not really. But it means he is alive, and I can use the sound like a beacon. Silence would mean something else entirely. So please, Emily, shush. Or better yet, go get help. The gardener, the coachman. Anyone and everyone, but hurry."

Closing her eyes, Imogene swiveled her head, trying to understand the echoes. With relief, she heard Emily's retreating footsteps, running across the bridge. Another sound caught her attention—shifting rocks—and her eyes flew open.

In the center of the great hall, Mr. Benjamin had joined her on top of the rubble. He was not on his knees but squatted, tilting his head from side to side and listening as she had been doing. Above him, the wall loomed.

"That is the most dangerous place to be, Mr. Benjamin. If the wall comes down, it will rain down on you directly." She was protected by the strength of the corner that abutted the tower.

"Indeed. If I could trouble you to warn me should the wall start to wobble, I would appreciate it. . . . If it wouldn't be too much trouble." He lifted his cheeks.

Imogene nodded, and while she did not return his smile, she did appreciate his attempt to lighten the situation.

"Or perhaps I should borrow your parasol," he said as he tilted his head lower.

Imogene snorted; it was half laugh, half sob.

"I left my stone-repelling parasol at the manor," she said after a moment of intense listening. "So seldom do I need it."

Leaning back, he squinted and then scuffled to the side.

"Your bonnet, then?" he asked eventually.

Imogene bent in the opposite direction, listening.

"I don't think the style would suit you."

"I have to proceed bareheaded, then." He scuffled again to another spot—and then sudden silence bore down on them.

Imogene waited. She swallowed and waited. Looking up, she caught Mr. Benjamin's gaze, and they stared at each other, waiting for Jasper to whine again. "Jasper!" she called. But nothing. No dog sound, and the hush continued far, far too long.

Jumping to her feet, swaying and then finding her balance, Imogene grabbed a stone and tossed it up and over the lip of the hole. She turned and grabbed another. Stone after stone, Imogene frantically grabbed, tossed, and turned. It was some minutes before the utter futility of her actions penetrated her frenzy, and she stopped, dropping the rock in her hands.

Closing her eyes, Imogene felt her knees wobble. She would have fallen had arms not come around her shoulders to prevent her from dropping to the ground. Imogene laid her head on the shoulder provided. "Jasper," she whispered in profound misery. Her trickle of tears became a torrent, and she turned her face into the coat to muffle her sobs.

Standing together, locked in wretchedness, Imogene lost her

sense of time; it no longer mattered. It felt like an eon of seconds when Mr. Benjamin stiffened and grabbed a sharp breath of surprise.

Imogene lifted her head, his reaction breaking into her grief-filled mind. "What is it?" she asked, pulling away and only just realizing how entwined they had become. She tilted her head and looked up at his expression.

He was smiling. Broadly. It was almost a grin. And then a burble of laughter burst from him, and Imogene wondered about his sanity. About to inquire, Imogene was instead directed to turn around.

"Look," he said, pointing to the corner occupied by the stone spiral staircase.

Imogene squinted into the shadows and, at first glance, saw nothing worthy of happy acclaim. Then two dark spots disappeared only to reappear in the blink of an eye.

With a gasp, Imogene stared, waiting for the two dark spots to blink again. And they did. "Jasper!" she screamed. Yes, it was a most unladylike sound.

Scrambling as best she could, Imogene rushed with Mr. Benjamin across the rubble, holding each other up as they tripped across the uneven surface.

Only Jasper's head could be seen peeking out from behind the central stone newel post. He appeared to be on the widest step where the entrance to the great hall had been. But he was not moving. As she got closer, Imogene could see that Jasper was panting. Was it anxiety or pain? He was so entirely covered in gray dust that it was hard to discern that his mouth was even open. She was not at all comfortable with his lack of enthusiasm. The only time Jasper was not high-spirited was when he was asleep. As she neared, the dog began to whine, but still did not move.

"I'm coming, dearest puppy. Almost there." With eyes on Jasper, Imogene spoke to Mr. Benjamin. "If you go round the other way, we can approach him from both sides. I'll take his head to comfort him until we can understand . . . oh." Imogene blinked. "Oh, Jasper, what have you done?" She was both relieved and concerned.

"His tail," Mr. Benjamin said as they looked at each other over the dog's back. "Well, it might not be too bad. We'll know better as soon as I move the rock."

It was not done easily. The rock was not a single stone but, in fact, a group of stones still mortared together—heavy and unwieldy. Still, Mr. Benjamin did not have to lift the weight far, just off Jasper's tail. Once free, Jasper jumped to his feet, tried to wag, and then yelped in pain. The tip of his tail was kinked and matted in blood. Imogene crooned as she half lifted, half dragged him out of the stairwell and into the fresh air and light. Once there, she laid him down and gave him a thorough inspection.

"Oh dear. He has a significant cut on his shoulder and is missing a patch of fur on his side. And, of course, his tail is quite mangled."

Mr. Benjamin knelt beside them, nodding as Imogene pointed out Jasper's terrible injuries. "Yes, indeed, he *was* very lucky."

Imogene smiled. "You are right. It could have been so much worse." She laughed; it almost sounded like a giggle. She was so very relieved.

"I will carry him if that is all right with you and Jasper."

"Your coat will be ruined. He is filthy and bloody and—Oh, I'm afraid—"

"Yes, rather pointless to be concerned about my coat now. Too late for both of us, I'm sorry to say. Your lovely gown is not at its best, either."

Imogene looked down, snorting at the understatement. Not at its best? Her dress was ruined beyond repair, stained with dirt and blood, and ripped about the knees, and her lovely cerulean sash was missing. She grimaced. "Mother will not be pleased."

"Under the circumstances, I'm sure Mrs. Chively will understand the forfeiture."

Imogene shrugged—rather handily; it was a shame that Emily was not there to witness the feat. "I'm sure you are right," she said, knowing otherwise. She would not allow thoughts of Mother's anger to ruin her euphoria. Jasper would be fine. That was all that mattered.

Placing his hands carefully under the dog, Mr. Benjamin lifted Jasper easily, despite the precious creature's weight of three and a half stone. Imogene guided them back across the rubble, providing support whenever rocks shifted beneath Mr. Benjamin's feet. Once up and over the lip of the hole, walking became much easier, and Imogene trotted alongside, patting and crooning to Jasper. It seemed to be unnecessary, because

Jasper was as content as any injured dog can be, no longer panting in distress.

They had just crossed the bridge and started to climb the hill toward the manor when they heard a hail. Imogene looked up and saw Emily and Mr. Beeswanger rushing toward them.

"Thank heaven," Emily said when she was near enough to be heard without the necessity of raising her voice. She stopped in front of Mr. Benjamin, stroking Jasper gently. "Well done, Mr. Benjamin."

"Jasper deserves the praise, not me. He cleverly stayed near the stairs and out from under the worst of the rubble. His tail suffered the most damage." He pointed with his nose.

"Oh, you poor dear," Emily said, leaning to look closer. "It's rather flat."

"This is a much happier outcome than expected." Mr. Beeswanger joined the group. He was winded, likely from the act of rushing across the lawn. Emily's father was an affable, somewhat portly gentleman, prone to laughing and jolly conversation, and brought comfort with his company. Not at all like—

"Imogene! What have you done?"

Imogene's heart sank at the sound of her father's voice. She took a fortifying breath and turned to look up the winding path to Gracebridge. Walking . . . no, marching . . . toward her, Imogene's father quickly set upon them. His expression was thunderous; his countenance had a tendency to be pinched and critical at the best of times, but he had added a ruddy complexion and piercing gaze to the ensemble.

And then, to increase the uneasiness of the situation, Mr. Steeple—Mr. Ernest Steeple—stepped out from behind her father, and Imogene was suddenly very aware of her disheveled appearance. She smiled awkwardly.

"Look at you," her father continued, speaking with a raised voice, despite having joined the company. "You are in complete disarray." He turned to speak over his shoulder. "I can assure you, Mr. Steeple, that this is a highly irregular state of being. Imogene is usually the epitome of a properly brought up young lady."

Without responding, Mr. Ernest stepped past her father and approached Imogene. He hesitated, and Imogene feared that he might try to take hold of her hands while greeting her. Instead, he bowed his head, and Imogene returned his greeting with a bobbed curtsy. She tried not to chew at her bottom lip.

"So good to see you again, Miss Chively. Are you well? You seem to have had a slight mishap." The breeze played with the hair that had fallen in front of his eyes. His grin was half self-conscious, half admiring.

Imogene nodded with a ghost of a smile. "Thank you, Mr. Steeple. I am as well as can be expected after—"

"After you brought down the castle." Imogene's father gestured toward the ruin, flailing his arms about.

"The erosion was significant, Mr. Chively. Likely made worse by the frosts of last winter—"

"Winter has been over for some months, Mr. Benjamin. I hardly think we can blame the weather for this disaster."

"Perhaps the ravages of time, then."

"What?" Imogene's father turned his head to stare at Mr. Benjamin. He added a frown to his stormy expression and a slight curl to his lip.

It was a clear display of condescension, and Imogene was insulted on Mr. Benjamin's behalf. No, more than insulted, she was peeved—yes, truly peeved. Here was a helpful young man in a ruined coat carrying *her* injured dog, and her father was not only ignoring this act of gallantry but also deriding the bearer. Still, Imogene knew better than to confront her father directly.

"Father, I made mention of the growing number of cracks and sagging floor yesterday." She had been assured that there was nothing to be concerned about—a great fuss for nothing were her father's exact words.

"Yes, well you should have explained yourself more fully, Imogene. Now the whole will have to come down. It's a danger to everyone."

His words unsettled her, as they were meant to. Shaking her head in distress, Imogene stepped forward as if to put her hand on her father's arm. "No. Please, Father. It can be repaired."

Leaning back, away from his daughter, Imogene's father lifted his chin—allowing him to look down his nose at her. "I would say not. Look at that mess. A piece of history utterly destroyed. If you had stayed away, this would not have happened. All that tramping about."

Mouth agape, Imogene glanced at Mr. Ernest, who exuded sympathy and confusion at the same time. She didn't wonder at his uncertainty. Her father's angry declaration made little sense; though, to point that out would only increase his ire. And yet she had to try—the thought of losing the castle entirely was just too upsetting to stay her tongue.

"But, Father, there is no need for—" Imogene began, but she was interrupted.

"No need for such drastic measures, sir. The west wall would require only bracing. The tower is undamaged, and once the storeroom is cleared of rubble, you can secure the remains of the foundation."

Silently releasing her pent-up breath, Imogene felt her heart swell with appreciation. Mr. Benjamin had picked up the gauntlet and was crusading to save her castle.

Father's lip curled higher, and he smiled in a most unfriendly manner. "Ah, I see. Know a lot about castle ruins, do you, young man?"

"Yes, actually."

"Oh?" It was amazing how much haughtiness could be instilled in a single word.

"Ben has been studying with Rudyard Newbury in Canterbury this past year. He is a first-year apprentice," Mr. Ernest explained, pushing the hair out of his eyes. "You have heard of Lord Penton, the legendary architect, I assume?" He turned to smile and nod at Imogene. His pride in his brother's prowess was evident.

Imogene returned her gaze to that of her father. His countenance underwent a gradual change as he mulled over the comment cum query. His brow lost the multitude of folds, lifting until he looked almost even-tempered. "Indeed, I have heard of Lord Penton. Your mentor? Indeed. Looking to make your mark in the world, are you? Erect a building or two?"

"That would be the ultimate goal, sir. Though it will be many years yet."

"Why are you not there now? In Canterbury with Lord Penton? Not playing truant, are you? Won't have any of that."

"No." Ben laughed easily. "Indeed not, Mr. Chively. I can rightly understand. No, Lord Penton has graciously allowed me the summer off. Rather unheard of, but I believe that Lady Penton insisted that her husband rest after completing the last project. I will be returning to Canterbury in the autumn."

"I see. And you think the old castle worth saving."

"Absolutely, sir. In fact, just before the floor gave way, I wondered if Lord Penton might be interested in knowing of your stonework, particularly where the great hall and tower come together. A masterful design."

"Really? The stonework?"

"Oh, indeed, finest I've seen."

Imogene frowned ever so slightly. Was there a tinge of sarcasm in Mr. Benjamin's reply? No, it was just her imagination—the gentlemen were nodding at one another without any display of rancor.

"Oh, well, we must preserve that then, mustn't we." Imogene's father stepped closer, one with the group again. "Yes, yes. Preserve it, we must. Might I ask a great favor of you, young man? Might you consider overseeing these repairs? Shouldn't take too long, I would think. Just a word or two to Mr. Opine, my land agent. Suggestions and whatnot. *You* are the expert. What say you?"

"It would be my pleasure, sir." Mr. Benjamin glanced at his brother with a smile and a wink before he looked down at the bundle in his arms. "At the moment, however, I believe this fellow needs attending to."

Imogene's father dropped his eyes to Jasper; he offered a startled expression, as if only just realizing the dog's condition. "Yes, indeed. He looks worse than Imogene, and that's saying something. The stables are the best place for him."

Imogene straightened. "Yes, Father, that's where we were headed." Laying her hand on Jasper's furry head, she scratched behind the dog's ear. She glanced at Mr. Ernest; he was watching her. Should she invite him along?

"Come up to the house, Imogene. You need to make yourself decent. I was just about to show Mr. Steeple my superb collection of snuffboxes. Come, everyone, we can leave the dog in Mr. Benjamin's capable hands. I'm sure he can find the stables."

"I would rather accompany Mr. Benjamin and speak to Mr. Marshal about Jasper's care, Father. We will follow you directly." The words were out of her mouth before Imogene could consider the consequences. She turned, hiding her self-conscious swallow and wide, horrified eyes from all but Mr. Benjamin, who was standing in the wrong place.

However, when their eyes met, Imogene did not look away in mortification . . . or disgrace . . . or discomfort. She didn't feel the need. If he had noticed her disagreement with her father, he gave no sign. He turned instead to his brother.

"Yes, we will away to the stable while you run up to the manor. You shall have to admire the snuffboxes for both of us, Ernest. How many do you have in your collection, Mr. Chively?"

"Oh, well, let me see now. Over fifty, perhaps as many as sixty."

"Most impressive, sir. I'm sure Ernest will want to see each and *every* one . . . and to know their entire history as well."

"Might we not wait until Ben's return?" Mr. Ernest offered the company a guileless expression. "It would be a shame for him to miss out. I'm sure they must be wonderful works of art."

"Ah, but that is far more your interest than mine. You know my taste runs toward brick and mortar. No, no, you gentlemen go right ahead. I shall appreciate the music boxes at another time."

"Snuffboxes," Mr. Ernest corrected his brother.

"Yes, just so." Mr. Benjamin grinned. His tone was cordial—too cordial.

Imogene highly doubted the sincerity of their words; they were funning. She would have appreciated the jocularity so much more if it were not for her father's presence and the possibility that he would be insulted. However, either oblivious to or simply ignoring the undercurrents of the conversation, Imogene's father started up the hill, expecting everyone to fall in behind him . . . which they did.

Except Emily.

"Might I join you?" she asked as she matched Mr. Benjamin's gait and direction. Leaning back, Emily glanced behind his back to Imogene walking on his other side. She lifted her eyebrows in her friend's general direction—several times. Imogene felt the stirring of . . . hmm, she wasn't entirely sure what she was feeling. Disquiet came to mind, or something in that order. Despite Imogene's frown, Emily grinned and straightened.

"I've seen the snuffboxes before. . . . Many times. I could even describe them to you, if you wish," Emily chatted as they skirted the manor.

Mr. Benjamin chuckled. "Thank you, no, Miss Beeswanger. Don't use the stuff."

"The snuff?" Emily interrupted and giggled.

"Just so." Mr. Benjamin chuckled again, softly this time. "I don't use snuff, and I'm not entirely sure why one would go to such lengths to beautify what amounts to a box—a tiny one at that." Then, glancing in Imogene's direction, he added, "I mean no disrespect."

"None taken, Mr. Steeple. I do not share my father's fascination. I prefer a larger canvas." Imogene frowned and glanced over her shoulder toward the ruins. "Oh dear, my sketch is still at the castle."

"I'm sure Sawyer will ensure your art supplies are brought up when they collect the basket and foodstuffs," Emily reassured her.

"Yes, I'll mention it to him when we get to the house."

Turning back, Imogene looked up at Mr. Benjamin and was surprised to meet his gaze. It was brief but enigmatic—a puzzled frown. "My brother mentioned your interest in art. But he did not tell me that you were an artist yourself. You have an enviable talent."

Imogene lifted one corner of her mouth in a half smile. She was rather pleased. Few persons, other than family or friends, had seen her work, and her family was less than impressed. Harriet, Emily's youngest sister, while appreciative of Imogene's abilities and lessons, was an easily impressed twelve-year-old. To hear such a compliment from someone who was, to all intents and purposes, a learned stranger was rather heady.

"Thank you, I quite enjoy—"

"Imogene has been drawing since her nanny put a graphite pencil in her hand," Emily interrupted, helping her out, filling in the awkward conversation.

Except this time, it was not awkward, and the rescue was unnecessary. Perhaps it was his easy manner, or his aid in rescuing Jasper, or that moment when Mr. Benjamin held her as she cried—yes, when she thought on it, that moment had broken down a barrier or two. She should have been in her highest state of embarrassment, but she wasn't.

Imogene did not regret finding solace in his arms—not at all. She had needed consoling, and Mr. Benjamin had provided it; it had felt natural. And rather pleasant. He had smelled earthy and manly and . . . yes, indeed, *quite* pleasant. Her heart started to beat faster with the memory.

Surprisingly, she was comfortable in his presence . . . and charmed. She wanted to talk with him, understand him better and—stranger still—have him understand her. She was filled with excitement, not fear, when he turned his eyes in her direction. It was a most unusual state to be in, something that she had never experienced before. Something she rather liked.

And as these thoughts raced through her mind, Imogene did her best not to regret that Emily had taken over the conversation, leaving her with an inexplicable longing.

chapter 3

In which Ben inadvertently
interferes with Ernest's wooing

Stepping across the threshold into the somewhat small but well-lit bedroom to which he had been assigned, Ben yanked off his starched neck-cloth with grubby hands. The long strip of white linen, which *had* been expertly tied, was now spattered with dirt. "I do apologize, Matt," he said to his valet as he dropped it into the man's waiting hand. The mess would require a fair amount of labor to see it returned to its former glory, but at least it was salvageable. His coat on the other hand . . . "Is there any hope for this?" He shucked the coat off his shoulders and passed it to his man as well.

"Of course, sir." Matt's doubtful tone belied his assurance. "Well, I will do my best. You will need it—can't get by on one coat. What would our hosts think?"

Ben smiled at Matt's horror. His valet was a young man and

fairly new to the job, and yet he was traditional in his views—taking pride in the manner and style of the gentlemen he attended.

"Is my brother dressed for dinner?" Ben asked as he pulled off his dirty vest and shirt before leaning over the pitcher and bowl. He scrubbed at the grime on his hands and then washed his face.

"Indeed," said a new voice. "Ready and waiting."

Ben turned to watch Ernest enter wearing a charcoal dress coat with a contrasting vest of vermilion; his neck-cloth was tied in a formal oriental knot, and his hessians shone.

"Well, well, doing it up proud." Ben nodded. "That should impress."

"You think so? I am uncertain. I seem to have her father's interest more than hers."

Smiling, Ben turned back to his ablutions. He knew that the *her* was none other than Miss Imogene Chively—who had risen in his estimation just this afternoon. "I was rather captivated by your Miss Chively today, Ernest. She forgot to be shy when the floor of the castle caved in. Showed a great deal of character while trying to get her dog out. Yes, I can see what appeals to you after all."

"There, now are you satisfied?"

"Yes, I will concede this was not the fool's errand I had labeled it. I will support your decision in the face of any objection from Sir Andrew."

"It wasn't Grandfather I was worried about, but Grand-mother."

"Oh, I don't think she will remain disgruntled when she meets Miss Chively. There is a winning way about your young lady that I think will shine through and sway Grandmother."

"And she is lovely, isn't she? Admit it now, Ben."

"Yes, I will concede that as well. But, really, you can hardly fault my doubt. Until today, I never saw her eyes or her face. She was always looking at the ground."

"She is shy."

"Yes, of that there is no doubt, and because of it, you will have to sparkle with wit to overcome that natural tendency. She definitely has a great interest in art and quite the talent. I'm rather envious of her ability." Which was, in truth, a gross understatement. "Now, let's see . . . hmm, do you know of Turner?"

"Who?"

Tossing his towel onto the mattress of the four-poster bed, Ben accepted a clean shirt from Matt. "Joseph Turner. He's quite a famous artist, Ernest. Really, you *have* to have heard of *him*."

"Even I've heard of him, sir," Matt commented while helping Ben into his vest.

"There you go. See! Even Matt has heard of him."

An excessive amount of silence emanated from the other side of the room.

"What?" Ben asked, looking toward his brother while doing up his buttons.

"Stonework?" Ernest shook his head and then raked his fingers through his hair.

"I beg your pardon?"

"His stonework? In the castle. Don't take down the castle, Mr. Chively," Ernest said in a high voice likely meant to represent Ben—though it sounded nothing like him. "The stonework is too important."

"Well, it worked, didn't it? The purpose of my comment was to keep Miss Chively happy—you would never have gotten so much as a smile from her if she was mourning the loss of her beloved ruins." Ben tugged down the corners of his sapphire vest, affixed the fob of his watch, and then dropped it into his pocket. "So now, not only will the castle *not* come down, but I will see that it rises from the ashes. Miss Chively will be ever so grateful."

"To you."

"To your brother, Ernest. I'm standing in your shadow." He snorted a laugh. "I barely exist to her father." Wrapping a clean band of linen around his neck, Ben tied the neck-cloth in a simple knot.

"Yes, but what happens when Lord Penton does not arrive and there is no interest in his *stonework*? The man will look at us with jaundice eyes."

"Well, Chively can't expect Penton to drop everything and rush into the country, especially when I stated that the old gentleman has taken a hiatus."

"There's no telling what he expects." Ernest lowered himself to the window seat and turned his gaze to the view. The roof of the old castle tower could be seen peeking above the trees.

Lifting his arms into his dress coat, Ben let Matt pull it on and then smooth out the shoulders. He was rather pleased with the reflection in the looking glass; he rarely took the time to dress for dinner—a habit that annoyed his grandmother and amused his grandfather. "Let's cross that bridge when we get to it."

"Hmmm." Ernest continued to stare out the window.

"She's not there, you know."

"Pardon?" Ernest turned a sheepish grin in his brother's direction. "Oh, yes. Well, no . . ."

"Well said." Ben laughed. "Let's go downstairs so you can make calf-eyes at the lovely Miss Chively in person."

Ernest was up from his seat and waiting at the door in a flash. "If we must," he said with mock nonchalance and another grin. "Tell me all about Turner on our way down."

Ben chuckled and shook his head. "Well, I'll give the basics. How's that?" And he ushered his brother into the hallway.

The upper corridors of Gracebridge Manor were not wide, but they were long and convoluted because they accommodated the irregular shape of the building and its many bedrooms. Ben and Ernest had been assigned chambers at the far end—far north end, if he was judging the direction correctly. It took a little navigation to wend their way to the noble carved staircase and allowed Ben to provide Ernest with enough information about Joseph Turner to give his brother something to talk about, if he found himself searching for a topic of which Miss Chively might be interested. At the top of the stairs, they lapsed into dignified silence—yes, dignified. That had been Ernest's request; Ben was not entirely sure how one was silent in a dignified manner, but he did his best.

While the staircase delivered them into a lovely reception room on the ground floor, complete with seating in front of a marble fireplace as well as the nearby window, the family could not be seen.

"This way, young sirs." Sawyer, standing beside the newel post, indicated a corridor to the left from which voices echoed. He was a tall man, with sharp features and a no-nonsense cast to his eye. Rather intimidating.

Ben nodded, with continued dignity, and allowed his brother to take the lead. It was a good sign that the general tone of the voices bouncing toward them was convivial. Proceeding to the far end of the corridor, they passed the library and billiard room as well as a large dining hall.

The reception room at the end of the corridor, however, gave no hint as to its size or décor until they passed through the double doors and were presented with a grand saloon. Two huge mullioned oriel windows lit the company in rays of sunshine and offered a spectacular view of—what else?—the old castle. The room itself was opulent in color, material, and trinkets—knickknacks that Ben could admire though not identify. However, the chimneypieces at either end were modeled with Tudor elements and quite impressive.

As much as Ben would have liked a closer look, he was forced to note the company in the room instead of the architecture surrounding them. A silent company—for the happy chatter was no more.

They were a party of ten; fortunately, only four of the faces were not familiar. The elder Chivelys stood with Mr. and Mrs. Beeswanger between them in a group by one of the windows. Well-dressed for what had been touted as a casual meal, it was still clear that the Chivelys had taken great care with their toilette. Mrs. Chively, in particular, had not been sparing in her use of jewels.

The younger members of the group had gathered by the ornate chimneypiece at one end of the room, where, if one could go by their positions, a young man enjoyed the attention of two young girls who looked to be around the ages of fourteen and twelve. The young man bore a striking resemblance to the Chivelys—blond hair, blue eyes, oval face—though there was a hint of merriment that was entirely missing in his father's gaze. This, of course, must be Percy Chively, Miss Chively's older brother.

Standing next to Miss Beeswanger, Miss Chively was a reflection of her parents in dress, though not in expression. Her eyes sparkled as much as the jewel in her necklace when their eyes met. A smile hovered on her lips . . . until her gaze shifted to Ernest, and she swallowed visibly, the promising curl to her mouth faded.

A lady of some indiscernible age between twenty and thirty sat sour-faced on the settee between the two groups. Her gown shouted mediocrity—an unembellished serviceable gray. This was likely the governess.

"Welcome, Mr. Steeple, Mr. Benjamin." Mr. Chively stepped forward, enunciating and projecting his words so that it felt more like a performance than a greeting.

Fortunately, the company laughed, and the atmosphere relaxed immediately.

"Chively, old fellow, no need to be so formal," Mr. Beeswanger called out.

Mrs. Beeswanger, who looked as genial as her husband, nodded with great vigor. "Indeed not." She stepped to the center of the room, glanced toward Mrs. Chively—who shrugged—and then back to Ernest. "The countryside lends itself to a far less decorous lifestyle—the strictures of society can be relaxed somewhat here. To that end, we"—she gestured to those around her—"are quite comfortable with given names for the younger generation, and if it would not insult your sensibilities, we would offer you the same casual address. A little untoward, perhaps, but we are all on good terms." The implication being, of course, that the good terms would soon include the Steeple boys. There was no hiding why they were visiting.

Ben glanced at Ernest, knowing he would be flummoxed. Ernest found great comfort in those strictures; they provided a template—expected behavior drilled into him since birth. Well, no, that was an exaggeration. Their regimented life had begun only when Sir Andrew and Lady Margaret had accepted the responsibility of two lads while their parents traipsed around the Continent. Still, five years of rules and regulations had been of comfort to Ernest . . . though not to Ben.

"Untoward, indeed, Mrs. Beeswanger," he said, stepping into the fray, allowing Ernest to gather his wits. "But a welcome deviation. Another reason to appreciate country life."

"Marvelous" was her reply, said with an exhalation as if she had been holding her breath.

Ernest's silence continued a tad overlong, forcing Ben to nonchalantly shift in his brother's direction and knock him shoulder to shoulder.

"Yes, yes, indeed." Ernest came to life. He turned toward Imogene, raising his voice slightly to include the offset group. "Call me Ernest. Benjamin prefers Ben."

Looking at Ben, Miss Chively smiled quite broadly. "Thank you, I shall. I'm Imogene." She turned and swept her arm back as if to indicate those standing with her, but her gaze moved as she did, falling on Ernest. She turned a bright shade of pink— that Ben thought rather becoming—then blinked and swallowed, all in silence.

Clearing her throat, Miss Beeswanger secured the attention of the room. "Ernest . . . Benjamin . . . please, call me Emily."

Ben noticed the use of his full name, pronounced slowly as if it were being measured, and he lifted the corner of his mouth, offering a weak smile. *Benjamin* was pretentious in his mind; it reminded Ben of his namesake, General Benjamin Steeple, a great-uncle of a stern and pompous repute. Not exactly a person he wished to emulate.

"These are my sisters, Pauline"—Emily gestured toward the older girl first and then, the younger—"and Hardly Harriet."

"Em," Hardly Harriet whined with a deeply entrenched frown and . . . yes, a pout. "You can't say that to strangers. It's not right."

"I beg your pardon," Miss Emily said, facing Ben, not her sister. "Harriet prefers Harry."

"Do not!"

"Percy Chively." The young man stepped forward with a nod, ignoring the teasing. "Everyone calls me Percy." He, like his parents, was focused on Ernest.

"There we go. The formalities of the night are over; we can enjoy—" Mrs. Beeswanger started to say.

A gravelly noise emanated from the settee. They all turned toward the sound and the person making it—by clearing her throat.

"Oh, dear me. I apologize, Miss Watson. Please, let me introduce Miss Bertha Watson, Pauline and Harriet's governess."

With introductions truly complete this time, the host and hostess dragged Ernest into their group—almost literally, for Mrs. Chively asked Ernest to walk her to the window, a distance of a mere ten feet or so. Ben, unfettered for a moment, drifted toward Percy's group. Though not interested in the man's bragging about his hunting prowess, Ben thought this discourse held more promise than a soliloquy about the weather . . . or snuffboxes. Catching Miss Imogene's eye, he winked, eliciting a light laugh from her. It sounded so enchanting that Ben was taken aback.

Looking down at Miss Imogene, Ben tried to imagine her as a member of the Steeple family and discovered that the prospect was no longer as unwelcome as it had been a mere day ago. In fact, the possibility was rather buoying.

"Lordy, Lordy, Ernest. I don't envy you your in-laws. . . . Possible in-laws." Ben chuckled quietly while closing the door behind him. He had followed Ernest to his bedroom for a private chat about the whys and wherefores of their evening.

"Really? How could you not be fascinated by . . . now let me see if I recall—the compound interest of debt, or was it the compound debt of interest? No, no, I'm quite certain it was the former. . . . Or was it the latter?" With a snorting laugh, Ernest shook his head and pulled off his coat. "What in heaven's name would give Mr. Chively the idea that I cared about the ins and outs of banking? His chosen occupation, not mine." Ernest frowned at the door until it opened briefly to allow Matt to slip in, and then he handed the valet the coat and limp neck-cloth that he had just tugged free.

"Well, I might have mentioned something."

"Ben, you didn't."

"Not intentionally. It was an innocent comment. We were talking of Musson House, and I simply stated that Grandfather already appreciated your opinion in regard to management of the estate. I was trying to impress the man with your competence; I did not know that he would take it as a sign that you were kindred spirits in all matters of economics. See, nothing untoward—all very innocent."

Ben smiled, for in truth he *had* known that Mr. Chively

would take the comment and run with it; though Ben had not expected the man to monopolize Ernest completely and leave his brother with no opportunity to woo all evening. Ben had meant to set his brother up for a boring conversation, not an entire night.

Ernest looked at Matt. "Does he ever make an *innocent* comment?"

"Not that I have observed, sir." Matt made no attempt to hide his grin.

"See?" Ernest offered Ben an ineffectual glare. "In our employ only a month and already Matt knows *that* to be a bouncer. Really, Ben, the point of this visit is to become better acquainted with Miss Imogene, *not* her father."

"Too true." Ben shrugged and dropped onto the window seat that was similar to the one in his room. It was, perhaps, the only similarity; this chamber was larger and much more lavishly appointed. "Well, tomorrow is another day in which Mr. Turner might still provide fodder for a lively discussion. The tutelage was not for naught."

"It felt like a waste. . . . Not the tutelage, the evening. If I hadn't seen that you were entertaining Miss Imogene, I would have called the night a *complete* loss. By the by, what were you talking about? She seemed fascinated. Extolling my virtues?" Ernest raised his brows in a hopeful manner.

"Mother and Father's Italian journeys. Might be an idea for a bridal trip."

"Oh." Ernest huffed a sigh as he unbuttoned his vest; he stared without focus above Ben's head. "Miss Imogene is of a retiring disposition, Ben. She's not a traveler. We can hunker into Musson House in harmony. Not stir beyond Chotsdown."

"That might be to your taste, Ernest, but I got the impression that Miss Imogene would enjoy a wider view of the world."

"No, no. You are mistaken. Miss Imogene was quite unhappy in London. Mentioned several times how much she preferred to be at home—in the country."

Ben frowned. He was not mistaken in Miss Imogene's interest. She had leaned forward with rapt attention, asked about the ruins in Rome, the canals of Venice, his parents' collections of paintings and sculptures—where they had been found, what was their condition, what subjects were depicted. The shyness from which she usually suffered was hardly evident. In fact, they had become so involved in their discourse that it had taken a nudge from Miss Emily to pull Miss Imogene out of her reverie.

Ben thought it likely that his brother misunderstood the nature of Miss Imogene's desire to stay in the country. A bashful character would not enjoy the squeezes of London balls and soirees, but a Continental journey with a husband at her side—well, that would be an entirely different matter.

Ernest became very still. "I have no cause for concern . . . do I?" He lowered his gaze.

"About what?"

Ernest continued to stare, his jaw tightened.

"What is going on in that pea-brain of yours, brother?"

"Miss Imogene hung on your every word. Don't think I did not notice."

"You just said that the evening would have been a waste had I not entertained your lady-fair."

"Yes. But she has never looked at me in such a way."

"Ernest, Ernest, Ernest. I helped rescue her dog and saved her castle from destruction. Of course she is kindly disposed to me. It was a traumatic afternoon, and you should admire her ability to step past it so quickly. She *is* impressive; no vapors, no histrionics. . . . Still, worry not, brother dear, she was not looking at me in *that* way."

"She was quite animated when you spoke," Ernest said with careful enunciation.

"True. But a shared experience does create a bond."

"A brother-sister bond?"

"Indeed." Ben nodded, happy that Ernest was coming around. "Be her hero tomorrow, and you'll be all set."

"How?"

"Ernest, you are so unimaginative! Let's see. Offer to carry her art supplies."

"Hardly heroic."

"True. But I don't recommend throwing Jasper down a well so that you might rescue him or setting the manor alight so that you might carry Miss Imogene from the flames. Perhaps jump into the fray when Mrs. Chively offers her daughter a particularly snide remark . . . which she does on a regular basis."

"That's not heroic, either."

"Really, Ernest." Ben shook his head in frustration. "I have little doubt that Miss Imogene would simply appreciate someone coming to her defense. As you must have observed, the Beeswangers are far kinder to Miss Imogene than the Chivelys."

"Yes I did. Perhaps they are too practical. Don't value her artistic abilities. Yes, I will talk to Miss Imogene about John Turner tomorrow. Prove that I, unlike they, appreciate creativity."

"Yes, yes, excellent idea." Ben rose to his feet and slapped his brother on the back as he headed for the door. "However, I think you will impress Miss Imogene more if you call the gentleman *Joseph* Turner instead."

IT IS DIFFICULT to maintain an air of indifference while one is rushing down a hallway in desperate need to talk to one's closest friend. It was just as well that Imogene was not trying to deceive those around her but simply to maintain her privacy. A privacy that was about to come to an end . . . as soon as she and Emily put good English oak between them and the rest of the household.

Imogene could hardly contain her disquiet; she needed Emily's opinion.

Had she noticed? Had her friend seen the way Ben looked at her?

Imogene was certain . . . almost certain . . . that Ben's interest in her was not of a brotherly nature. Had he not stared at her throughout dinner? Had he not engaged her in a discourse of which she, and she alone, could be a part? Had he not reached out to touch her as they sat at the table? And then he had split his dessert, offering the sweet, delectable seed cake to her and Emily when Imogene declared it her favorite.

How could he flirt so openly with her when Ernest was watching from the other end of the table? It was a most uncomfortable situation—made worse by the fact that she quite enjoyed Ben's company.

What was she to do?

"Oh, Imogene, we have so much to discuss," Emily said. A mere step or two behind Imogene, Emily grinned with excitement.

"Let us hurry," Imogene said, though to hurry more would necessitate running. Even without her mother's watchful eye, Imogene could not do something so undignified.

It seemed an age before Imogene could close the door to their shared bedchamber, though in fact it was but a moment or two.

"I can hardly believe it." Emily was the first to speak, unaware of Imogene's troubled thoughts.

"Indeed," Imogene squeaked. She walked over to the bed and then, changing her mind, strode over to her window seat. Even that did not appeal. How could she sit still when every fiber of her being was tense with concern? She wanted to fling back the shutters and fly away, soar high into the sky until all the worries and complexities of the evening disappeared.

She paced instead.

"It has happened," Emily said as Imogene passed by for a second time. Grabbing her hands, Emily leaned back, and they spun together in the center of the room. "I am in love!" she shouted . . . quietly.

Imogene gasped. Had she not been caught in the momentum of their spin, she would have tripped. "Oh, Emily! That is wonderful." Could she mean Percy? No, probably not. They had known each other forever, and he had paid Emily no heed this evening. Surely, she didn't mean *Ben*.

Imogene stopped twirling. "Who . . . ?" She suddenly found it difficult to form words.

Fortunately, Emily did not notice. She threw her hands up and began to twirl on her own. "Can you believe it? Never would I expect to attract the attention of such a splendid young man. But we have so much in common: our interests, our pursuits. Yes, we will be laughing and chatting into our dotage. Oh, Imogene, I feel as if I could slay dragons—I know the knight is supposed to slay the dragon, but . . . well, I feel as if I could, too. Life is a marvel, don't you agree? Can you imagine, Imogene, we are going to be sisters as well as fast friends? You shall be Mrs. Ernest Steeple, and I will be Mrs. Benjamin Steeple. Can you think of anything more glorious?"

Imogene swallowed. "What makes you think that Ben might be entertaining romantic thoughts about you?"

"Oh, Imogene, did you not see? It was glorious. . . . I love that word, don't you? Yes, glorious. He stared at me with growing affection all through dinner. He spoke to me, and me alone. Did you not notice how he answered my questions about Florence? And then Benjamin reached out to touch my arm as we sat at the table. Yes, that was when I began to hope that he was mine, but I knew for certain when he offered me his seed cake after I declared it to be my favorite. He claimed to be sated, too full to eat even a morsel. But I knew the truth; it was a sacrifice—for me. How could I not return such glorious affection? Imogene, I am so very happy."

Imogene stared wide-eyed. Emily's words were an echo of Imogene's thoughts. Was Ben attracted to them both? How was that possible? This was terrible—a disaster in the making.

chapter 4

*In which hands and fluff are subjects
of a deep discussion*

"I know what you are going to say—that Benjamin still has to complete his apprenticeship and that I will have to be patient."

That was not what Imogene was going to say.

"Though we might be able to marry earlier; I am not aware of his financial situation. We could rent a cute little cottage. . . . I could suffer a snug little place for a year or two. Though I would probably not do well without a carriage. Yes, we would have to rent a place with enough room for horses."

Imogene breathed deeply through her nose. "Oh," she said with great intelligence, sitting heavily on the mattress of her four-poster. She exhaled a deep sigh of relief, though an unsettling whisper of disappointment wafted into the air with it. "I don't think you can be certain of Ben's feelings, Emily."

Imogene felt wretched, watching the change in her friend's face. It progressed from happiness to puzzlement, followed by disbelief, a hint of anger, and then resignation. Silence filled the room. Imogene rubbed at her forehead, reluctant to explain. The hush stretched into several minutes.

"Did I misread Benjamin?" Emily finally asked. "Have I presumed too far?"

"I believe so."

"But . . . no, I'm certain. He looked at me with such kindness and interest, Imogene. He seemed taken with everything I uttered. He even laughed when I described my muddy boots. It was a banal story. . . . But he laughed. Why do you think . . . ?" Emily swallowed, unable to continue.

"He laughed and chatted as easily with Pauline and Harriet as he did with you. Even offered Miss Watson a kind smile and comment." Conjuring up his face, Imogene watched him grin in her mind and felt an unwelcome quickening of her pulse. She turned her face to the dark window. A somber reflection gazed back. "It would seem that Ben is quite adept at making *everyone* feel special."

"Oh." There was a pause and then a deflating sigh. "How utterly and completely . . . disappointing." The rustle of Emily's skirts warned Imogene of Emily's approach. She dropped onto the bed beside Imogene, bouncing her slightly. "Being charming is not a bad trait," Emily said softly. "But I am sorry. . . . I thought his smiles were for me."

"I'm quite certain they were. Nothing can diminish that. It was the interpretation that was askew."

"Oh, Imogene, when I think on it clearly, Benjamin paid heed to you, as well. How uncomfortable you must have been."

"In what way?"

"To think that Ernest's brother was trifling with you. You must have wanted to melt into the floor."

Imogene snorted a laugh. "Actually, I find Ben such easy company that I have not wanted to melt in some hours. I was not embarrassed." It was true enough; she had been puzzled and anxious but not embarrassed.

"Still, what a fine kettle of fish that would have been. Thank the heavens your father did not notice. He would have been furious. Only a firstborn with a sizable income for you."

"Ernest Steeple's inheritance matters little to me, Emily. If I never feel my heart race when our eyes meet, then no matter what my father demands, I will not marry Ernest."

A sharp rap sounded on the door just before it opened to admit Emily's personal maid. The young woman stepped across the threshold with a broad grin, closing the door behind her. "My gracious. Look at the Friday-faces. Whatever has brought my girls down?" Kate bobbed her brows up and down and offered a cheeky look. "Trouble with the gentlemen?"

As Kate advanced into the room, her expression faded into bewilderment. She was close in age, with straight dark hair—firmly secured in a cap—and an elfin face. Her position as Emily's personal maid was a new one, having only just been elevated from housemaid before the Season started. Whenever Emily and Imogene were together, Kate helped them both. Mrs. Chively thought it frivolous but did not interfere.

Emily nodded. "Trouble indeed, Kate. I thought Mr. Benjamin had singled me out. His gaze was so penetrating it made me breathless, but Imogene cautioned, and rightly so, that Mr. Benjamin is generous with his attention, that she, Pauline, and even Harriet were the beneficiaries of the same." Emily sighed again.

"Ah, a ladies' man." Kate pulled Emily to her feet and turned her around so that she could reach the buttons that ran down Emily's back. "If only there were more of them in the world . . . Nothing compares to the teasing of a ladies' man. Charmers . . . through and through. Makes you want to float away."

"Kate! You know of . . . charmers?" Imogene sat up straighter.

Emily turned, making it impossible for Kate to continue working on her buttons.

Kate laughed. "My experience is by way of three brothers and their friends. You learn a thing or two when they are pulling at your hair. The charmers get away with it."

"This is marvelous." Emily's eyes were full of excitement again. "Kate, tell me what to do?"

"Do?"

"Yes, I . . . well, I am quite taken with Mr. Benjamin. I would like to encourage mutual interest, if you know what I mean."

"Oh yes, indeed. I do." Kate nodded. "You must learn to flirt."

"Yes, exactly." Emily's expression was once again full of hope and anticipation. "Tell me. Tell me."

Still sitting on the bed, Imogene listened to Kate's advice to Emily. She laughed when Kate took Emily's fan and showed her how to bat her eyes across it, use it to tap lightly on an arm or shoulder, and snap it to garner attention.

"Sashay, Emily," Imogene suggested as her friend sauntered across the floor. "A little more sway," she said as they dissolved into a fit of giggles.

It was all quite amusing, and yet a touch of melancholy stole its way into Imogene's high spirits. She preferred not to examine the cause too closely. It was good to know that Ben had not singled her out for romantic attention as she had feared. He had simply been true to his character: friendly, kind, and beguiling. He was a charmer. A very good match for Emily.

Directing her thoughts to Ernest, Imogene recalled the gentleness of his smile and his calm manner. The memory was pleasant, but it did not make her heart race. . . . Still, there was time.

With a sigh, Imogene reached around to unclasp her necklace. She wound the chain around the topaz pendant and closed her fist around it, concentrating on the feel of the cold stone.

THE NEXT MORNING, Ben stepped into an empty dining room with a grumbling belly. He had been up early to visit the castle and speak to Mr. Opine about the repairs, and now he was quite prepared to break his fast. The other gentlemen were already up and away. Mr. Chively felt that dawn was the most productive time to fish, and he had dragged Ernest and Mr. Beeswanger along with him. Ben's reprieve was born from his agreement to see to the ruined ruins.

A generous breakfast had been laid out on the sideboard, enticing him with the delectable aromas of ham and fresh breads. Though there didn't seem to be a pot of coffee or . . .

"Oh."

Ben turned with surprise, in time to see Miss Imogene enter the dining room and then take a half step back, straddling the threshold into the hallway.

"Ah, Miss Imogene," he said, placing his half-filled plate on the table and then executing a formal bow of his head. "How are you this morning? Up early?" He smiled and was pleased to see a like expression spread across her face as she stepped farther into the room.

"I am well." She winced as though some thought of an unpleasant nature had flitted through her mind, and dropped her eyes to the floor. "Thank you." Her voice was slightly muffled. "I believe the other ladies are keeping town hours."

Ben puckered his brow. This would not do. He was certain that he had made headway with Miss Imogene yesterday. Helped her to feel comfortable in his company. He needed to extol his brother's virtues since Ernest was not here to do so. . . . And talking to the crown of her lovely head was of little use.

Tipping his head to the side, Ben squatted, trying to look up into her downturned face. His antic elicited a smile and then a laugh, and then, more important, she lifted her head.

"Whatever are you doing, Mr. . . . Ben?"

"Well, I am trying to hold a conversation with a lovely young lady, full of wit and wisdom . . . and enamored with dogs and castles. But it would seem that something on the floor has caught her full attention." Bending down, he made a show of picking up a spec of lint from the floor. "There. I have it, Miss Imogene. Worry no more, it has been found."

"And what, pray tell, is *it*?"

"I think it's a bug." Offering the lint to her, he was surprised when she took it without hesitation and then proceeded to examine it.

"An unusual species. Often disguised as fluff."

"Rare, indeed."

"Indeed." Imogene chuckled and dropped the *rare bug* on the floor with a jaunty look. "We'll send it home."

A laugh burst from Ben before he could temper it, and he stared at Imogene with admiration. Few returned his teasing so readily. "Come, let us break our fast," he said, waving toward the sideboard—actually, her sideboard.

At first she hesitated, and then with a nod, she grabbed a plate and piled it with a healthy helping of kippers, toast, preserves, and tomatoes. They sat at the table across from each other, silent for several minutes, but it was a companionable silence born from the necessity of eating. Eventually, Ben raised his eyes to find Imogene staring at him with a quizzical look.

"So, your brother is angling with my father and Mr. Beeswanger?"

Ben had the impression that this question was not the cause of her puzzled expression. "Yes. They left rather early. I heard a fair amount of stomping down the hallway. Ernest is not light on his feet when he is tired—and a sport that requires a dawn rising is his least favorite."

"He could have stayed abed."

"I don't think your father gave Ernest a choice. Enlisted him last night. Your father seemed quite determined to have Ernest's company. I find it somewhat odd being that the entire purpose of our visit—well, there is no hiding the fact that Ernest wishes to know *you* better. And yet he is being thwarted at every turn. Is there something about you that your family is trying to hide?" His query was stated in a playful tone, and yet Imogene stilled and grew pale.

"Whatever do you mean?" Imogene asked, clearly expecting ridicule of some sort.

Realizing his mistake, Ben smiled and reached across the table for her hand. "Let me see now." He uncurled her fist. "Ah, good, good. Four fingers and a thumb on this hand. And . . . yes, this one as well." When he looked up, he was pleased to see that her color had returned and that, in fact, Imogene's cheeks were a lovely shade of rose . . . pink . . . now they were red . . . crimson.

"Might I have the return of my hands, Ben?"

Ben looked down to see that Imogene's hands were encased in his. He rather liked the way they fit together; then he realized that he had been holding them overlong. "Oh yes, indeed. Are these yours?" He let go with a laugh that sounded a little forced even to his ears.

"Since birth," Imogene replied with a grin. Her heightened

color was most becoming. "I also have ten toes and . . . the normal set of appendages."

"Splendid. I shall share the good news with Ernest." Though having said so, Ben thought he might not share the holding hands aspect of their conversation. "Not entirely sure why then—"

"It's my insanity."

It was Ben's turn to blink in surprise. "Pardon?"

"Yes," she continued, as if unaware of Ben's astonishment. "My family believes anyone deeply interested in the arts is not rational . . . and boring. I think that might be more the crux of the matter. They believe Ernest will tire of my conversation; after all, Father certainly does. He, my father, that is, is all about numbers and business. We have little in common."

Despite the light tone, Ben was fairly certain that Imogene was stating the hurtful truth. A lack of appreciation for her talents—enviable talents—would explain much.

"Well, I certainly know the value of your artistic abilities . . . and so does Ernest." He shrugged, trying to express his understanding and sympathy—a lot to convey with such a small gesture, but it seemed to do the job, for her face brightened.

"Chocolate, miss?"

Both Ben and Imogene started, turning toward the tall, liveried footman who was standing at Imogene's elbow. He held a polished silver pot in each hand. "Or coffee?"

"Chocolate. Thank you." She watched as her cup was filled and then waited as coffee was poured into Ben's cup. "Did you find out about Jasper and the hounds, Greg?"

"Yes, miss, Mr. Sawyer sent Roger to check. The message came back that all was well. Jasper's hobbling around just fine—and eating as much as ever. As to the hounds: the chickens did not get into the kennels again. The noise was . . . Well, it seems that a bone had been hung from the rafters just far enough above the dogs' heads that they could not reach it. That's what set them off, miss. The terrible racket that you heard."

"I see. A bone hanging from the rafters. It has been removed?"

"Yes, miss."

"Excellent. Tell me, Greg, have the Tabards arrived?"

"Yes, miss. They arrived late last evening."

"Of course. Thank you." Imogene nodded, and the footman placed the urns on the sideboard and then took a position between the windows, standing stiff and ready to serve if need be. Imogene scrubbed at her forehead.

"Tabards?" Ben asked.

"Yes." She pulled her hand from her face to reveal a smile that did not reach her eyes. "Yes, the Tabards are the other family that we visit with over the summer. Cousin Clara is no longer with us, but Mr. Tabard and his son, Jake, have arrived. I imagine you will meet them this evening."

Ben could see she was hesitant to say more. "And . . . ? Does this have something to do with the hounds?"

Imogene shrugged—rather prettily. If Ben hadn't seen her bite at the corner of her lip just before lifting her shoulders, he would have been convinced of her nonchalance.

"Whenever Jake and Percy get together, they have a

tendency to get into mischief. Tying a bone above the heads of the dogs is just the sort of lark they would get up to."

"Pranks? Always in the suds?"

"Yes, indeed. They make a mull of everything!"

"Hard on a younger sister."

Imogene's smile broadened, and it not only reached her eyes but shone through. The transformation was astounding. . . . And Ben swallowed, entranced.

"I have learned," she said, "to stay out of the way."

"A very good strategy."

"I believe so."

They stared at each other for several minutes—it was a natural break in the discourse—until Imogene looked to the mantel clock. "Oh my, where has the time gone? I want to get my studio ready before Harriet gets there. I had better put a little hustle on." The footman was behind her, pulling out her chair, before Ben could even acknowledge the statement. And then she paused. "Are you off to see to the old castle?"

"No, I was there earlier. Mr. Opine had it well in hand and required little of me." Ben stood, without the footman's help, and followed her to the hallway. "I thought I might take a closer look at the chimneypieces in the grand saloon; they were impressive. In the classical style—"

"Well, actually, they are reproductions added only five or so years ago. In fact, well . . . if you are interested . . . then you might. Yes, a better example you will never find . . . I think . . . perhaps."

She stopped in her tracks, turned, and waited expectantly.

Ben puzzled for a moment, reran the dialogue back in his head, and decided that it really didn't make sense. "I apologize, Miss Imogene, but I am not entirely sure of what you are speaking."

"Oh . . . oh. I beg your pardon. We were talking of chimneypieces, and my mind jumped ahead. Dear, dear." She leaned back momentarily, then lifted her chin and nodded to some unasked question. "Yes. Perhaps the better chimneypiece to see is the one in my studio. It came from the old castle. It is a fine example of typical Elizabethan craftsmanship: embellished columns, pilasters, and engravings. It's almost a shame that it is hidden away in my studio."

"Except that you appreciate it—I can see that—and you have the opportunity to show any of us who are greatly interested."

"Are you?"

Ben stared again—no longer sure if Imogene was being enigmatic or if he was having a problem thinking. His brain seemed to have lost its train of thought. "Am I what?"

Imogene laughed. "Greatly interested?"

Ben stared at pretty Miss Imogene Chively in her soft blue dress that accented her lovely blue eyes and agreed readily. "Most definitely," he said, no longer sure of the topic. "Very interested."

As they made their way to the attic level of Gracebridge Manor, Ben made a concerted effort to clear his thoughts and regulate his breathing. He talked of Ernest. There was no sequence to his soliloquy; he began with an anecdote about Ernest's first pony, threw in a story about a winning hand at a London card party last week, and then mentioned Ernest's cataloguing abilities whenever their parents sent newly purchased art from Italy. He thought of mentioning Ernest's interest in Turner but changed his mind—he would let his brother enthrall Imogene with his Turner knowledge—whenever Ernest returned from the lake.

Imogene, not surprisingly, contributed little to the conversation, but when she did, her subject was Emily: her love of dance, her interest in horses, and her affable character. Even the discussion about Italy brought with it a reminder of her best friend, as Imogene's only comment was that Emily had always wanted to go to Florence.

The stairs narrowed with each ascending staircase as they headed toward the pinnacle of the manor. However, when they entered the room that Imogene called her studio, he was surprised. It was cavernous, in length and height—made all the more impressive by the windows at either end and the skylights worked into the peaks of the dormers at the back of the manor.

This was not the dusty garret he had expected but a wonderful room full of the natural light needed for rendering true color. There were two easels under the skylights, an ornate desk between them, and a scratched table with two spindle-legged chairs in the center. Other than a couple of covered chairs ruined by shattered silk, the room was full of canvases. Some sat on the floor, and many hung in a crowded hodgepodge on the rough walls.

"Your father may not understand your talent, but he has

certainly provided you with a haven. This room is amazing—especially this!" Ben made a beeline for the Elizabethan chimneypiece in the center of the far wall.

Imogene snorted a laugh. "This was originally my grand-mother's studio. She had the fireplace moved here—draws far better than the small one that it replaced. Before she passed away, Grandmamma insisted that the room, in its entirety, be mine. She also provided an allowance to purchase any supplies I might need. She knew Father would not support any costs associated with art."

Ben nodded and sighed in understanding. Turning back to the shallow hearth, he examined, and marveled at, the engravings on the mantel. Though somewhat worn with age, it *was* a fine example. He ran his fingers across the grooves, noting the depth, assessed the weight ratio of the pilasters, and admired the angle of the chimney to provide a strong draft. After a while, Ben pried his gaze away from the stone and glanced around, focusing on the artistry of the canvases around him.

The paintings were in various states of completion. On closer examination, there was little doubt of two artists. Their styles and subjects were very different. One preferred big sky landscapes—and were often half-finished—while the other offered intimate scenes of plants, vistas of the castle, and various manors. He stopped in front of one painting to admire the architectural details, marveling at the talent and ability to render a mansard roof with such precision.

If only he could do as much—half as much—he would no

longer have to worry about Lord Penton. He could sleep through the night secure in his apprenticeship, comfortable with his future—a future that slipped out of his grasp every time Lord Penton suggested that a drawing would serve better than notes. What would the old gentleman do when he discovered that Ben could not draw? What use is an architect who can't render his designs?

"That's Shackleford Park," Imogene said as she came to stand beside him. "Emily's country home. Newly built—I believe just a decade or so old."

"It is quite impressive. You can see where the architect has tried to provide balance and function—the mullions, the intricate brickwork . . . more than a hint of a French chateau. The square towers are perfect foils against the central round entrance. Yes, very impressive."

"The Beeswangers are very proud. Love to take guests around, pointing out the details. I'm quite certain that they would be more than happy to show it to you. Give you a full tour. We go to Shackleford *en masse* in a few weeks. . . . You and Ernest could join us."

"We could not impose."

"I doubt it would be an imposition. Though you might wish to be shed of us by then."

Ben shifted so that he could face Imogene and offered her an amused smile. "Most unlikely." It was more probable that Ernest would be inordinately pleased to continue the acquaintance, if he knew his brother. Glancing back at the painting,

Ben felt the tug of envy again. "Your talent for perspective and detail is remarkable."

"Thank you—"

"I'm here!" a voice gleefully called from the doorway. "Good day, Mr. Ben."

"Good day, Hardly Harriet," he said with a broad grin, pleased when his greeting brought out a smile and giggle from the little girl.

"Funny, I like it when *you* say it. Emily always sounds—"

"Are those your sketches?" Imogene asked.

Harriet Beeswanger walked deeper into the room and dropped the pile of papers, which she had been hugging to her bodice, on the table. "Yes. I did just as you told me, Imogene. I spent the whole time you were in London drawing. Come see." Looking up, Harriet nodded at Ben. "And you, too, Mr. Ben." Searching through the pile, she pulled out a piece of paper—a depiction of a cat-shaped doorstop. "Look. This is my favorite." She passed it to Imogene with pride.

It was a black-and-white pencil sketch that, though simple, showed definition and shape.

"Well done, Harriet. Your shadows are perfect. Now do you believe me?"

"Yes, I suppose . . . but when can I use color?"

Imogene laughed in a freer manner than she had as yet within Ben's hearing, and he quite enjoyed the sound. It was infectious—though Ben refrained from joining the merriment as he did not know the context.

"I started teaching Harriet to draw last summer," Imogene

explained as she smiled down at the girl and then continued leafing through the sketches. "She wanted to paint horses right away, but I told her she needed to start with something less complicated. Pencil sketches, concentrating on shadows to make an object stand out."

"And I have done it, haven't I?"

"You have indeed. You have done an exemplary job. I think it is time to work on perspective."

"Not color . . . or horses?"

"Not quite yet."

Harriet sighed but readily pulled out the chair. She sat wiggling with anticipation, her eyes shining.

"And I think it is time for me to leave you two ladies alone." Ben bowed formally, eliciting another giggle from Harriet and a gentle smile from Imogene. "Thank you for showing me the chimneypiece."

At the door, he looked back and watched for a moment as the two put their heads together while Imogene explained the next lesson. Drawing what you see, not what you know. Frowning, Ben recalled all the drawing masters that he had had over the years. None had explained the process so simply . . . or so clearly . . . as Imogene was doing for Harriet.

He felt a stirring of hope. Was it possible that all he needed was the right teacher? Could Imogene Chively succeed where the others had failed?

As he descended to the first story, Ben considered how he might go about asking for her help. Naturally, spending time in Imogene's company would require his brother's agreement first. But that was not the worst of it. He would have to admit his failing to a pretty young lady with a shy smile and a talent that would put all his masters to shame. He would have to swallow his pride and watch the admiration in her pretty blue eyes diminish. The prospect added a touch of the dismals to an otherwise uplifting morning.

chapter 5

In which Ernest steps into the light,
metaphorically speaking

Watching Ben leave from the corner of her eye, Imogene sighed in resignation. There was no favoritism—not for Emily, not for herself. From their meeting in the dining room to moments ago, Ben had been affable, a gabster, considerate, and, well, most excellent company. He had stared at her hands overlong and hesitated before leaving, but she had a feeling those were merely the usual lapses of a young man in thought. Percy's head was regularly in the clouds.

As to Emily . . . well, her friend might be disappointed that Ben showed only a moderate interest in the anecdotes of her, but it was more likely that she would see his lack of favoritism as a boon or even a challenge. She would not be disheartened; she would flutter her fan with even more panache.

When Emily joined Imogene in her studio just after

Harriet had skipped away, Imogene noted that Emily had donned one of her most becoming gowns. The soft teal, multiple collars, and lace-covered décolleté served to bring the eye up to Emily's face. Her color was high, naturally so, and . . . yes, she had a matching fan in hand.

"It would seem the gentlemen have disappeared," Emily said with raised brows.

"You mean Ben, of course," Imogene said with a smile as she collected the objects Harriet had been tasked to draw. "Did you try the castle?"

"I thought of it. . . . But I don't want to appear too bold—as if I am setting my cap at him. I would rather Benjamin come to me."

Laughing, Imogene removed her painting apron. "You might not see him until dinner, then."

"I will keep my fan at the ready, just in case." Emily sashayed across the floor, looked back over her shoulder, and then raised her fan to cover all but her eyes.

"Oh, well done!"

"Thank you." Emily ruined the mysterious effect by breaking into a grin. "I have been practicing. You'll have to try it with Ernest."

Imogene's smile froze. "Perhaps," she said as lightly as she could, and then led the way to the stairs.

IMOGENE SPENT THE rest of the day trying not to think about either of the Steeple boys. She stayed sequestered through the afternoon with the ladies idling on the patio. Emily read, Imogene sketched, the younger girls played a string game, and the mothers gossiped. It was a normal summer day. Even when Jake threw a bucket of water from the window, soaking Pauline, nothing seemed out of the ordinary.

And yet, as much as she tried, Imogene could not get either Ernest or Ben out of her mind. It was the height of ridiculousness, for dwelling on the matter didn't help one iota. She did not know how she felt about Ernest—that could not change until they spent some time together. And as to Ben, she had to discover a way to *not* find every move he made, every twitch of his brow, or every smile . . . appealing. It might be simpler to admit a modicum of awareness and attribute it to the possibility of being related—by way of marriage—someday. . . . Oh dear, that brought her right back to Ernest.

"Where *are* the gentlemen?" Emily asked in an excessively casual tone partway through the afternoon. She met Imogene's gaze and grinned. "Shouldn't they be back from the lake by now?"

Mrs. Beeswanger turned and squinted into the shade where Emily and Imogene were seated. "They have been back for some time, my dears. I believe they are with Mr. Tabard, playing billiards. Jake and Percy have joined them as well."

Emily frowned. "Really? You would think that they would want to be out of doors on such a fine day."

"Perhaps they had had enough of the sun and warmth. Gentlemen feel the heat so much more than us ladies."

Emily huffed and went back to reading.

It was a quiet afternoon.

THE GAIETY OF the evening impressed Imogene as being entirely false until dinner was complete. Ernest and Ben had indeed met the Tabards, and while Jake was the same age as the Steeple brothers, they had little in common. The conversation at dinner was awkward, a few comments about the winning shots at billiards and the catch of trout that had made its way to the table. Even Ben's attempt to engage Miss Watson in an intellectual discourse about natural history was strained.

When Emily suggested an impromptu dance, the idea was quickly taken up with relief. The footmen were instructed, and the entire party retired to the music room, where the carpet had been rolled out of the way and the furniture set against the walls.

The elder members of the group collected at the far end of the room, near the open windows, to enjoy the draft and watch and appreciate the grace and high spirits of their fledglings. Without a word to anyone, Miss Watson sat at the piano and began to play.

It was a somber piece, not at all suited for dancing, but the company smiled politely and then encouraged her to choose something a little more lively. She complied readily enough, and, at last, the room was filled with merriment as eight young people prepared to be frivolous. Though Harriet should have been abed, Mrs. Beeswanger allowed that she might stay up another half hour . . . or so.

Standing awkwardly beside Ernest, Imogene tried to keep her eyes on Miss Watson but found they kept wandering toward

Ben . . . and Emily. She watched Emily practicing her fan flirting but looked away when he laughed and asked her for a dance. Imogene stared at the floor for some minutes, until she realized that a pair of well-shone hessians was in her field of vision. When she looked up, Ernest smiled.

"Would you care to dance, Imogene?"

Though his words were few, his expression was kind and patient, encouraging a welcome sense of enthusiasm in Imogene. She laid her hand on Ernest's arm, and he led her to the center of the room. It was just as well that there were only four gamboling couples, as the space would not have accommodated more. Country dances involved skipping the length of the room, switching partners, hopping, and leaping. As it was, there was much bumping and hilarity. Most contact was accidental— though Jake's tripping over Percy's foot might have been intentional.

Throughout the evening they changed partners. Ernest proved to be a good dancer, considerate of her toes and not overly chatty as they passed each other. Imogene found this informal manner of dancing far more to her taste than the elegant balls of London, where every move and every partner was scrutinized by the tittle-tattle Ton. Here, those watching wore indulgent expressions and participated in the levity, if at a distance.

It was good to see Mr. Tabard smile, a rarity since the passing of Cousin Clara. Tonight the old gentleman grinned broadly as Jake danced in circles around Emily—perhaps he was remembering the days when Cousin Clara teased about Jake and

Emily making a match of it. He clapped out of rhythm, stomping his foot one minute, slapping the other gentlemen on the shoulder the next. His loud guffaw echoed throughout the room.

It was good to hear.

In appearance, Jake favored his mother. Mr. Tabard was a reedy figure with an abundance of shoulder-length hair—gray, of course—and a slight stoop. While his son was short and stocky, with an appealing grin—complete with dimples—and mischief in his eyes. Only when their faces were in repose did the similarities of the two gentlemen emerge: the narrow shape of their faces, large noses, thin lips, and the aspect of melancholy.

Partway through the evening Harriet was sent to bed, with protest, leaving an odd number of dancers. The extra gentleman should have waited until the end of each set to take up a partner, but when his turn came, Percy would have none of that. Cutting across the lines, and generally making a nuisance of himself, Percy managed to tangle the company up so thoroughly that the steps were completely confused, and the parents called for a break.

"For Miss Watson's sake, if none other," Mrs. Beeswanger said with a smile. "Perhaps refreshments are a good idea."

Collapsing into a chair, Imogene was quite glad of the rest; while not particularly tired, she was very thirsty. Not surprisingly, Ernest took the seat next to her. Across the room, Emily joined Ben, with Pauline on his other side. Percy and Jake headed out of doors for a breath of fresh air. Imogene thought their departure had more to do with Percy's newly acquired to-bacco pipe and Mama's dislike of smoking.

"The country suits you, Miss . . . Imogene." Ernest smiled down at her.

Feeling her comfort slip away, Imogene straightened, shifted to the edge of her chair, and stared at a painting on the far wall. "Thank you." Would that she could think of something further to say . . . but her tongue did not cooperate.

"Do you enjoy the paintings of Turner?"

"Most certainly." Imogene nodded.

She could hear a *tap-tap* sound and turned to see Ernest's toe bouncing on the floor . . . as if *he* was nervous. Looking up, she met his gaze, briefly, and then she dropped her eyes to his waistcoat—a very nice shade of red with crested buttons . . . dapper. But why was he not talking?

The silence between them continued for some minutes. In the background, Imogene could hear a smattering of Emily's discussion with Ben and parental murmurs from the far end of the room. However, the lack of conversation with Ernest was proceeding to uncomfortable.

Finally, he spoke.

"I would like to apologize, Imogene. I am a fraud."

He sounded so serious, and upset, that Imogene lifted her face to puzzle the matter out. "Whatever do you mean? I . . . beg your pardon . . . but . . ."

"I am not who you think me to be."

Glancing around the room, Imogene met Ben's gaze; he smiled, nodded, and then returned to his conversation with

Emily. She turned back to Ernest. "So you are not Ernest Steeple of Musson House, grandson of Sir Andrew Steeple?" When his expression did not change, she added. "I see. You are, in fact, a vagabond wandering the country—impersonating young gentlemen in order to secure lodging . . . and a dance." This time, Imogene was rewarded for her levity.

Ernest Steeple burst into a loud, rich laugh that brought a smile to everyone in the room—curious looks, as well, but she ignored those.

"No, indeed," Ernest said, catching his breath. "I have been trying so hard to find a subject in which we share an interest that I have represented myself as a gentleman of the arts."

"But you are not?"

"No, in fact, I am. But not painting. I have little to no knowledge of fine art. . . . Ben has been trying to educate me ever since I met you." He took a quick breath. "However, I am interested in literature."

"You are a poet? Or an essayist?"

Another hearty laugh. "Would that I were. No, I'm afraid it is much worse than that. . . . I am a reader. Nothing that I like better than quiet days of contemplation and the written word." He breathed deeply through his nose and then sighed. "I realized that I wasn't being fair. If we are to know if we suit, I have to be honest. So the truth is now before you. I will no longer maintain the facade of being an art aficionado." He stared at her for a moment, the corner of his mouth lifting in a quirky—rather appealing—smile. "Please tell me that you have done the same. It will make me feel so much better about my deception."

Imogene frowned ever so slightly. She was confused. Staring into the eyes of Ernest Steeple, she felt her heart stir; this young gentleman might not be a charmer, as was his brother, but that did not make him any less engaging. It was merely a different sort of charm. Ernest's allure was not flashy but understated and gentle.

"I have indeed been cutting shams, Ernest." It was the first time that she had used his name comfortably. "I cannot say if I enjoy the paintings of Turner . . . as I have seen only *one*." Again, Imogene was rewarded for her sauciness by a broad grin. She thought she might enjoy getting to know Ernest, after all. She appreciated his honesty, and his laugh was rather captivating.

THE NEXT MORNING, Ben stood at the bottom of the main staircase, leaning on the newel post, trying to look casual. Sawyer had walked by several times, eyeing him with speculation, but said nothing. Campbell's book *The British Architect—Volume Two* was not providing the distraction he needed as he pulled out his pocket watch every few minutes to check the time. Harriet had come down from her lesson a full quarter hour earlier, and yet there was still no sign of Imogene.

"Steady on," Ernest said without looking up from his own book. He was relaxing with the historical novel *Waverly* in the sitting area by the window. The large entrance doubled as a reading room.

"Easy for you to say. . . . You are not going to expose your darkest secret."

"No, I did that yesterday."

"Hardly. Admitting that you know nothing of art doesn't qualify. Perhaps if you had told Imogene that you snore, then that might—"

"I do *not* snore." Ernest's protest was mild. He sighed and continued to read.

"Who snores?"

Ben turned to find Imogene standing on the landing looking down at them with curiosity.

"No one. No one. Just giving Ernest a hard time, is all. Yes indeed, that's all."

"Brotherly banter, then?"

"Yes. Indeed." Ben shifted to stand out of the way—closer to the unlit fireplace, no, a little more toward the hall, yes, there. Perfect. He lifted his chin and realized that Imogene had descended and was now watching him from a distance of a mere six or seven feet.

"Is anything amiss?"

"Yes, I mean, no. Might I have a word with you?" Without allowing her time to decline, Ben gestured to the empty chair opposite Ernest. Once she was seated, Ben lowered himself onto the cushioned window seat between them.

This was the best arrangement. All seats were occupied,

discouraging others from joining them and . . . and he could head for the door if he felt the sudden urge to flee.

"Are you quite all right?" Imogene looked genuinely concerned.

"Not entirely." Ben shook his head, surprised that this conversation was proving to be so difficult. "Since I was a child . . . No, that might be going back too far. When Lord Penton took me on . . ." Scrubbing at his face, Ben pursed his lips for a moment and began again. "I was hoping that I might solicit your help."

"Of course."

"You don't know to what I am referring yet."

"Indeed not, for you are being rather enigmatic; however, if there is something that I can do that would assist you, then of course you can count on me."

"Told you," Ernest said, looking over his book at the two of them.

Imogene sniffed a laugh and turned back to Ben. "Apparently, Ernest told you that would be the case. So perhaps you might now enlighten me about my role."

Ben smiled back, feeling a modicum of tension drain from his shoulders. "It is a familiar role for you." He sat up straighter and took a deep breath, preparing to let it all spill out—to get it over with. "Might you be prevailed upon to take on a new art student?"

"Gladly. Teaching is a pleasure."

"Excellent. Then might I ask you to teach *me* to draw?" Ben held his breath. He stared at her, waiting for Imogene's eyes to cloud over, censure to change her expression, ridicule . . . mockery . . .

"Of course."

Ben blinked, certain it could not be that easy. "I want nothing more in life than to be an architect. But one has to have some ability to render if one is to be a success."

"Of course."

Ben frowned at her smile and continued to explain. "When Lord Penton took me on, I was not entirely honest. I indicated to him that I had some talent."

"You out-and-out lied, Ben," Ernest said unhelpfully.

"Yes, well, there might have been a little prevarication." Ben glared at his brother, who glared back in silence. "Fine. I offered a bouncer."

Ernest lifted his brow at Imogene. "He lied."

Imogene nodded and then turned back to stare at Ben, considering for some minutes.

As expected, her expression began to change. But not in the direction that Ben anticipated—not censure but calculation, not ridicule but understanding, not mockery but concern.

"It will take a considerable amount of practice," she said at last. "I can help you in the time we have, but, Ben, you will not be able to create a masterpiece in a day . . . or a week . . . or even by the end of the summer, for that matter."

"I don't need to create a masterpiece—not this year, at least. I need to be able to sketch various elements of a building. Small pieces. A cornerstone. A cornice. A sill or a doorway. Up until now, I have written out descriptions. . . . And Lord Penton has noticed."

"Ben's previous drawing teachers were talented in landscapes, seascapes . . . you know, vistas. They did not—could not—concentrate on architectural details," Ernest explained.

Imogene smiled. It was a beautiful sight, offering hope. "My forte."

"Exactly," Ernest and Ben said together.

"And you would prefer word not get back to Lord Penton."

"Exactly . . . or at least not get back to him until I can demonstrate *some* skill. Not a secret *per se* . . ."

Imogene's gaze shifted to the window behind him. "It would be too apparent were you to join Harriet. . . . But I often sketch at the old castle. . . . And you were asked to oversee the repairs. Yes, that might suit." She turned to Ernest. "Would you care to join us?"

"If you don't mind. I will bring my book and not disturb you."

Ben watched as Imogene smiled shyly at Ernest and felt a twinge of the oddest sensation. Had he not known better, he might have called it jealousy.

THE AFTERNOON PROVED IDYLLIC. There were just enough clouds to offer interesting shadows; it was not too hot to make them uncomfortable but hot enough to discourage flies. The scent of flowers wafted on the breeze, and the elm offered shade and cover. Hence, no distractions—save one.

Jasper.

Ben had arrived first at the rendezvous point on the hill overlooking the castle, waiting anxiously. Now that the worst was over, in regard to revealing his lack of talent, Ben could concentrate on the process . . . and worry instead about whether he would *ever* be able to draw adequately. Imogene had joined him shortly thereafter with paper and graphite pencils.

They were discussing Ben's first subject when Ernest arrived with Jasper. It was a masterful stroke. Imogene was quite distracted—completely forgetting to be uncomfortable in his presence. In fact, she was so pleased to see that Jasper was improving—if somewhat less bouncy—that she treated Ernest as if he had had something to do with Jasper's recovery, when, in fact, all he had done was release the dog from his compound and lead him to Imogene. Ernest had done just as Ben had suggested—found a way to look heroic in Imogene's eyes.

It was most irritating.

"But it's just a rock." Ben looked at the gray form that Imogene had placed in front of him.

"You have to start somewhere. And I need to know what you can do." She widened her eyes and pointed, looking quite owlish. "Draw!"

"Easy for you to say."

"Draw!"

Ben grumbled under his breath but set to work.

At first, the indistinct mass looked entirely like a nameless shape . . . until Imogene showed him that one side of the rock was pointed, that there was a shadow in the sun's lee, and that it was rough on top. The more she pointed out, the more the shape became a rock, and Ben started to understand why Imogene kept saying, "See, don't look."

He had no idea how long they sat under the tree focused on the bloody rock, but when he eventually lifted his head, Ernest and Jasper were asleep, both snoring softly. Imogene, however, stared at him with a gentle smile—though he did not understand why.

He frowned his question.

Wordlessly, she lifted his paper from his knee and held it up.

There it was—a rock. The drawing would not win any awards, but without a doubt a rock in shape and definition.

"Success," he said, causing Ernest to stir and mumble in his sleep. "Success," he said again, this time in a whisper.

"Yes." Imogene looked proud.

And then he frowned. It had taken him hours and a lot of intervention from his teacher to draw a simple object. A simple, irregular object. Nothing even remotely as complex as a cornice, let alone as intricate as the chimneypiece in Imogene's studio. He sighed.

"This is going to take a long time."

Imogene's smile faded slightly until it took on a wistful appearance. "I'm afraid so."

STANDING THE SKETCH against the glass above the window seat in his bedroom, Ben stood back to stare at it. He was pleased, too much so. Really . . . it was just a rock.

"Lovely, sir," Matt said, entering the room. He had Ben's evening waistcoat and fresh neck-cloth in hand. "A bird, right?"

Incensed, Ben whirled around to see the amusement in Matt's eyes. "No, indeed," Ben replied loftily. "It's a glen, with children playing in the grass. Here we have a little boy"—he pointed at the rock's shadow—"teasing his sisters while a horse runs through the background. It's all symbolic."

"Symbolic for a bag of moonshine?" Matt asked, trying to maintain a serious expression—with little success. He placed his load carefully on the bed and then opened the wardrobe door. "Do you wish to change your watch this evening? Perhaps the silver fob—" He lifted a chain out of the small box that housed Ben's pocket watches, fobs, and rings, but it caught on the edge and tumbled from his grasp. Bending to pick it up, Matt said with a muffled voice, "What's this?" He rummaged behind the leg of the wardrobe. He stood and then glanced over his shoulder at Ben.

Ben met his quizzical gaze. "Is something amiss?"

"I'm not entirely sure. Though I am surprised that you are in possession of a lady's necklace." Matt turned with the silver fob in one hand, a topaz necklace in the other.

Recognizing it as the one that Imogene wore on the evening of their arrival, Ben stepped forward, taking it gingerly. "Odd. It belongs to Miss Imogene." He frowned down at the pendant, trying to understand how it came to be in his room. And why.

"To say the least, sir."

Ben looked up. "Pardon?"

"Odd. And dangerous."

Ben snorted and then realized that Matt was in earnest.

"Why would you say dangerous?"

"If the housemaid found it here . . . in your room, where it has no business . . . it would look like thievery. Or that Miss Imogene . . . well, you know . . . visited."

"Matt!"

"Exactly so, sir. You now understand my concern."

"Indeed." He continued to stare at it for some minutes. Then he shifted closer to his evening coat, which hung over the desk chair, and dropped the necklace into the pocket. "I'll give it back to Miss Imogene this evening." He wanted it out of his possession as soon as possible.

Matt nodded and turned back toward the wardrobe, but not before Ben saw that the valet's frown had deepened.

"This will not fall on you. I will make sure of that." Ben watched Matt nod, though the man did not turn around. "I suspect this is yet another lark by a couple of mischief makers. They are likely unaware of the repercussions. Tomfoolery is all."

Despite his words, Ben was certain the two troublemakers he had in mind would know exactly what the accusation of thievery would do to Ben's reputation. He would be asked to leave forthwith, and likely Ernest would be given the boot as well. This was not the work of a couple of rascals—this was spiteful.

chapter 6

*In which the words "dreadful" and "secret"
are bandied about*

"You are so very clever, Imogene. That will do very nicely.
Pending parental approval, of course, but it will certainly
do the trick. Especially since we have been forbidden to cross
the bridge to the old castle until the work is complete. Clever,
clever girl."

Imogene shifted her gaze from her own reflection in the
looking glass to that of Emily, who was standing behind her.
"Clever?" Imogene laughed. "Not the usual description of my
character."

"Only by those who know you not. I would never omit such
an obvious trait."

Kate's grin and nod brought Imogene's eyes back to the
maid, who was combing out her hair, preparing to twist it into

an upsweep. Imogene watched Kate work out the tangle of knots formed during a restless night of tossing and turning.

"Well, I have yet to put the idea to the boys. It might not be to their liking . . . or other plans might have been made."

"Last night, I believe I overheard your father suggest a visit to the oast house. He seemed to think Ernest would be interested in the process of drying hops. I did not discern *any* enthusiasm."

"Oh dear. I'm sure a picnic by the abbey will be more to his taste . . . their taste. Especially since the weather is being so obliging. Ben can examine the ruins and Ernest can—"

"Make calf-eyes at you without any interference."

"Really, Emily, I am nervous enough in his presence without—Oh." Imogene frowned on recollection of the previous evening: the easy manner of their conversation about Sir Walter Scott, his rich laugh when Pauline suggested that he try his hand at playing the bagpipes, and the way in which he included Harriet in their discourse. "Strange."

"What's strange?"

"Hmm? Oh, I beg your pardon. I just realized that I am far more comfortable with both the Steeple boys than I ever would suppose after such a short acquaintance."

"I think everyone noticed."

There was an edge to Emily's comment that Imogene didn't quite understand. "Did they?"

"If I didn't know you better, I would think that you were trifling with Benjamin as well as Ernest."

"Oh, Emily, that is nonsense."

"Yes. I know it is. . . . But something was going on, Imogene. Benjamin kept looking at you, trying to get your attention. And then, after dinner, he sat next to you . . . and passed you something."

Imogene sighed deeply. "Yes. I'm not really sure what to do about that. Percy and Jake have been up to their usual tricks, but this cuts a little too close to the bone. Ben found my topaz necklace in his room. I didn't even know it had gone astray until he handed it to me."

"Wonderful! I knew you wouldn't flirt. . . . I mean, that's terrible!"

"I quite agree. Father would not have looked favorably on Ben at all had he known of it. Would have assumed the worst and had Sawyer see him to the door. It would have been a horrid scene." Shifting her gaze back to her friend, Imogene noted Emily's tight lips. "I can talk to Percy, but there is no reasoning with Jake. He's much worse since . . ."

"Since Cousin Clara died. Yes, there is a nasty look in his eye these days. As if he is greatly irritated by the entire world. Should I speak to Mr. Tabard?" Emily asked. "Although, I'm not certain the old gentleman is quite right yet, either."

"I'll try my brother first."

"It will do no good. He listens only to your father."

"Too true." Imogene met Kate's eyes in the looking glass as she sighed. "Idle young men, Kate, a breed unto themselves."

"Too true." Kate nodded solemnly.

The morning proceeded much as expected. Despite asking Sawyer and Greg, and sending Roger to the stables, neither Percy nor Jake was located, and Imogene was forced to defer her discussion about the topaz necklace until later. However, Ernest and Ben were far less elusive. They were sitting in the dining room, noses in the newspaper and coffee at their elbows. It was almost as if they had been waiting for Imogene and Emily to break their fast.

"Mr. Chively had a dispatch from the bank earlier this morning," Ernest said as he folded *The Times* and set it aside. "It will tie him up for a good part of the day." This was not said with any inflection of disappointment.

"Oh, that is unfortunate," Emily said with a big smile turned toward Ben, who was peeking over his newspaper. "It will be up to us to keep you busy, then. And it just so happens that we have a splendid idea."

Little convincing was required. Ernest and Ben were kindly disposed toward the idea of setting out on a picnic after Harriet's lesson. Carden Abbey, it was agreed, would make a *splendid* destination; the Beeswanger landau was chosen as the vehicle to take them the four miles past the village; and Emily offered to arrange the baskets while Imogene was busy in her studio. It was implied, though not stated, that in seeking the use of the family carriage, Emily would also obtain the necessary parental approval. One set of parents would do. Emily would avoid Imogene's mother and father; they were seldom amenable to anything they had not conceived.

THE FOUR SET off on their adventure just after the strike of twelve. Mr. Fowler needed little in the way of direction. He had been coachman for the Beeswangers for some years and knew the roads around Fotheringham well. Two large baskets of foodstuffs—along with a smaller one for Mr. Fowler—were strapped to the back, as well as a satchel of art supplies.

As they rolled along, Imogene rehearsed various scenarios in her mind of how she and Ben might continue their drawing lessons unbeknownst to Emily. Most involved subterfuge or misdirection, but all leaned heavily on prevarication. She and Emily had shared confidences since childhood, and not doing so now felt wrong. Still, it was not her confidence to reveal. However, all her anxiety proved to be pointless—as most anxiety usually does.

With the boys facing the girls and the carriage hoods folded back so they might all enjoy the cooling breeze, conversation was, at first, very general. They discussed the abbey's history, the various shops in Fotheringham, and the conviviality of the day. Then Ben took the bull by the horns.

"Now that we have you away from the house, Emily, we must swear you to secrecy." Ben's tone was light, almost playful.

Imogene wondered if he was going to mention something other than his inability to draw. Gone was yesterday's discomfort—hardly any hesitance.

As expected, Emily looked puzzled. She turned toward Imogene, an unspoken question in her eyes. Imogene smiled wanly and looked back at Ben, waiting.

"Our picnic is going to include drawing lessons."

"Oh." Emily's expression was less than pleased.

"Indeed," Ben continued. "My skills are not what I would like them to be. Imogene has offered to help."

"Goodness." Emily laughed a sigh. "Such a relief. I thought for a moment that you were going to suggest that we all partic-ipate. I must assure you, I have no talent, no talent at all." She looked over at Imogene, touched her arm, and then turned back to Ben. "What is the secret? I will swear. . . . But I must know what it is about before I do so."

Ben laughed. "That was it, Miss Emily. The secret is that Imogene is to be my teacher."

Emily shook her head and shrugged at the same time. She was clearly confused. "So it is no *great* secret, then."

Ben laughed again. "Apparently not."

With a sigh of her own relief, Imogene nodded. It was evi-dent that Emily did not understand the significance of an ap-prentice architect not being able to draw. . . . And Imogene was not going to enlighten her. But the path was now clear—the lessons could continue with impunity.

"Yes, that's very nice." Emily leaned across the blanket for a closer look at Ben's sketch, bringing her shoulder in contact with Ben's. She tapped her fan on his paper, hummed her approval, and then turned her head to look up at him. Their faces were mere inches apart. "Beautiful," she said, taking a deep breath, trying to look up at him through her lashes.

Flirtation at its finest.

Imogene wondered if she should take notes.

"Thank you. Almost done." Ben shifted the paper out from under Emily's fan. He continued to frown, adding an additional line here and there. "Imogene, there is a problem. The edge is not clear, and the ivy . . . well, it looks more like . . ."

"Cracks." Emily nodded, unaware of the insult.

Ben cleared his throat. "Yes, apparently the ivy looks like cracks."

"But very nice cracks," Emily clarified.

"Indeed. My ivy has the appearance of very nice cracks." He gave Imogene a long-suffering look.

Imogene chuckled, setting her own sketch aside and leaning across from the other direction—without touching Ben's shoulder or batting her eyelashes.

They were lounging in the shadowed grass next to what used to be the chapter house of Carden Abbey. It was a ruin now, abandoned during the Dissolution of the Monasteries in the sixteenth century. Many of the stones had been carted away over the years until all that remained were the arches of the cathedral and parts of the monks' meeting room.

Ben was attempting to draw one corner of the room. Ivy had grown up and over the half wall, creating a lovely tableau that had appealed to Ben immediately. Imogene had suggested something simpler or even a portion of the wall; that would be more in keeping with his present skill level . . . but—well . . .

"This is dreadful!"

Imogene straightened and caught the paper, with its accompanying board, just as Ben attempted to pitch it into the grass.

"It is not dreadful," she said as she righted it and then studied the sketch. Not dreadful but quite grim. Ben had overworked the piece to the point that it was a mass of gray lines with no definition. "Merely indistinct," she added. And the scale was off-kilter, too, but she would deal with that at a later date. "An easy fix. Watch." With a few deft strokes—darker strokes—the wall gained dimension—though there was little she could do with the ivy.

Ben huffed a sigh. "Yes, that's better—but . . . I will listen to you next time. Something simpler."

Imogene nodded. "You can't run before you can walk."

"Speaking of walking, can we?" Emily's expression was bright and hopeful. She shifted as if she were about to rise. "I am stiff from sitting overlong and would so enjoy a little stroll around the abbey." She winked at Imogene while she reached for her parasol.

With a nod, Ben untangled his long limbs, stood, stretched, and then offered Emily a hand up. "Shall we?" he asked like a true gallant. Once he got Emily to her feet, Ben pulled her arm through the crook of his, and they set off across the grass.

"And you?" Ernest inquired. Unlike the rest of the company, he had relaxed in the sun—under a wide-brimmed hat, of course. Sitting on the ruined wall nearest the group, Ernest had a placid expression as he swatted languidly at a pestering insect. As usual, he had brought a book. "Would you care for a meander?"

Glancing down at her unfinished sketch, Imogene hesitated. She seldom left her work incomplete, and yet the prospect of a stretch held enough appeal that she looked around for her parasol, too.

Soon they were arm in arm, swaying in unison at an easy gait. They took the path opposite the one Ben and Emily had chosen, and so for a time the couples were out of each other's sight. It would have caused shock and consternation had Mama been aware of this little breach, but Imogene had no intention of informing either of her parents.

Chatting comfortably, Imogene was quite content, and she tried to imagine what it would be like to be married to this kind, handsome young man. Ernest was all that she had ever imagined in a husband: quiet, calm, and while not actively interested in her art, he did not dismiss it as worthless, either. He had the approval of her father, which was a major accomplishment in itself, and most important, there seemed to be great affection in his eyes when he looked her way. She felt comfortable in his presence, which was a surprise. While she let him carry the weight of the conversation, she could comment without nervousness and self-doubt. Yes, it was all very pleasant.

Then, as they rounded the arch leading to what had been the nave, the sight of Emily laughing and Ben smiling—oblivious to all but each other—gave Imogene pause. Her belly clenched, and she felt a sudden need to turn away. Lifting her gaze back to Ernest, she concentrated on his mouth and his delivery of a Lord Byron poem. Imogene knew "She Walks in Beauty" well enough, and by focusing on each individual word, she found the strength to push back the distress that threatened to overwhelm her sensibilities.

It took some minutes for Imogene to recover her equilibrium and bury her yearning. When she did, Imogene turned her head again toward Emily and Ben, noting her friend's high color, her broad grin, and the way she leaned closer than was likely considered proper. Imogene smiled, happy for her friend. And if the tableau blurred a little with unshed tears, she would blame the brightness of the sun.

"MIGHT I SPEAK to you, Percy?" Imogene asked while reaching for her brother's arm, giving him no chance to refuse. She had dressed quickly for dinner and rushed to the bottom of the main staircase so that she might have this very conversation. She could hardly allow him to escape at this juncture. Naturally, Percy complied, though Jake, who was at his elbow, thought the invitation included him, which it did not. Still, she could hardly quibble.

The trio stepped out of the way in the event that others might wish to continue down the corridor toward the grand saloon and the predinner gathering. They stood in front of the large unlit hearth in a loose triangle. The boys' eyes sparkled as if anticipating a laugh; Percy and Jake seldom took Imogene's frustrations seriously.

"What do you think of my pendant?" she asked with no preamble. Imogene had worn the topaz necklace as an accusation and to show the miscreant the failure of his lark.

Percy's foolish grin faded, and his mouth curled in distaste. "Really, Imogene, what a boring topic. I have never thought it particularly attractive."

"Yes, but are you not surprised that it is once again in my possession?"

"Hardly. Who would want to borrow such a thing?"

Jake snorted in support of his friend and, though he said nothing, made it plain he thought Imogene one of the silliest girls in Kent.

"No one *borrowed* it," Imogene snapped.

"There, see? I said as much. Not even worthy of a conversation . . . so why are we talking about it?"

Imogene glared at her brother to little effect. "Then you had nothing to do with my pendant vacating my jewelry case and hiding in another room?"

"Nothing at all. What would be the fun in that?"

And with those words, Percy and Jake looked at each other, shrugged, and left Imogene standing by the fireplace unable to answer his question.

"Are you well, my dear?"

Imogene turned her frown toward the first step of the staircase. "Yes, of course, Mr. Tabard," she said before realizing that her folded brow told a different story. She took a deep breath and adopted a calm demeanor.

"Were Jake and Percy giving you a hard time?" Mr. Tabard puckered his lips, likely trying to adopt the disapproving appearance of Cousin Clara, who had always been the one to rein Jake in.

"No, no. I'm just having trouble understanding something. I'm rather puzzled."

With a sigh and a nod, Mr. Tabard offered his arm, and they strolled down the hallway. "Life *is* a puzzle, my dear," he said in a blousy tone. "Or so your cousin used to say. Puzzling and unpredictable, and needs a steady hand at the helm." He patted the top of Imogene's hand as they approached the grand saloon. "So very glad to know that Jake was not the cause of your confusion. Yes, good to know. Clara would have been terribly disappointed."

Imogene's frown returned unbidden. "Indeed, she could not abide malice. . . . Percy and Jake's antics are seldom *purposefully* cruel."

That was the difficulty. For when she considered the theft, she no longer saw the stamp of two young men intent on mischief. The incident did not offer any amusement. No, the accusations that could have followed would have been serious, with far-reaching consequences. Even if Percy and Jake had taken a dislike to Ben or Ernest, to see one of the Steeples falsely accused would be out of character. The blame could also have been laid at their valet's doorstep . . . or Kate's . . . or the housemaids'. It would have meant dismissal and an upheaval downstairs. No, this was not a prank of the same sort as a spider in her bed, a dousing, or teasing the dogs.

But if Percy and Jake were not the instigators of the theft, then who was?

It was a question that occupied Imogene for a majority of the evening—certainly from the soup to the jellies. Ernest tried to draw her out with a conversation about the abbey, which was a brief diversion from her troubled thoughts. But unfortunately, as soon as the beauty of the day, Carden Abbey, the countryside, and the horses had been exhausted, Imogene's mind doggedly returned to the puzzle.

Who had stolen her topaz necklace, and why had it been in Ben's room?

chapter 7

In which a question about <u>the</u> question is questioned

"Is today the day?" Ben asked Ernest as they waited in the yard for the carriage to be brought around. It was too fine a day to linger indoors: warm with a fragrant breeze, layers of clouds playing with the sun. This was the fifth dry day in a row; it would have been a miracle in Chotsdown, where Musson House hunkered on the coast.

"The day for what?"

"Toad! What is the purpose of this visit—all this excessive civility? Is today the day you ask Imogene to marry you?"

Ernest shifted his balance and turned to stare at the sky above the stables. "That's a rather personal question."

"You are hedging. I take it to mean the answer is *no*." Ben shook his head in disbelief, and he considered offering Ernest a snarl, but his brother was still staring at nothing. The effort would have been wasted.

"Haste is not necessary."

"Not necessary? Brother dear, we are off in two days. You are running out of time." Ben watched Ernest shift again. "Feeling uncertain?"

"I believe that Imogene is not quite ready. We have only begun to know each other."

"Have *you* changed your mind?"

Ernest's head snapped around, and he frowned at Ben. "How can you even suggest such inconstancy? You know me better than that."

"Well, you better get a wiggle on." Ben held up his hand, waving two fingers in front of Ernest's face. "If you don't, you will have to wait until the Chivelys return to London in the autumn. Someone else may push you to the back of the line by then." His words were meant as a jest, but Ernest didn't smile. "Though it's unlikely," he added lamely.

"I have decided to wait a little while longer." Ernest nodded, agreeing with himself.

Ben huffed in frustration. Ernest had never rushed toward change. In fact, when his brother had become suddenly enamored with the shy Imogene Chively in London, Ben had thought that Ernest had overcome his aversion to impulsiveness. Accepting the invitation to dwell among strangers, even if only for a seven-night, he thought to be a sign of Ernest's tremendous attachment. . . . But now he hesitated.

"Well, you might get permission to write. Her parents

should be amenable. And your prose is quite eloquent in a blousy, boring sort of manner."

"Thanks ever so."

"Still, it will probably impress your lady-fair and give Imogene . . . and you . . . the time—"

"No need." Ernest's expression lightened—with a decided twinkle to his eye. It usually spelled trouble.

"Oh Lud. What have you done?" Looking across the yard, Ben watched a chicken round the stable corner. Where was the coach . . . or the ladies, for that matter?

"I have accepted an invitation."

Another chicken joined the first, and they set about scratching in the dirt.

"Have I accepted, as well?" Ben could finally hear the clop of hooves on cobblestone. The landau would soon follow the chickens.

"Most certainly. You were very pleased to accept."

"Was I, indeed?" Ben harrumphed, returning his gaze to his brother. "You realize, Ernest, that I cannot traipse after you all summer. I have my own pursuits."

"Of course, but this fits in handsomely with your plans."

"Does it?" He waited, hoping to be convinced—since it would seem he had little choice in the matter.

"Yes. The Beeswangers have asked us to join the company at Shackleford Park. Apparently, all are to Tishdale within a fortnight. This visiting back and forth over the summer is a decades-old tradition."

"Yes, I had heard something in that order." Ben tried to

maintain his glower. He did not want Ernest to know that he actually did approve of the idea. Not only would Ben get a chance to appreciate the architecture of the Park, but Imogene could also continue his drawing lessons. It would do rather nicely.

"That will give me more time to ready."

Ben laughed. "To ready yourself or Imogene?"

"Both, I imagine."

Ben continued to chuckle as the door at their backs squeaked open.

"Ah, there you are," Emily said as she and Imogene stepped across the threshold. She was pulling on a pair of soft yellow gloves that matched her gown and the ribbon in her bonnet. Imogene was dressed in blue—a light sky sort of blue . . . that had an identifying name that eluded him. "Cerulean?" he asked, pointing to her skirts.

She smiled. "Azure."

Emily glanced up at Ernest with a lifted brow—either puzzled or surprised—and ignored the exchange. "I'm afraid Pauline and Harriet have decided they are not interested in the view from Foxhill after all. So once again, it will be just the four of us." She tried to turn down the corners of her mouth as if she were disappointed but was less than successful.

"That's a shame," Ben said without conviction. "The girls had seemed quite taken with the idea at luncheon."

"Yes, well, Mama thought that a little shopping in Fotheringham was more to their taste." Emily tipped her head to the side, offering Ben a saucy grin. "The offer of sweets and new ribbons can quickly change one's mind about a lovely vista."

Ernest laughed. "Indeed."

During this exchange, Mr. Fowler had pulled the carriage to a neat stop in front of the group, alit, and come round to help his passengers into the landau. He waited patiently beside the stepping-block, doing his best to appear unaware of the conversation.

Ernest nodded a thank-you to the elderly coachman, offering to hand up the ladies in his stead. Emily was seated easily enough, but Imogene required more attention. Well, not really, but Ernest made a process of the deed—almost ceremonial.

Taking her left hand in his, Ernest cupped Imogene's elbow with his right. He led her to the carriage and provided support as she negotiated the tremendous height to the block, and then onto the step and into the vehicle. Unfortunately, his hold was a tad overlong; she had to turn around and ask Ernest to release her. She stared at her hand with what appeared to be a troubled expression for some moments—standing across the threshold—until Emily called, breaking into Imogene's thoughts.

It did not bode well.

By the time they were all seated comfortably, Imogene's color had receded from the bright red of embarrassment and Ernest had no idea that he had caused Imogene any anxiety. Ben understood Ernest's desire to touch Imogene—opportunities were few and far between—but he had done himself a disservice.

Ben sighed inwardly as the carriage rolled through the Gracebridge gates and out onto the main road. Perhaps Ernest had the right of it: Imogene was not yet ready to accept his proposal of marriage, and Ernest was not yet ready to ask. Ben did his best not to be pleased with this realization, and he refrained from considering why that might be so.

IMOGENE STARED AT her hand, aware that she should be involved in the discourse about the passing scenery, but she was unable to join the trivialities. She was instead locked into a loop of unanswerable questions.

When Imogene had dressed for the outing, she had chosen to adorn her gloves with her turquoise ring—a little accent of blue-green. As a gift from her grandmother, the finely worked silver and stone held tremendous sentimental value. . . . But now that she thought upon it, it had monetary value as well.

"Would you say topaz or turquoise more precious?" Imogene turned to Emily beside her, interrupting her friend's observation that the buttercups were particularly yellow this year.

For several minutes, the only sounds in the carriage were the crunch of the wheels on the road and the clop of the horses' hooves. Emily blinked, frowned slightly, and glanced to the other side of the vehicle, where the Steeple brothers were seated.

"I'm not entirely certain," she said. Though it was clear Emily was not certain about the question, either.

Following her friend's gaze, Imogene observed that Ernest and Ben were looking at her as if her conversation was odd . . .

which it was since they were not privy to her thoughts. And yet, even as she watched, Ben glanced down at her ring and nodded—clearly perceiving the source of her non sequitur.

"If I were to hazard a guess, I might say the turquoise." Ben nodded in the direction of her hand.

"And that is relevant in what manner?" Emily asked.

"Ah yes." This time it was Ernest who nodded. "Yes, why would a thief take a topaz necklace when there was a turquoise ring sitting next to it?" It was clear that Ben had shared the incident with his brother, as Imogene had done with Emily.

"Or both?" Ben observed. "It was but a moment's work—no need to choose one over the other. Both would have brought the thief some reward."

"Or the entire box, for that matter." Emily touched Imogene's skirts to garner her attention. "Your jewelry case is not large, it could easily fit beneath a coat . . . or in a reticule. And my case was in the same room—a different drawer, but to a thief, what is that?"

"Exactly," Ben said. "And yet this person took only the topaz necklace. And then after going to the effort, dropped it in my room. A very inept thief, to my way of thinking. Are we quite certain this was not a prank?"

Imogene appreciated Ben's avoiding her brother's name outright, but it was clear to all to whom he referred.

"I cannot be sure, but Percy's protest rang true. He and Jake derive their amusement from watching the discomfort of others—not kind, very immature, and incredibly irritating—but . . ."

"Might they not have found amusement when I was accused of theft?"

"Too far, even for Percy and Jake."

Ben lifted his brows. "Really?"

"You are not convinced." Imogene sighed. Unfortunately, she could not defend her brother any more than she already had; she was doubtful as well. She was going to have to make further inquiries downstairs. Silent and often ignored by the unwise, one of the housemaids might have seen someone in the vicinity of her room, someone who had no business there. She could but hope it was Percy; a nasty practical joke was preferable to thinking a thief, or worse, was in their midst.

The journey to Foxhill was not onerous to the passengers; a mere half hour took them to the base of the *mountain* and an additional quarter hour saw them wind back and forth to the top. The horses, however, were tired and glad of the rest. Mr. Fowler had wisely brought feed bags and led them to a small pond, where they could drink and enjoy the shade.

Arm in arm, the two couples crossed the open meadow and approached the precipice. Emily swayed her skirts as she walked, twirling her parasol ever so slightly; she leaned in Ben's direction. Imogene followed with Ernest at a respectable distance. Her skirts did not sway. Imogene had no idea how to— perhaps longer steps . . .

"Oh dear," Imogene gasped as she tripped, glad to have Ernest's arm for support. Pitching over the cliff would have put a decided damper on the day.

"Careful," he said kindly, offering her a wink.

Imogene tried not to blush and stared after Emily and Ben once again. She did her best to ignore the bright smile Ben offered Emily as they chatted quietly. Emily laughed, and Imogene swallowed in discomfort, changing her focus to the glorious view.

Now standing ten feet or so from the edge, Imogene marveled, as she always did, at the distance that could be seen. While the angle did not offer a bird's-eye view of Gracebridge, the church steeples of Fotheringham and—off to the south—the oast houses of Cuppard were clearly visible.

The patchwork of fields, hedges, and lanes inspired, and Imogene felt a yearning to commit the scene to canvas—which she had not brought. It had been a conscious decision not to do so. She could hardly stand there painting while requiring Ben to sketch his next lesson. His frustration would have sapped him of his creativity. Hardly helpful.

"It's a child's block," Ben growled, as Imogene had expected.

"Three actually," Imogene said as she pulled two more from her satchel and laid them on the blanket. They were seated, as they had been the day before, Ben sharing the blanket with Emily and Imogene. Ernest lay in the grass on his side, slightly set off from the group, reading.

"You would do well to stop arguing with your teacher, Ben. She knows what she is about." Ernest's eyes never strayed from his book.

Ben harrumphed and then caught Imogene's watchful

expression and laughed. "Thank you, Miss Chively. I would love to draw three children's blocks. Let me see, we have *R*, *T*, and *A*." He laid them out so they formed the word *rat*.

"Harder than you might think. This is the beginning of perspective." She rearranged the blocks to spell *art*.

"Have I jumped ahead of Hardly Harriet?"

"You have indeed." Imogene laughed and then glanced at Emily's speculative frown. "It's your fault," Imogene explained. "You introduced your sister as Hardly Harriet, remember?"

"Yes, of course. That was not the reason—never mind." Emily shook her head at some inner thought, shrugged, and then shook her head again. "I think I will give it a try as well. Drawing, that is. As I have said before, I have no ability. . . . But it might prove to be amusing. Do you have enough supplies?"

"Of course." Imogene reached back into her satchel. "Would you care to join us, too, Ernest?"

"No, no. It would be a prodigious waste of time."

"Read to us then, old man," Ben said in a commanding manner. "Entertain us while we work."

Ernest offered an impish smile. The reason was apparent when he began to read.

"Lud, Ernest! Byron?" Ben rolled his eyes. "You are reading Byron?"

"Shall I continue?" Ernest asked, turning his wide-eyed, innocent look upon Imogene.

"Absolutely." Imogene laughed again, agreeing as much to please Ernest as to irritate Ben. Though she had no idea why that thought was so appealing.

As expected, Emily's aptitude was poor at best, and she made herself more of a distraction to Ben than a fellow student. Imogene listened to their playful banter, glanced at Ernest— who had lapsed into silence after reading only a page or two to the company—and watched the clouds roll in. At first, the layers of cumulonimbus occasionally hid the sun, but as they grew in number and the temperature dropped, Imogene knew they were in for a storm. Her suggestion that they head back to Gracebridge *tout suite* required little persuasion when a distant rumble echoed across the fields.

Heading down the hill proved to be more difficult than going up, as the horses were skittish. Walking beside the carriage may not have eased the nerves of the bay geldings, but it made Mr. Fowler—and, in truth, the company—more comfortable. It also delayed them somewhat, so there was now no doubt of the change in weather.

By the time they arrived back at Gracebridge, the wind had begun to bluster in earnest.

"We'll get off at the stables, Mr. Fowler," Imogene suggested to the coachman. "That way you can take care of the horses right away. . . . And I can check on Jasper." None was surprised by her proposal, as she had mentioned a desire to see how Jasper fared at breakfast.

"If you wish, I can take your art satchel inside while you are with Jasper." Emily glanced at Ben. "I'm sure Benjamin would not mind carrying it for me."

Imogene was unclear as to how that meant Emily was taking charge of the drawing supplies, but she refrained from addressing the issue. She nodded and headed for the kennels. "Thank you," she called over her shoulder.

"Ernest, be a good fellow and give Emily a hand with the satchel. I, too, would like to see how Jasper is faring." Ben's voice became louder as he spoke, joining Imogene just as she opened the door to the smaller of the barns.

Imogene did not hear Emily grumble, but she was almost certain that she would have.

Once inside the kennels, Imogene ignored the noisy barking of the hounds, bypassing their enclosure and making her way to the back wall. However, the gate to Jasper's kennel was open, and the St. John's water dog was not within. Worse still, Mr. Marshal did not know where the dog might be.

With a sinking feeling, Imogene stood once again in front of the small barn, looking around. She scanned the inner yard, the active stable, and the fields beyond. She considered calling for Jasper, even though it would have been a breach of decorum, but refrained—temporarily. If Jasper had been let loose, it was likely that he would head to the old castle, her favorite haunt. Calling from the stable yard would be pointless.

And just as they walked past the edge of the stables and Imogene could see across the lawn and down the hill to the ruin, she heard a most welcome sound. A very excited bark.

"Ah, there he is," Imogene said with no little relief.

Ben stood at her side, looking up at the sky; he nodded. "I'll get him. You should get inside before the storm hits." He started down the hill without waiting for an answer. "Your father expressly—"

"Forbade me to visit the old castle. Yes, I know, but this isn't a visit. . . . It concerns Jasper." Lifting her skirts to a height just shy of improper, Imogene rushed to catch up . . . and then passed him. Shouting his protest, Ben raced after her, and the game was on. Not surprisingly, Ben crossed the moat bridge first, though Imogene was not far behind. They stood for some minutes wheezing and trying to catch their breath, merriment in their eyes as they enjoyed the exhilaration of the vigorous exercise. Yes, that was why they continued to stare and smile at each other. No other reason. At all.

"Jasper," Imogene called when she had the breath to do so and the will to look away. The dog continued to bark but still did not put in an appearance.

The castle island was deserted, devoid of workmen. It was likely that Mr. Opine had hustled the crew indoors, out of the impending storm. Heaps of rock sat near the bridge, waiting to be carted away. A lone shovel leaned against the crumbling wall, looking forgotten.

Imogene was impressed by the progress. Over half of the fallen floor had been cleared, and huge beams had been used to brace the leaning wall above it. She wouldn't be banned much longer.

Following the sound of Jasper's barking, Imogene realized the dog had returned to the staircase. How he had done so was a puzzle, as several lengths of lumber had been propped across the arches leading to the great hall. Yet that explained why the dog had not come when he had been called.

"Silly pup, always getting into trouble." Imogene sighed as

she leaned over the top board, squinting at the floor. The line directly to the stairs was dangerously close to the collapse, but if they kept to the wall . . . no, there was no need to take the chance. "It would be safer to go through the castle's south wing and then up the inner tower stairs," Imogene called over her shoulder, trying to be heard above the cacophony of an excited dog and the rumbling thunder. "There's a door to the top landing. I can lead the way."

"The storm will be on us by then," Ben said as he shifted the boards to the side. "You stay here. I'll just run over and get him. I'll be right back."

"No," Imogene shouted as he stepped confidently through the arch. Without a second thought, Imogene jumped forward, grabbing his coat. She pulled back, falling in the process, dragging Ben with her.

Ben grunted in surprise as he fell on top of her and released a stream of words that Imogene had never heard before. "Why in heaven's name did you do that?" he finally asked.

"I apologize," Imogene said, feeling uncomfortable with her ill-considered haste. She pushed against his weight, gasping for breath. "Could. You. Get. Off? Oh, thank you." Struggling to sit and then stand, Imogene accepted Ben's hand as he pulled her to her feet.

"I beg your pardon," she started again as she straightened her skirts, doing her best not to meet his frowning stare. "But it seems rather foolhardy to rush onto a cracked floor with no idea of its integrity." She heard him sniff.

"You are quite right."

Raising her eyes, Imogene smiled, expecting to see an easing of Ben's frown, but he had already looked away.

"Let's use this," he said as he lifted one of the boards that had barred their way only moments earlier. "It will distribute my weight." He didn't wait for Imogene's assent but stepped up to the arch once more.

Squatting, he placed the board on the stones and began sliding it forward. It scuffed and scraped along the floor as expected until its full length was nearly stretched to the base of the stairs. Then there was a great snap. Gravity yanked the board from his hands as it tumbled six or seven feet to the floor below in a shower of stone.

"Well," Ben said, staring at the newly formed hole. "That's disappointing." He stood, dusting his hands together. "So what was that other suggestion?"

"Going through the castle?"

"Yes, that was the one."

A flash of lightning, followed almost immediately by a clap of thunder, urged Imogene to hasten. Pivoting, she hurried around the corner of the south wing and into a side door; Ben was on her heels. She rushed through the dark, empty rooms to where the wing joined the tower. Up a few steps, over a landing, and then they could make their way up two flights to the door that originally led from the tower into the impressive great hall. They emerged breathless, but just where they needed to be.

Jasper greeted them with buckets of enthusiasm. He leaped high in the air, looking more like himself than he had in days. . . . But he was not free. Someone had tied him to one of the tower's wall braces.

"Why would anyone tie . . . ?" Imogene folded her brow into deep trenches and glanced over her shoulder at Ben.

"He must have been in the way," Ben suggested. "And they forgot him in the rush to get out of the storm."

Imogene nodded but was not entirely certain that was the case.

Releasing Jasper took longer than one would expect. The knot had been pulled so tight that it was soon apparent they would have to cut the rope, not untie it. Ben ran back for the shovel and then used it like an ax while Imogene held Jasper out of the way.

By the time the rope was frayed enough to break, and the shovel completely ruined, the sky had opened up, and the storm was in its glory. Clinging to each other, they slowly made their way back up the hill, buffeted this way and that. Their progress, or absence, must have been noted, for Mr. Marshal and Ernest met them at the crest of the hill. With Jasper headed back to the kennels and Imogene secured between the Steeple brothers, they at last made it to the front door.

Family and friends wearing matching worried expressions greeted them in the hall, and, unfortunately, just as Imogene opened her mouth to assure everyone that all was well, she sneezed. There was nothing to be said after that; Mother would not allow Imogene to do anything other than take to her bed.

And so it was that Imogene found herself alone in her room all evening, listening to the rain on the roof and wondering how Jasper came to be in the ruin and why workmen would tie the dog to a brace rather than return him to his kennel.

More important, she wondered if Ben . . . no, Ernest . . . missed her company.

chapter 8

In which Imogene and Emily rush to the door ...
with elegance and grace, of course

Being sequestered had one benefit—though only one that she could conceive. Imogene could avoid the long-winded sermon of the Reverend Harris the following morning. The good Reverend had a tendency to preach fire and brimstone, yelling from the pulpit one minute and whispering the next. It was all very dramatic. . . . Or it would be if it were not the same every Sunday. Imogene was never entirely certain that the words changed—so repetitive was his diction.

The greatest loss was, of course, Emily's company. Mrs. Beeswanger, in the interest of protecting her daughter from the possibility of ill health, had rearranged the bedrooms. Emily was now sharing with Pauline, while Harriet was placed on a trundle bed with Miss Watson. No one was very pleased with the change, but, as it would be of short duration, they all made the best of it.

Before he left, Ernest sent Imogene a lovely three-page note full of flowery language. He expressed his disappointment that he would have to wait a full fortnight before seeing her again, but he thanked the heavens that the Beeswangers thought to invite him and Ben to Shackleford Park. Such a great and wondrous kindness. Until that glorious, fateful day, Ernest would wait impatiently and anticipate their marvelous reunion.

On the bottom of the third page, Ben had added a sketch—a small drawing of a dog and a few scrawled lines explaining that the tangle behind the dog represented the ruins and the moat.

By the time Imogene was allowed up and out of her shuttered, stuffy room, all the company had gone. Her sneeze had not developed into anything more than a runny nose and a mild sore throat, certainly nothing resembling a deadly contagion. Storm in a teacup, Imogene decided with no little asperity.

The manor seemed inordinately quiet. Not only were the Steeples, Tabards, and Beeswangers gone, but their servants were as well. The opportunity to question Matt or Kate about the topaz necklace would now have to wait until they all arrived at Shackleford Park. But would it matter by then? Betty, the Chively housemaid, had seen nothing out of the ordinary.

"So many strangers about the place, miss, there were no telling where everyone were *supposed* to be."

The idea that Percy and Jake were part of the riddle remained in the back of Imogene's mind for some days;

tenacious thoughts that also laid the blame of Jasper's misadventure at their feet. There seemed nowhere else to put it.

As the days passed, Imogene spent more and more time in her studio doing very little painting. She was restless and preferred to design lessons for Harriet and Ben instead. She tried not to think of Ben and Ernest overly . . . with little success.

Fortunately, Ernest was in her mind nearly as much as Ben. While she did not have the excuse of trying to teach Ernest how to draw, he was the one to whom her Father continually referred at dinner. Quotes. Ernest said this, Ernest said that. Father attributed many adages to Ernest . . . none of which Imogene had heard the young man utter. It mattered not; managing other people's lives had always kept her father happy.

Imogene ignored it as best she could.

"YOUR EYES ARE brighter than the sun. I cringe in your shadow," Ben stated with one arm outstretched, as he swayed with the rhythm of his black thoroughbred, Lancelot, and kept a firm grasp on the reins with the other hand.

"No."

"I promise to love you until we are old and gray, shriveled and shrunken."

"No."

"I will do anything to win your heart: swim the widest ocean, slay a dragon . . . read a book."

Ernest sighed, rather deeply. One could hardly blame him;

Ben had been gleefully offering proposal advice for the past hour. It helped to ward off the monotony. They had been on the road to Shackleford Park for the better part of three hours, and Ben was restless.

"No."

Ben looked around surprised. "What? Oh yes, no dragon slaying. They are hard to come by these days."

Ernest sighed again and gave him a long-suffering look. It wasn't as effective as it might have been had his brother not been swaying on the back of his white-starred thoroughbred, Arthur. It was not his usual bob but a tired side-to-side sort of motion, not in the least dignified.

Ben grinned. "Enlighten me, then. How are you going to go about it?"

"I haven't thought on it overly."

With a snort, Ben shook his head and dropped his arms. He knew *that* to be a bouncer. He had seen his brother's crumpled efforts collecting under the desk in the Musson House library. In truth, Ben did not envy his brother this step toward matrimonial bliss. If Imogene's answer were a certainty, then—perhaps—the matter of how to propose would not be as worrisome. But as best as Ben could tell, Imogene was well on her way to friendship, but would it go further?

Recollecting her shy smile, Ben frowned and ignored the slight acceleration of his heart. It did not gallop or even run but merely trotted—signifying nothing more than an interest. And why would he not be interested in this gifted artist who made his mouth go dry when he thought of her standing in the rain, her gown clinging to her every curve and a look on her face that invited . . .

Invited cold reflection . . . that she would soon be betrothed to his brother and a most welcome sister-in-law. What a happy family they would be. Yes, the Steeples and the Chivelys getting together for Christmases and baptisms. Somehow the thought of baptisms brought a hitch to his calming thoughts, and he forced his mind to other topics, again.

Looking behind him, he saw that Matt's cart was lagging behind, and he pulled up Lancelot to wait. He heard Ernest do the same but did not look over until he heard his brother clear his throat—as if he were about to broach an uncomfortable subject.

"I was wondering," Ernest started to say, then paused and started again. "Well, I know it to be an imposition as it is and to ask further is . . ."

"Spit it out, brother. You are being mysterious, and it does not suit you."

"I was wondering . . ."

"You said that already."

"Yes, but I still don't know."

"Don't know what?"

"I saw that Emily was somewhat taken with you, and I wondered if you felt any affinity toward her, because if you do, that would be wonderful and marvelous and all that. But if you are just being charming—because that is what you do—I was wondering if you wouldn't. It might cause Imogene a difficulty with Emily—being a friend and all. And I was wondering . . . I know I asked you to accompany me—and I can't tell you how very much I appreciate your support and I could not do this with you—but I was wondering if you wouldn't."

"That didn't make any sense whatsoever."

Ernest looked crestfallen and then laughed. "It didn't, did it?"

"No."

Taking a deep breath, Ernest began again, speaking slowly—whether the purpose was to make himself clear or to settle his tumbling thoughts, it was not apparent. "I could not help noticing that Emily is rather taken with you."

"I noticed that, too. Unlike Imogene, Emily is not shy."

"Yes, just so. I would not wish Emily to be hurt, not only for her own sake but it would upset Imogene prodigiously. They have been fast friends all their lives."

"Ah, you want me to be standoffish around Emily."

"No, not at all. But perhaps a little more guarded. Unless all your *tête-à-têtes* are your way of getting to know Emily better . . . that she has imposed on you . . . that you *are* interested in her . . . conversation. Then that would be another matter altogether. Not that I am asking for a confidence, I . . . I . . ."

"You . . . you . . . are floundering again."

"Yes."

Seeing that Matt had caught up to them, Ben pulled Lancelot's head around and heeled him into a walk. "I will be a little more prudent in my conversations with Emily so that neither she nor anyone else will make any assumptions. Emily is a very amiable and worthy young lady, and I enjoy her company immensely; however, I am not interested in being riveted as yet. Only at the start of my apprenticeship, if you recall."

Riding alongside, Ernest nodded. "Of course. Though, long betrothals are not uncommon in circumstances such as these."

"Yes. Well, I shall keep that in mind."

Ernest sighed as if a great weight had been lifted from his shoulders.

"Don't get too comfortable, brother of mine. If I am not mistaken, Tishdale is dead ahead . . . and then on to Shackleford. And you still don't know how you will propose. Have you considered throwing yourself at her feet and begging?"

"No."

Ben laughed and continued with his absurd suggestions.

SHACKLEFORD PARK, TISHDALE, KENT—
LATE JULY 1817

As EMILY AND IMOGENE meandered through the great rooms of Shackleford Park, Imogene could not help but reflect on how much more there was to impress in this elegant estate than at Gracebridge Manor. The affluence of the Beeswangers was patently obvious: from the quality of their furnishings and tapestries to the number of rooms and the large staff.

When their mothers and Cousin Clara had been school chums, there had been little difference in their social or monetary stature, and while each had married a gentleman, Mr. Beeswanger's prosperity was decidedly more significant. It was not to be wondered at; Ralph Beeswanger inherited his fortune under the guidance of an exemplary land agent, and that fortune had grown.

Mr. Chively's success came from an unexpected source: Cousin Clara's husband, Mr. Tabard. Myles Tabard had inherited an estate weighted by debt. Without knowledge or management skills, Mr. Tabard could not prevent Greytower Hall from slipping further and further into the mire until Imogene's father stepped in to help. It had not been an altruistic gesture on the part of John Chively. It had been a sensible business arrangement: one that brought both gentlemen success.

In the process, Imogene's father had discovered a skill for organization, management, and banking; he had found himself a career. There was none more horrified than his wife. Olivia Earlton Chively had not been brought up to support a husband in trade. . . . But after a few years of prosperity, Imogene's mother had decided that banking was not unlike being a magistrate or a bishop. The social censure she had felt initially was tempered by large gatherings at the newly acquired London townhouse. And while Lady Scatney and Mrs. Redger might refuse to acknowledge them, Mother was on the best of terms with Mr. and Mrs. Alma, who were well-placed members of the Ton. Such was the complexity of proper society.

"I thought this might make a good study," Emily said, pointing to the cornice above one of the windows in the dining room.

All of Emily's suggestions involved rooms in the front of the house near windows. She was watching, as was Imogene, for the arrival of two young gentlemen of the surname Steeple.

"Yes, actually. I think that would do much better than the one in the billiard room. And a corner of the chimneypiece in the library rather than the whole. I'm not sure that Ben is quite up to the entire piece yet. . . . And we don't want him frustrated."

Imogene smiled at Emily to show her appreciation for her friend's careful consideration of subject matter. It was apparent that she had spent a great deal of time considering Ben's artistic needs. But Emily had already turned away and was watching the drive again.

"What's that? Oh yes . . . I see . . . I see . . . Bother. I believe it is one of Papa's deer. They are always munching on the hosta. Most inconsiderate." She sighed and turned back to Imogene. "So there we have four projects for Benjamin to sketch."

"Five, actually, if you include the newel post of the backstairs. Well done. Simple enough but excellent practice—very practical examples of architecture. This is more to his purpose."

"As to the medallion in the great hall—Oh, horses. Yes, look. A carriage. It's them. I know it's them." Emily made as if to desert the window and rush to the front door, but a movement outside caught her eye. "Oh, Percy has seen them as well. And he's waving with great enthusiasm. Dear me. He is too pleased. It has to be the Tabards. Only—"

"Jake. Yes, only Jake would get such a greeting from my brother." Imogene sighed, as did Emily, and they laughed at each other's foolishness. Imogene watched as Emily turned back to the window to verify that the carriage did indeed disgorge the Tabards.

Sighing again, though silently this time, Imogene observed that the passage of time was a boon for those whose sensibilities had been clouded by unformed emotions. A fortnight had proved to be just the right span of time for her to set her thoughts to rights—to realize that her attraction to Ben was fleeting. It was born from a misinterpretation of his charm. She had been interested in him merely as a result of believing he had been interested in her. When he hadn't been . . . interested.

Ben was his own man. Enjoying the company of others . . . not Imogene in particular. That was as it should be—for Ernest was the gentleman Imogene should consider. And she had. Ernest had so many stellar qualities that Imogene had made a list of them . . . a list she repeated every time her traitorous thoughts veered toward Ben.

Ben Steeple was not for her. Any attachment he formed, if he formed an attachment, would be toward Emily. They were better suited by far, both being in possession of outgoing characters, both enjoying opportunities to laugh, and both finding life an adventure.

Ernest was quiet, as was Imogene. He thought before he spoke, and he was not impulsive. Imogene had even detected a slight shyness in his manner. Yes, they were much more suited to each other. Peas in a pod.

Imogene sighed.

"Oh, look!" Emily fairly shouted. "Two riders and a cart."

Her gaze was focused at the far end of the drive, past the opulent flower beds and the manicured lawn.

Yes, indeed. Two large black horses with tall, broad-shouldered riders were approaching at an easy trot, followed by a pony cart. It would seem that the Steeple brothers had, at last, found their way to Shackleford Park.

Imogene joined Emily in a rush to the door. Though they exited the manor with decorum and grace, of course.

PULLING HIS HORSE to a stop behind the Tabard carriage, Ben alit and passed the reins to a waiting groom. He was greeting Mr. Tabard when the front door of the manor opened to let loose two excited and squealing girls. Ernest's horse shied and stepped back. Ernest quickly brought it under control and dropped to the ground, passing his reins as well.

"Hello, ladies." Ben bowed deeply to Pauline and Hardly Harriet. Their enthusiasm was artless and delightful. Never before had Ben and Ernest been beneficiaries of such a reception. Even at Musson House, where their grandparents were usually pleased by their return, the greetings were unexceptional. "It has been such a long time. Harriet, I believe you have grown."

"Silly. It's been only a fortnight." Harriet grinned her reply. "I haven't grown a bit."

"Welcome to Shackleford Park," a voice drifted from above.

Ben lifted his eyes to find Emily standing regally on the top step, resplendent in a pastel green gown with frilly things along her hem. On her right was an equally lovely Imogene, in mauve, with lace covering her . . . above her bodice. Both young ladies looked the epitome of sedate modesty, both smiled benignly. Imogene's smile hinted of reserve, while Emily's hinted of mischief.

"Thank you," Ben and Ernest said at the same time, and they all laughed.

Ben turned briefly to see Mr. Tabard looking at him with curiosity, while Percy and Jake simply nodded and took themselves off.

"Come inside," Emily said grandly. "All has been prepared." She gestured first to Mr. Tabard and then to Ernest, allowing his brother to follow Imogene. The girls ignored protocol and pushed ahead, giggling all the while.

Ben watched the company enter the manor from where he stood. Just before stepping across the threshold, Imogene turned to look over her shoulder, and she smiled. This was a true smile, an unselfconscious smile—one that offered a continued friendship. One that Ben was very glad to see.

"Benjamin?" Emily queried, likely puzzled by his inattention and lack of movement.

Glancing toward her, Ben realized that he was rather pleased to see Emily, too . . . and that the use of his full name did not rankle as it had at Gracebridge. And while he was not aware of any acceleration of his heart, Ben thought that his keenness deserved a little exploration. In deference to Ernest, he would not flirt. . . . But that did not mean he had to ignore Emily's company. They might suit just fine—and then wouldn't that be a happy situation? Yes, suddenly Christmases and baptisms held much more appeal.

"Might I stand back for a moment or two? I would like to take in the entire facade of Shackleford Park before entering," Ben called over his shoulder, even as he stepped around the departing carriage and horses and onto the lawn.

He turned to see that Emily's smile no longer reached her eyes; the mischief had faded. "Yes, of course," she said. Grabbing a handful of skirts, she moved toward the front door.

"Would you care to join me?"

Emily's head snapped around. She paused as if considering and then hopped down the stairs, walking out to where he now stood facing the manor. "Yes, of course," she repeated quietly. She stared up at him for a moment and then turned toward the manor.

Shackleford Park was without a doubt a beautiful building, and though Ben knew it to be at least a decade in age, the manor could have been mistaken for new. No wear on the stone, no rot in the sills, and no mold on the lower floor. The blue mansard roof sparkled in the sun, and tower caps pointed straight to the sky. The architect had done a masterful job. The effect was understated elegance.

"So . . ." He waved his hands in the general direction of the east wing—and then the west.

"So?"

"Tell me about Shackleford." A quick side glance to Emily allowed Ben to offer her encouragement—in the way of a saucy grin. He couldn't help it; that was the way he grinned. If Ernest had a problem with it, then . . .

"As you likely know, the manor was built in 1807 by Lord Harold Lestor," Emily began, and proceeded to explain the ins and outs of Shackleford, adding a few anecdotes from her own childhood memories.

They stayed out of doors, slowly strolling across the front of the building, for some time—at least a quarter hour or so. Emily used words such as *gable* and *pediment* to describe the windows and various embellishments. Ben wondered if Emily had known the meaning of those words a fortnight ago, but he was rather flattered that she might have gone to the trouble of studying up on his favorite subject.

It was a very pleasant interlude that did bode well for the visit. And Ben found himself not only anticipating exploring Shackleford but getting to know its occupants as well.

Looking over her shoulder, Imogene squinted at the looking glass, trying to see the pearl buttons running down the length of her back. She had managed all but the last few. Now she could neither reach the rest nor see them. Cream on cream. Who thought that a brilliant idea?

"Mama," she said with a snort into the empty bedroom. And then she huffed, pulled out the vanity chair, and flopped elegantly onto the edge of the seat. It was a beautiful silk gown, with tucks and ribbons, one made for her Season in London and far too grandiose for the country. Still, Mama had insisted. Imogene had to make the right impression.

She could have argued that if she had not already made that impression, Ernest would not be back in their company. Imogene sighed instead.

Mama did not realize that they—she and Ernest—were trying to get to know each other, assessing character, not affluence. Mama thought it the same thing, but it most certainly was not. Imogene wanted to know Ernest's interests, his pursuits, not how to lead him around on a short leash—whatever that meant.

With another huff, Imogene rested her elbow on the small table and then her head in her hand . . . and huffed a third time. She could huff as much as she wanted without reproach or queries. She was alone. There was no need to double up in Shackleford Park; there were plenty of rooms, enough to accommodate all the guests and then some. Imogene was installed in a room that had been hers to use every summer for almost ten years—a room that seldom heard huffing. This was a change.

This was a new Imogene, waiting for Kate to help with her dress and put up her hair. This was not the Imogene of a few hours ago, looking forward to an idyllic stay at a country estate, a relaxing visit that included getting to know Ernest Steeple. No. This was a foolish girl, a befogged girl. A young lady with a noodle for a brain. A ninny. A dunderhead. A . . .

She could call herself names all evening, but nothing could alter the unalterable.

It took a moment—a mere moment—for Imogene to look down on the Steeple brothers and realize that while she thought very highly of Ernest, her foolish, foolish heart had practically thrummed out of her chest when Ben had looked her way.

Ben, not Ernest, had stolen her heart, and she had to get it back. Whether she gave it to Ernest upon its return remained to be seen. First things first: purging Ben.

But how did one go about doing such a thing? The person Imogene would normally turn to for such advice was Emily. However, this was *not* a question for her closest friend. No. Emily would be hurt, or furious, or never wish to speak to her again—or all three—if she learned that Imogene harbored deep feelings for Ben. Emily had all but started the guest list for their wedding—as if Ben had no say in the matter. As if the mere fact that Emily wished to marry him meant that Ben would wish the same.

Could she speak to Mama? Never. Cousin Clara would have known what to do. But . . . Imogene huffed again. Mrs. Beeswanger . . . no, Emily's mother might not be pleased, either.

"That was a big sigh, miss," Kate said as she closed the door behind her. "I hope it weren't 'cause I were a bit longer than expected." She handed Imogene a piece of folded paper. "I'm putting curls around Miss Emily's face. It's a little fussy."

Imogene sat up straight, meeting Kate's eyes in the mirror. "No. No, indeed." For a moment, she considered asking Kate, but that would put the maid in an untenable position. Even without using names, it would be obvious to whom she was referring. No, Imogene would have to do this on her own. "I was deep in thought, is all."

Kate smiled.

It was a knowing smile that made Imogene grit her teeth and look downward for a moment. She focused on the paper in her hand.

"What's this?" Imogene lifted it so that Kate could see it in the mirror while she finished doing up the buttons.

"Don't know, miss," she said, glancing at the paper and then back down at the gown. "Found it under your door. A love note, mayhap?"

Imogene scoffed, flipped it open, saw Ben's name, and flipped it closed. "Hardly," she said as casually as one could when one was suddenly out of breath.

Watching Kate's head nod without looking up, Imogene struggled for calm. Not only had Ben's name jumped to the fore but also the word *love*. She would wait to read the note, wait until Kate finished her hair and left to check on Emily's curls.

Waiting.

Still waiting.

Why did an upsweep take so long!

Imogene smiled and thanked Kate for her hard work. She really had done a wonderful—

There, the door was closed.

Imogene paced around the room—briefly. Sitting on the edge of her bed, she swallowed several times, breathing deeply. After a moment of trying to steady her nerves, she gave up and flipped the note open, reading it quickly.

My dearest, dearest Imogene,

*Now that we are reunited, I find it
impossible not to express my true feelings. We
are so often together, but while walking with
Emily, my thoughts are of you——you
alone. In vain have I struggled. It will not
do. My feelings will not be repressed. You
must allow me to tell you how ardently I
admire and love you.*

Benjamin

Gasping, Imogene hugged the note to her bodice. She stared across the room, not seeing the far wall but *his* face. Her beloved! Tears of joy threatened to spill, and she swallowed against the excess emotion—exhilarated beyond reason. She could hardly think straight. She wanted to run from the room, shout his name, and fling herself into his arms. The thought sent her heart racing and her knees shaking.

Giving the note an extra squeeze, Imogene held it up to read again. This time she whispered his beautiful declaration. By the third reading, she grew bold and spoke the words aloud.

And then she stopped . . . frowned and swallowed the sudden lump in her throat.

Imogene reread the note a fourth time but *not* out loud, not even a whisper. And as she did, her heart stopped pounding. She no longer gasped for air, and her exhilaration faded into weariness.

This was not what it seemed; this was not a love note from Ben—or Benjamin. She had seen his distinctive scrawl on the bottom of her letter from Ernest; this handwriting was not in the least similar. There was no sketch anywhere on the paper, and the prose was awkward, as if being made to fit the context. In fact, the words were familiar. And the more Imogene thought about it the more she was incensed; this passage was from *Pride and Prejudice*—one of her favorite Jane Austen novels.

How could they? Imogene knew the villains of this horseplay: Percy and Jake, without a doubt. They likely thought this funny. Imagined Imogene running to Ben agog, only to be rebuffed and made ridiculous. Would they watch, waiting to laugh, waiting to mock, waiting to see her brought low?

Had Percy recognized the expression in her eyes when they had greeted the new arrivals? It mattered not; she would give no satisfaction.

Folding the note, Imogene tore it in half, then quarters, then eighths. She continued to shred the paper until it was a littered mess at her feet. And then she turned to the looking glass and practiced smiling. But as much as she might try, the anger stayed in her eyes.

chapter 9

*In which an unremarkable excursion
is interrupted by a challenge*

The atmosphere of Shackleford Park was remarkably different from that of Gracebridge Manor. Considering it was merely a backdrop change—like a stage play—and the actors were the same, the change was indeed . . . um, remarkable.

Perhaps when Mr. Chively was no longer called upon to impress, to be the best of all possible hosts, he found the ability to put a smile on his face. Or was it the news that Lord Penton was indeed interested in seeing the old castle's stonework? Mrs. Chively's affable expression hinted that she preferred playing the cherished guest to that of hostess. Her biting asides to Imogene were fewer and not as sharp.

Still, if Ben were to note the most significant difference in the transplanting of the company to another country estate, it would be Imogene's behavior. She was acting rather oddly. It was as if she were angry, seething, in fact, and yet he had not witnessed anything untoward. It was a puzzle. Something must have occurred between their arrival and dinner as she seemed to be just fine—quite pleased, actually—a few hours earlier. Yes, odd.

Doing his best to stay out of trouble—not too charming with Emily, pleasant to the governess, and engaging with the young gentlemen—Ben found his eyes settling on Imogene, finding her behind every chair, within any group, or imitating a statue by the window. And every time their eyes met, they blazed, as if he had caused the affront. . . . And he was fairly certain that he had not. It was rather disquieting.

When the party finally went in to dinner—and what a spectacular dining room it was—Imogene was seated far enough away that Ben could ignore his concern and dedicate his conversation to Pauline and Mrs. Chively. It was not stunning dialogue. Something about shoe roses preoccupied Pauline, and Mrs. Chively thought the Jessons might visit Gracebridge in the autumn . . . whoever they might be.

However, despite being two seats down on the other side of the table, Imogene mentioned him several times in her conversation with Ernest. Ben couldn't help but notice . . . his ears perking up like a dog's whenever she named him.

"Really? Ben doesn't like green beans? How odd. Who doesn't like green beans?" she said as Ben pushed the limp green vegetable to the side of his plate. "But I suppose he could be forgiven; it is an inconsequential flaw." She sounded almost disappointed.

Several minutes later, Ben's name entered the discussion again.

"So Ben has never read Jane Austen. Excellent. Very good to know. I thought as much." Ernest assured her that though his brother was practically illiterate, Ernest had enjoyed every word of . . . some novel Ben had never heard of.

And then later: "Wednesday. That's a shame; Wednesday's child is full of woe," Imogene had said when Ernest had laughingly declared what day of the week Ben had been born on. Ben had been chuckling with Pauline at the time.

Yes, it was all rather . . . odd.

Ben would get to the bottom of this in the morning. While naught had been said—too many ears, listeners, people about—there was an unexpressed agreement that the two couples would meet to break their fast and begin the art lessons anew.

The next day saw Ben and Ernest lingering in the morning room, coffee cooling at their elbows. By the time all the gentlemen—except Mr. Tabard—had set off on their various pursuits, Emily and Imogene entered the room ahead of the other ladies, who were still keeping town hours. Breakfast was a quiet meal, as all four were exceptionally aware of Mr. Tabard.

Looking over his paper, Mr. Tabard appeared to be well aware of them, too, and the studied silence. "Have I done something wrong?" he asked with a slight frown. "I assure you it was quite unintentional. Clara was always getting after me for my absentminded ways. . . . What did I do?"

"No, no, Mr. Tabard. All is well," Imogene said.

"I will admit to finishing the last of the toast. . . . But I'm sure you can ring for more."

"Yes, indeed." Emily nodded and then lapsed into silence again.

Mr. Tabard looked from one face to another. "I can vacate the room if you like?" he said eventually. He tucked a long strand of gray hair behind his ear and returned his eyes to his newspaper. Clearly, the offer was not heartfelt.

"No, no, Mr. Tabard." Emily chuckled without humor. "We are all but done. And I wish to show Benjamin the cornice in the dining room."

"Didn't he see it yesterday?" he asked without looking up.

"Indeed," Ben interjected. "I need a closer look."

They left the old gentleman lost in the latest issue of *The London Times*.

Closing the tall door to the dining room, art supplies waiting on the corner of the table, Ben rounded on Imogene.

But Emily was faster. "What is *amiss*, Imogene?"

Imogene lifted her brows and stared wide-eyed from Emily to Ben to Ernest and returned to Emily. All stared back. Slowly a flush crawled up her cheeks until Imogene's entire face resembled a beet. "Naught. Why do you ask?" She swallowed with some difficulty and turned her eyes to the window.

"You are not acting yourself, Imogene." Emily approached, putting an arm around her friend's shoulders. "You would not say last night, and it kept me awake a full five minutes, tossing and turning. Has something happened?"

Imogene tittered awkwardly, turning back to the company. There was a sharp edge to the sound, but the storm in her eyes had disappeared. She offered Emily a weak smile, the blush fading. "I apologize. I was the brunt of more buffoonery, and it took longer for me to calm down than it ought to have."

"Percy and Jake?" Emily asked.

Imogene nodded.

"What did they do?" Ernest looked as angry as Ben had ever seen him.

Imogene shook her head. "Nothing damaging. Mockery. The folly is now mine, for holding on to the annoyance for so long. I am certain they are off on another lark, having forgotten all about it. I have long since learned not to react; it only urges them on."

"You did react," Emily said, correcting.

"Not to Percy and Jake. They enjoy melodrama. They were likely hoping for a scene." Again, she looked from face to face, this time with a bashful smile. "Only my nearest and dearest noticed."

Simple words, but they did the job, for Ben was fairly certain they were meant to ease the tension in the room. Ernest grinned, Emily nodded, and Ben . . . well, he was a little too pleased to be included in this select group. He also tried not to notice that Imogene had given two young men of a short acquaintance—not her parents—that distinction.

WHILE IT WOULD seem the day started out poorly, it did not progress in the same manner. The morning was spent as

139

Imogene preferred: art lessons for Ben, art lessons for Harriet. Both were coming along, though not with any speed. It was a pace that Ben found frustrating no matter how much Imogene repeated that practice and time were the only roads to success.

After luncheon, a walk in the park was suggested. Emily wanted to show off the extensive grounds of Shackleford, which included an artificial lake. Imogene had made the mistake of calling it a pond one time and had been rather firmly corrected. Surprising vistas and delightful alcoves had been planned to offer a changing tableau for those wandering the acreage, as well as a boathouse and a folly for exploration. It would take many hours to meander through the wondrous creation in the tradition of Capability Brown—landscape designer extraordinaire.

The weather was obligingly benign—no oppressive heat, no dark clouds, and no howling wind—only a gentle breeze fluttering everyone's hair while starlings wheeled overhead. Quite romantic, in a crowded sort of way. The entire younger generation, all eight, had decided the excursion worthy of their time . . . even, to Imogene's great displeasure, Percy and Jake.

"Look at the ducks," Pauline called loudly, as if she had not seen ducks before. Watching Ben, she gestured, somewhat needlessly, at the lake.

They were wandering as a collective—no couples, just an ever-changing arrangement, stopping and starting and surging as they circled the lake, climbing over hill and dale with delicate steps. The only constant was the twirling of lacy parasols protecting the young ladies from the sun.

Although Jake *borrowed* Emily's parasol briefly so that he might sashay across their path, simpering and squealing in a scornful parody of womanhood. Ben retrieved it for her with a polite but stern request. Jake had not appreciated his tone and said as much, but he relinquished the parasol nonetheless.

Imogene hid her smile with a quick glance to her right, only to encounter Ernest's steady gaze. They grinned at each other with approval and camaraderie—aware of the true nature of Ben's derisive tone.

Jake, in his frustration, grabbed a stick from the ground and swung it fiercely at the grass. Seeing him as an immature pup and not a young gentleman of nineteen, Imogene shook her head at his behavior and then blinked. For a moment, only a moment, Jake's face had gone into repose, and a terrible sorrow had sculpted his features. It was so profound that she had to swallow against the sudden tightness in her throat.

It was a reminder. Jake's need to hurt others was brought on by his own ache—his own pain. No excuse, but an explanation. Poor Jake. This was his first summer without the calming presence of his mother. How terribly he must miss her; they all did, but none more so than Jake and Mr. Tabard.

Glancing again at Ernest, she saw him frown. He was aware that something had changed but knew not what or why. Imogene shook her head ever so slightly. "Later," she said quietly. She was no longer angry.

The rest of the outing might have been a pleasant but unremarkable affair had the conversation not veered toward horses—in particular the ones on which the Steeples had arrived. Harriet had been very impressed with Ben's black thoroughbred.

"Lancelot, a noble name for a noble beast," Ben said with no little pride. "A steadier ride you will not find, or a better jumper." By now they had circled the lake, and he paused to look up at the manor from a distance.

"Except, perhaps, Arthur," Ernest added, stopping beside him, "who is from the same mare. They look alike but for the star."

The company joined the brothers staring across the lawn, though Imogene was fairly certain that the girls had no idea why the procession had come to a standstill.

"Not a match for Honor," Percy argued, citing his chestnut Oldenburg with white socks.

"Shall we test it?" Jake asked, his eyes sparkling with mischief again. "A race. A country race."

"No, I don't think that is—" Imogene started to say, but her protest was lost in the enthusiasm of the moment as all four young men decided it was just the thing. Even Hardly Harriet was excited, not realizing—one would hope—the dangers of riding pell-mell over gates, stiles, and hedge groves.

Within moments, Imogene and Emily were left alone, staring not at the manor but at the backs of the young gentlemen rushing up the hill toward the stables, and two young girls trailing after them.

"This does not seem wise," Emily said with a sigh.

"Certainly not when Ernest and Ben are on edge with Percy

and Jake as it is. I expect some posturing and a fair amount of one-upmanship."

"Indeed." Emily sighed again. "A recipe for disaster."

Fortunately, the Beeswangers got wind of the young men's intent and suggested a delay. After all, it was too close to dinner, and Cook could not hold off the buttered crab, which was always a favorite; the race was postponed. Stomachs trumped sport . . . but only until the next afternoon.

BEN ENJOYED RACING. And in this case, there was no doubt of a win. Ben merely needed to decide by what degree he should trounce Percy and Jake. If he had any competition in this race, it would be his brother. . . . For in truth, Lancelot and Arthur were not only from the same stock but also the same trainer. There was little between them—and Ernest had as good a seat as he.

While itching to prove his prowess and start the day with a healthy workout, there was a delay . . . again. Imogene and Emily had to set a course. There was no need for their fussing. It wasn't as if Ben and Ernest were wet behind the ears—country races were part and parcel to a proper gentleman's upbringing—but Ernest was courting and trying to impress. So they acquiesced.

As Ben sketched a corner of the library's chimneypiece, Imogene and Emily discussed the race route. And then, while Imogene was giving Harriet her lessons, Emily took Ernest and

Ben around in her barouche, showing them the ins and outs and roundabouts of the chosen route. It was tedium in the extreme. . . . But he smiled, and Ernest smiled. Percy and Jake shook their heads and declared they knew the route, which they probably did—giving them the advantage.

At last, when Imogene and Emily could interfere no more, the four excited horses were brought out of the stables and walked to the edge of the cobblestones. The Chivelys, Beeswangers, and Mr. Tabard had taken up position in the west wing conservatory, whence they could see the side of the stables. Harriet had a red flag in hand; she would shout the start.

The first part of the course would take them down the hill toward the lake, veering off at the bottom onto a country lane, across a narrow bridge, then curve to the left, over a gate . . . sharp turn to the right, or was it left, too . . . hmm. It was a little hard to recall the middle of the race, but Ben was certain he would recognize it when he got there. Fairly certain. Perhaps the markers hadn't been a waste of time after all.

Ben pulled himself atop Lancelot as the horse danced away from the groom, affected by the high spirits of those around him. The atmosphere was carnivalesque and Ben thought that the habit of country visits was not such a mundane enterprise after all.

And then Harriet dropped her flag. "Go!" she shouted.

All four riders heeled their horses into a gallop. All four surged forward, finding purchase on the edge of the cobbled yard. In a clump, they raced for the bottom of the hill—Jake and Ernest between Ben and Percy.

Caught up in the excitement, the horses, like their riders, reveled in the speed—the exhilaration of competition. As they turned onto the smaller lane, Ben pushed ahead with Percy, squeezing the other two behind—but only by a length.

Thundering toward the bridge, Ben realized that Percy was trying to force Lancelot into the water. With a laugh, Ben took Lancelot splashing through the brook and up the bank. He had almost caught back up when Ernest barreled past him.

Ben was incensed; he was in third place!

Up and over the first gate, he watched Ernest catch and then pass Percy. As the lane widened, Ben was hard on Percy's heels, and from the sounds of it, Jake was hard on Ben's heels. It was still anyone's race.

In a burst of speed, Ben took the next gate ahead of Percy and Ernest, placing him in front. He patted Lancelot's broad neck and stared down the lane, looking for the markers. Sure enough, there was one on the right. He would have to slow down to make the sharp turn.

Percy had a different strategy. Racing past—too fast to make the upcoming turn—he left the road early. Percy took Honor over the hedge at a full gallop, raced across the field and then up and over the hedge on the other side. Cutting the corner. A country race was about finishing, not the exact route.

Following Percy's lead, Ben urged Lancelot up and over the hedge; it was an easy jump for an experienced horse of seventeen hands. Ben leaned back.

Lancelot screamed and balked, turning so quickly that Ben was launched into the hedge rather than over it. Hitting the shrubs, he rebounded back onto the lane, landing hard on his knees and tumbling into a roll. He came to a jarring halt on his posterior and sat for a moment, dazed, confused, and . . . dazed.

Pounding hooves almost overwhelmed him as Ernest pulled up short, Arthur snorting in protest. Ben continued to reflect on which direction was up and decided he didn't need to stand as yet.

"Ben! Ben, are you all right?" Ernest shouted.

Ben blinked and was going to suggest that shouting was not necessary when Jake shot past them, riding neck-or-nothing. Ben turned his head to watch Jake sail over the hedge, and then he shouted to his brother. "Go!" A race had to be won. "Go!"

"Are you all—?"

"Go!" Ben shouted again. "Win this bloody thing!"

In an instant, Ernest pulled Arthur around to get a running start over the hedge, and then he, too, was gone. The sound of thundering hooves receded until Ben was left with only the rustle of the wind in the trees and a plethora of songbirds creating enough racket to warrant a frown.

As breath returned to his lungs, and his heart slowed to a normal rhythm, Ben assessed the situation. He was *very* pleased to see that Lancelot had taken himself over to the other side of the lane and was nibbling on the grass. The horse looked none the worse for wear, though he was twitching and throwing his tail about. Ben would check thoroughly as soon as he stood . . . whenever that might be. He thought it an admirable idea to determine the damage *before* moving.

Fortunately, it was a short list: bruised knees, mostly protected by his leather breeches; scratches, predominantly on the right side of his head; a cut on his temple, though not deep, since the trickle of blood was already stopping; and last, but most definitely not least, a tender posterior. Not bad, considering he could have broken his neck.

Now, having finished his inventory, Ben thought he might stand; it wasn't as difficult as he thought it might be. Even walking was acceptable after the first few steps.

Those steps took him to Lancelot.

Ben ran his hand over the horse's legs and back and under his belly, checking the girth. All looked fine. Lancelot bumped him with his nose and went back to his grazing, still twitching.

Knowing that he was lucky, that the incident could have been so much worse, Ben was rather baffled as to *why* it had happened. It was most unusual for Lancelot to balk. The horse loved to jump.

Shaking his head, he shrugged, straightened his coat, and dusted off his shoulders. He found his hat, and as he straightened, his eye fell on the edge of the saddle pad and a small bump, indicating something underneath. Nothing should be underneath a saddle pad!

Reaching up gently, Ben touched the bump. Lancelot danced away, nickering. "Easy, boy, easy." Ben tried to lift the pad but had to loosen the girth before he could raise it enough to get beneath. When he did, his fingers explored and found a burr—a small, prickly burr. He stared at it for some minutes, noticing the flecks of lint and horsehair caught up in the tiny spikes. He dropped it into his pocket and tightened the girth again—though not as taut this time. He would not get up on the saddle. There was likely a sore spot, bruise, or even a small cut where the burr had rubbed until Ben had made it unbearable by shifting his weight.

"Poor Lancelot. That's no way to treat a fine creature like you, now is it?" Ben rubbed the long black nose thoughtfully and then reached for the reins again.

Strolling back up the lane, Ben retraced the route in a loping stride that in no way matched the fury coursing through his veins. He was glad of the long walk back to the manor; it allowed his rage to crest and ebb, settling into a deep, seething anger. Had he seen Jake or Percy before that, there would have been fisticuffs. Ernest would have joined the melee without question, and the mill would have seen them to the door *posthaste*. Ernest would have lost his ladylove because of Ben's temper—being in the right would not make a difference.

Once through the gates, around the curves, and across the bridge, Ben spied the Shackleford towers through the trees; he did not hurry but allowed the tranquillity around him to erode his anger. While he ascended the hill, he heard a great roar of approval, cheering, and clapping. It would seem the race was won.

Within moments, a figure in skirts appeared at the top of the hill and quickly approached. As Emily got closer, her worried expression provided another salve to Ben's mood. By the time they were near enough to speak, Ben was once again a clear-thinking gentleman—a clear-thinking gentleman who had every intention of seeing burrs stuck to the backsides of two empty-headed sots who deserved to be thrown into a gutter of sewage. . . .

"Benjamin. Benjamin, are you all right? You look quite terrible," Emily said as she rushed toward him. Then she quickly added, "A wounded knight sort of terrible, of course. Looking brave and—"

"I am fine, thank you, Emily. Might look a little worse for wear, but I will be able to put most of it to rights with some soap and water." Then he took a deep breath. He did not want to shout his next words; the burr was not her fault. "Our miscreants have been at it again. Quite adaptable, these fellows. And cavalier. Thought nothing of putting a burr under Lancelot's saddle pad."

Emily stopped and put her hand to her mouth. "Oh good Lord, no. You could have been killed."

"Or Lancelot could have broken a leg. It was an idiotic and perilous thing to do."

"That's it! I will have them here no longer." She whirled around as if she were going to march up the hill and have it out with Percy and Jake once and for all.

This was something Ben planned to do, and had been planning to do since he found the burr. Forgetting himself, he touched her arm to garner her attention. Emily gasped and whirled around. They were now standing very close together. . . . And Emily had closed her eyes.

Leaning into him, she lifted her mouth, and Ben forgot why he was angry. Suddenly he was confused; he knew Emily was hoping he would kiss her, and the thought was tempting, but they were standing in an open field where anyone could see. He shifted to look around her and waved casually to the group waiting at the top of the hill.

"Emily. Emily!" he whispered sharply in desperation. "Smile at the family."

Her eyes flew open, and she stared at him with wide eyes. "Are they watching?"

"Indeed." Ben lifted his cheeks, shifted, and waved again.

"Oh dear."

"Exactly."

Doing as he had suggested, Emily slowly turned and waved . . . while heaving a heavy sigh. "Please don't thrash Jake, Benjamin. I know he deserves it, but Imogene pointed out that he is not himself right now. He is still grieving."

"And Percy's excuse?"

"He has none. Thrash away."

"Thank you. I think I will."

chapter 10

*In which enthusiasm for an idyllic respite
by the lake is thoroughly dampened*

The climb up the hill was neither arduous nor overlong; it was, however, unpleasant because they were watched the entire length. As Ben and Emily drew nearer, laughter could be heard, carried on the wind. Percy's and Jake's guffaws carried the best—though Ben might have been a tad oversensitive. He found the sound markedly irksome.

Once at the top of the incline, the families stood back so that Ben might lead Lancelot to the stables. There was a great deal of meaningless chatter around him; he ignored all until he entered the yard and a groom stepped forward. Passing him the reins, Ben requested that the coachman see to the horse's loin.

"Was he injured in the fall?" Ernest asked.

"No. Actually—"

"Parted company." Jake laughed. "Beautiful stepper, and yet

you parted company. Not the top-sawyer you thought, eh? Such a shame you missed it, Percy. It was a sight!"

"Appreciating the fruits of your labor?" Ben turned to face Jake square on.

"My labor? I had nothing to do with it, my friend. This was all on you. Trying to jump before your horse was ready."

"I think the fall had more to do with the burr than the hedge, don't you?"

Jake stilled, finally realizing that Ben was seething. "What burr?"

"The one under his saddle pad? Know anything about it?"

Pushing his shoulders back, lifting his chin, Jake scowled at Ben. "I most certainly do not. I don't care a wit about your hide, Mr. Ben Steeple, but I would never do anything to harm a horse, and I heartily resent the implication. Did you hear that, Percy? Next he'll be accusing you."

"It has crossed my mind." Ben's voice was edged with frost.

"Well, cross it *off* your mind. Neither Percy nor I had anything to do with your spill." And with that, Jake harrumphed, glared at the company as if they had done something other than serve as witnesses, and marched toward the manor. Percy looked daggers at Ben and then followed.

"That was uncalled for, Mr. Ben. I believe you owe Jake and Percy an apology," Imogene's father said as the group shuffled away in discomfort, leaving only Imogene and Emily standing beside Mr. Chively.

Ben pulled the burr from his pocket, presenting it on his

open palm. "It was under Lancelot's saddle pad. Do you have another suggestion?"

"Yes, young man. The pad could have picked it up drying in the grass or some such. There was no need to accuse Percy or Jake of mischief. You might wish to withdraw your accusation."

"I did not accuse, Mr. Chively. I merely asked if they knew whence came the burr. And Jake assured me that he did not know." Ben's voice dripped with derision. "It is up to each of us to decide if we believe that assurance."

"Really, young man, your manners are as suspect as that burr. Boorish behavior. You are a guest here . . . invited solely on your *brother's* merit."

Ben glanced at Imogene with a set down on his tongue and saw her eyes wide with distress. It stopped him short. He blinked, gulped at the air, and swallowed his spleen—with difficulty. "I beg your pardon, Mr. Chively. The fall has clearly rattled my brain, and I am not thinking rationally."

"Clearly!" Mr. Chively harrumphed—not unlike Jake had done—and nodded, walking away without another word.

"Oh dear," Imogene said.

"Oh dear," Emily echoed. "Worry not, Benjamin. It's no more than bluster. Your question was reasonable to those of us who know the true state of affairs. I'm sure Mr. Chively will come around." Linking her elbow to that of Imogene, she pulled her friend forward. "My parents certainly understand. They mentioned trying to keep Percy and Jake out of mischief before you arrived. Mr. Chively is, and always has been, indulgent and overprotective of Percy. His heir, you know." Her last statement was said in a fairly good imitation of Mr. Chively's imperial tone.

Imogene, looking over her shoulder, nodded just before they disappeared around the corner of the stables.

"Well, the *race* was entertaining," Ernest said, staring after the ladies.

"Who won?"

"I did," Ernest said with a sigh.

Ben laughed and slapped his brother on the back. "Well done! That's the best way to thwart our villains. Beat them at their own game."

Ernest smiled, though the worry never left his eyes. "Think I should propose soon, before we outstay our welcome."

"WHY ARE YOU SKULKING?"

Imogene jumped and whirled around without thought, despite recognizing the voice. "Oh, Emily, you gave me such a start." She laughed weakly, holding a hand to the top of her bodice. "Did I really give the appearance of skulking?"

They were standing at the bottom of one of the twin circular staircase towers that curved past the main floors. Emily must have come around behind Imogene, though the carpeted stone had offered up no betraying sound.

"Looking into the hallway before stepping across the threshold is certainly . . . odd." Emily's laugh was strong and genuine, and she hooked her arm through Imogene's. About to stride forward, she hesitated and spoke in an exaggerated whisper. "Where are we going?"

"The stables," Imogene whispered back, grinning, glad to have company.

"An unusual destination being that you are not dressed for riding and we will be called to ready for dinner soon."

"Perhaps a trifle unusual. However, asking your coachman to come into the manor would be odder."

"There is that." She pulled Imogene forward, adopting an easy gait. "Still, that begs the question, why do you need to speak to our coachman? Should we go through the conservatory? It's faster."

"Excellent idea." Imogene nodded. "Father is quite put out about the burr. I heard his indignant comments to Mother and Mr. Tabard. They all seem to be in agreement."

"Which is?"

"That Ben was a poor sport, a cad; that it was the height of rudeness to accuse Jake and Percy of cheating. I thought I might talk to your coachman and see if it was even possible that the burr was picked up from the grass, as my father asserts."

"You know it's not."

"Indeed. The pad would have been brushed before being used."

"More to the point: Were the boys in the stable as Lancelot was being saddled? And if so, would they have known which horse was Ben's?"

"They would have known. Most definitely. Lancelot is quite distinct, and all saw Ben arrive."

"This was not an accident."

"Indeed not."

It took little effort to run everyone down that had been in the stable earlier in the day, preparing for the race. Imogene had cause to appreciate Emily's presence for more than her companionship; the men did not hesitate to tell the daughter of the house how they felt about the dustup.

Mr. Fowler was deeply offended. The insult, of course, being that anyone—namely, Father—could suggest that his grooms had been so lax or inept or foolish as to saddle a horse with a burr. Mr. Fowler went on at length until his ire was fully spent and he returned to his duties. The grooms were a little more prudent in their language, but there was no doubt of their pique, too. As to the question of who was around during the saddling, it would seem that all the gentlemen of the house were in and out of the stables at some point, laughing and chatting and milling about—including Percy and Jake. No one had seen anything suspicious.

"Doesn't help in the least, does it?" Imogene asked as they walked back to the house. They were taking the longer route to the front door to allow time to discuss their complete lack of knowledge. It mostly involved chuntering.

"Skulking about?" a voice asked as they passed through the portico and into the vestibule.

Imogene turned with a smile, recognizing the voice. "Oh, Mrs. Beeswanger, you gave us such a start." Like mother, like daughter.

"I beg your pardon," came the jovial reply. "I thought to add some levity—your countenances were decidedly sour. Is something amiss?"

"No, Mama. Not really. We were just to the stable, hoping to understand . . ."

"Ah yes. The burr. Such a to-do. Let me guess. Mr. Fowler has assured you that the burr was not placed under the saddle pad, in carelessness or intent, by him or any of his grooms."

"As you say." Imogene nodded several times. She looked over to see Emily doing likewise and Imogene continued for a few more bobs.

"That was expected. The man knows what he is about—been a coachman for decades. Don't trouble yourself, girls. Put your pretty smiles back on your faces. Mr. Beeswanger is ready to ring a fine peal over those boys. . . . As it would seem that no one else is about to call them to order." Mrs. Beeswanger sighed—rather heavily. "There is no excuse for such behavior at their age. Clara would be horrified." Reaching out, she squeezed their hands reassuringly. "Now, off you go. Time to dress for dinner. I have a special treat for our entertainment tonight. I have hired a string quartet to play Haydn. It will be a lovely evening—little fodder for the boys to cause mischief."

As Mrs. Beeswanger had predicted, the evening was indeed lovely and mischief-free, lulling the company into complacency until the next afternoon.

IMOGENE LOOKED DOWN at her soft lilac skirts and lifted a lady beetle onto her palm, blowing softly so that it would take wing.

Ernest sat on the blanket beside her, saying little and yet breathing in a very controlled manner . . . as one does when one is trying to build up courage to ask a question.

The inability to speak his mind was not, in fact, Ernest's fault. Imogene had deliberately requested that the blanket be placed in the shade of the willow near the shore of the pond . . . lake. The proximity to dearest Mama and Mrs. Beeswanger, lounging nearby in chairs brought down from the manor, was not a coincidence. Imogene was well aware of the older ladies' preferred resting place, and she had used that knowledge to her advantage. The advantage of preventing Ernest from offering her his hand—something he was unlikely to do with others listening.

Imogene was desperately afraid that Ernest would rush his proposal, ask her too soon. She was not ready to say yes . . . but neither was she ready to say no. She was in a quandary.

Despite Ben's lack of appreciation for green beans, Imogene had yet to discover a horrible trait of his that would usurp his charm and make all his actions suspect. In fact, she had found no reason to not be in love with him—knowing that Emily wanted to call Ben her own should have been enough for her heart to cede victory and look to greener pastures. But her heart, apparently, had a mind of its own.

It was a confused metaphor, and yet it spoke to the essence of her indecision.

Imogene had to turn her thoughts once and for all from Ben and decide on Ernest by his own merit. She should not favor his suit simply because he was Ben's brother or that he could take her away from the intolerable control of her father; that would not be fair to a gentleman who saw more in her than she did in herself. She would not use him to continue her art studies. Nor would she accept him in the fear that there might never be another suitor.

It was only fair to judge Ernest as a possible husband when they had more times like these. Sitting quietly together, watching Emily and Ben rock sedately in a lake boat while Percy and Jake swam on the far side and Father, Mr. Beeswanger, and Mr. Tabard stood by the boathouse chatting. Yes, the air fairly wafted with peace and companionship. Lazy summer days . . . relaxation and calm . . . days conducive to happy thoughts—

Ernest cleared his throat.

"Please," Imogene said quickly. "Shall we talk of nonsense? I have just started reading a ghoulish book full of dire warnings and haunt—"

"Imogene, I would like—"

"To speak of other things. Let us not be serious"—she glanced at him under her lashes—"when family is about."

"It is family that concerns me. . . . Ben has lost the charity of your father."

"My father is in and out of charity regularly. That is certainly not cause for concern . . . or hurry."

"Imogene—"

"Please," she said, near to a whisper. But he heard.

"Of course, we will wait if you prefer to."

Imogene sighed in great relief. "Is it too much to ask?"

Looking down at her, no longer gulping at the air, Ernest

smiled. It was a kind, indulgent smile that reached his eyes, and they shone with caring. Her heart skipped a beat, and warmth, not born in embarrassment but something much more agreeable, spread throughout her body. It was a heady sensation, and Imogene grinned.

This was the *very* reason for delay. This sensation offered the possibility of a happy union: this, and the knowledge that Ernest Steeple was an honorable gentleman with a great capacity for compassion. What more could one need in a spouse?

A scream rent the air, and a great splash broke Imogene's trancelike state. Jumping to her feet, she ran to the lake's edge in time to see Emily's head bob up out of the water. She took a deep breath, stood, and then screamed again, this time in rage.

"How could you? You know I can't swim." Charging through the water as best she could, encumbered by her skirts in the waist-deep water, Emily snatched at Jake and Percy—who easily swam to the far side of the overturned boat.

Ben, hatless and equally sodden, grabbed Emily's arm and said something to her. She spun around. "But look! Just look what they have done!"

"Sorry, old girl. Meant *you* no harm. Got a burr in my breeches and had to lash out." Jake's smirk was not attractive.

If Imogene hadn't known better, she would have thought Emily near tears.

And really, it was not to be wondered at. Emily's beautiful white gown was ruined, covered in mud, reeds draped over shoulders, and a lily pad hung from her bonnet. Ben looked no better; though his dark coat hid the dirt, his shirt and cream pantaloons did not. Water dripped from his hair and down his face. He said something to Emily that gave her pause. . . . And she began to laugh.

Standing together, sharing a joke, ignoring the taunts of Jake and Percy, Ben and Emily rendered the prank toothless—childish and unworthy. Ben offered Emily his arm in an exaggerated gesture, as if they were standing in a ballroom and not in the middle of an artificial lake. With elbows hooked together, Emily removed the lily pad from her bonnet, took hold of her skirts, and sloshed to the water's edge.

Ernest offered them a hand up the bank while Imogene returned to the blanket. She tossed books, hats, and parasol aside, then she pulled it up off the grass. It could be used as a wrap should Emily be cold. Before Imogene turned back to the lake, her gaze fell on the mothers, who were staring at the commotion.

Mrs. Beeswanger's expression was excessively bland, while Mother was soundlessly chuckling. "These boys. What will they think of next?"

"That was an expensive gown, Olivia."

"Oh dear. I do beg your pardon, Diane. I will send Gabriella to look at it—my *French* maid is a treasure. She will be able to set it to rights, I am certain."

"Thank you for the offer, but if Kate is unable to recover that dreadful mess, then I will simply have another one made. It won't be *too* much of an imposition." Mrs. Beeswanger glanced at Imogene, winked, and then turned her face back to the lake.

"It is such a shame that boys mature so slowly. They can try one's patience."

Imogene's eyes grew wide, expecting her mother to take umbrage in defense of her son, but she said nothing. Imogene turned back to the sodden couple and pretended she had not overheard the caustic remarks.

Emily survived her soaking with little repercussion. Most important, she did not sneeze upon her arrival at the manor and, therefore, was not sent to while away the rest of the day in bed. Percy and Jake, however, did miss the duckling braised in sherry, and Miss Watson's stirring rendition of Bach's piano concerto in D Minor that evening. Nothing was said of their absence, and there were no empty place settings at the table. However, there was a slight chill in the air whenever Father addressed Ben . . . or Mr. Beeswanger, though it was not overt.

"I APOLOGIZE FOR my father, Ben. Since the burr incident, he has been rather beastly to you. The cold shoulder and all that . . ."

Ben and Imogene had set up their art lesson in the conservatory the next morning, not to sketch the beautiful calla lilies but the ironwork holding up the glass roof. A table had been repositioned with chairs pulled next to it, and they had set about their sketching with great concentration—well, Ben concentrated; Imogene was as unperturbed as ever when attending her art.

"Father has never been a warm or amenable person. Grandfather Chively was much the same."

"It is no never mind to me," Ben said, glancing up at the ceiling and then back to his paper. "The Beeswangers are quite the opposite, going out of their way to make me feel welcome. It is a shame that your father does not enjoy my company when it seems likely that we will be relate—" Ben grimaced at his very near *faux pas* and redirected the conversation.

He made a slight growl in his throat as the rod he was drawing looked anything but straight. Iron was not known to be inconstant or malleable. Imogene leaned over his shoulder—smelling of roses—and, using her own graphite pencil, redrew the lines in two quick strokes. She made it look so easy. "Thank you," he grumbled as she sat back. Scratching above his ear in frustration, Ben sighed, and then he traced her lines, trying to understand where he had gone wrong.

"You are doing very well, Ben. Making great progress."

"That is very kind of you to say so, but the evidence"—he waved at his paper—"says otherwise."

"Practice makes—"

"Yes, I know. You have said as much before, again and again. I will do as you suggest. . . . But I wonder if I will ever be good enough—soon enough."

Silence emanated from the other chair, and Ben looked up to see Imogene shaking her head at him. "Yes?" he asked.

"You must throw away all these doubts; they do not help in the least. You have such an affable manner about you until you start to sketch. Can you not throw away your expectations and simply enjoy the process?"

"Enjoy?"

"Please do not tell me that you have an aversion to drawing."

Ben shifted in his seat, suddenly uncomfortable. "Of course not." When was the last time he actually appreciated this necessity? "Merely an aversion to inept drawing."

"I would rather you squander paper than have your vexation affect your work. Perhaps it would be best to start again."

Ben quickly turned his paper over. Recalling Imogene's lesson on how to measure using the long edge of the graphite pencil, he closed one eye and stared at the ceiling for some minutes. When he began this time, he did so from the center, working his way out.

They sketched in silence, companionable silence, for a quarter hour or so, with Imogene casually looking over to his progress but saying nothing. This time the iron rod looked like the support it was meant to be, and the ridge didn't veer off in the wrong direction. Another quarter hour and Ben lifted the paper to view it at arm's length.

"Well. That is nearly, if I do say so myself, nearly recognizable." He turned for Imogene's reaction, pleased to see her grin. It was only a small sketch, five or six inches in diameter, but it illustrated the two most important aspects of the ironwork to his way of thinking—the supports and how they were joined. He would worry about the useless curling embellishments later.

"Might your enthusiasm for drawing be returning?"

"I believe it has." To prove his words true, Ben looked around for another subject. Should he sketch the vent? Perhaps the transom? He decided on the door and set to work. "You have a gift for teaching, my dear Miss Imogene." His words were imparted with far more warmth than he had intended. Shifting, not so much to see the transom above the door better but to avoid looking at his brother's ladylove, Ben imagined Imogene to be flying her colors. He regretted bringing her to blush.

He stole a peek, apology on his tongue. . . . But there it stayed.

There was no doubt of Imogene's discomfort—she was busy pulling at the leaves of the *Ficus benjamina* beside her, staring at nothing—but her complexion was not ruddy; her expression was pensive, not embarrassed.

"Imogene?"

"Hmm?"

"Is all well?"

"Yes, indeed. I am merely thinking."

"I believe that to be evident. Might those thoughts be of a disturbing nature?"

For several minutes the only sounds in the brightly lit conservatory were the scratches of his graphite pencil, birds twittering from nests in the iron rafters, and the wind whistling under the door to the garden—and the rustle of leaves being yanked free and shredded.

"No. Not really. Why do you ask?"

"You are decimating that poor plant."

"Pardon? I'm . . ." Looking down, she laughed and shook the detritus from her skirts. "I will blame you if Mrs. Beeswanger complains."

"Me?"

"Yes, indeed. If you had not complimented me on my teaching ability, I would not have been distracted."

"I'm not sure I follow."

"I shouldn't wonder. I am making no sense."

She turned back to her drawing—a large, beautiful rendering of the conservatory, which included foliage, ironwork, and glass—so well depicted it seemed possible to walk forward into the picture despite the fact that it was black and white—

"I have a most impractical dream."

"Ah . . . yes, having to do with your art. A showing in London perhaps? Acclaim? Not to be wondered at, really. You have an amazing talent. Perhaps we can find you a patron. I could speak to Lord Penton."

Imogene laughed in true amusement; it was a pretty carillon. "Thank you, no. A great fuss would be mortifying. Acclaim? No, indeed. A showing? No, and no again."

"I am getting the impression that you are less than enthused with the idea of renown. I'm rather astute in these matters. I understand small nuances . . . such as the word *no*."

"Very perceptive."

"Indeed. So if a showing is *not* to your taste, what has caused your consternation?"

"Foolishness. A flight of fantasy that is part ridiculous, part delusion, and entirely impossible."

"All the best dreams are."

"Oh, Ben, is there no seriousness to you?"

"Absolutely. I seriously dislike green beans."

Imogene chuckled and shook her head, finding more amusement in the comment than Ben thought warranted. She finally calmed, blinked, and then spoke in a rush. "I dream of having a school one day—an art academy for drawing and painting. I know I am young, inexperienced, and without funds, but dreams are, by their very nature, unattainable. Yes, there, you may laugh now."

Ben looked up from his sketch with no inclination to comply. "That is a most exemplary dream, Imogene."

It was . . . without a doubt. But where did Ernest fit within this dream? Was his brother waiting in the wings for nothing?

chapter 11

In which Ben is inundated with sentiment and doubt

With a deep sigh, Imogene stared at Ben as if trying to read his expression, as if trying to find the barb in his words. They stared at each other for quite some time, until Imogene's mouth curled up ever so slightly. Then her eyes widened, she blinked again, and she leaned back.

"Please ignore my ramblings. I don't know why I spoke. Only Emily is aware of this idiocy." A sudden flush colored her cheeks with crimson, and she looked vastly uncomfortable. "I spoke out of turn. A bad habit of mine."

With a laugh, edged with resignation, Ben shook his head. "I would never accuse you of speaking out of turn."

"Be that as it may, I would prefer it not to be bandied about."

"No bandying, I swear."

"Not even Ernest."

Ben's brow furrowed for a moment, and then he nodded. "As you wish."

Looking relieved, Imogene smiled her appreciation. "And you? Do you have some terrible secret that should never be exposed?"

About to argue over her definition of a terrible secret, Ben swallowed his retort and followed, instead, down the frivolous path she had taken. "Besides my dislike of green beans? Ah yes, I must confess to a decided lack of appreciation for the latest statue my parents sent from Italy. Carved by a great artist, or so I am told—but the boy is naked, with odd little wings sprouting from his back and a quiver full of arrows. Now really, what is that about?"

A giggle drew their attention to the door leading into the manor. "Cupid. That sounds like Cupid, Mr. Ben."

"Ah, I think you might be right, Hardly Harriet." Ben smiled at the young girl and then turned to greet Emily.

"Are you ready?" Emily asked, staying at the door while Harriet skipped over to the table.

"I believe so." Ben collected his sketches and dropped them into his string-tie folder, pushing them to the center of the table, out of the way. They were not ready for the scrutiny of a twelve-year-old. He glanced at Imogene; she watched him with a half smile and a rather enigmatic expression.

"Scout out our location for tomorrow's lesson," she said, lifting her cheeks. Ben could have been mistaken, but it seemed as if her tone had a forlorn quality to it, though he did not know why.

"Yes, indeed. I am sure there will be plenty of choices."

Emily had promised Ben a lengthy tour of the manor, top to bottom. He was quite looking forward to it. Turning toward Emily, he paused to admire her generous smile and pretty curls. Indeed, there was much to appreciate at Shackleford Park; he would have to thank his brother for the introduction some time. He was beginning to realize that young ladies and an architectural apprentice were not as mutually exclusive as he had once believed.

As he was just about to step across the threshold, Ben looked over his shoulder, expecting to see the charming tableau of two heads together as Imogene started Harriet's lesson. However, Imogene was not looking at her next student, she was looking at her last.

She was staring at Ben.

Their eyes met and held. The rest of the room, the rest of the world, fell away, and there was nothing and no one to consider—just the two of them staring at each other for an eternity or two. Was it forever or a moment? And then Imogene frowned, breaking the spell.

Ben turned away. Listening to the pounding of his heart, he tried to breathe again and swallowed against the pain in his gut. He gestured Emily ahead because he could find no words to speak. He was a raw bundle of sentiment and doubt.

"Do you want to start in the attics or the cellars?" Emily asked in a perfectly normal tone, as if the world were the same as it had always been.

"Let us start in the cellars," Ben said in much the same tone, even adding a smile and a wave for her to take the lead.

No one could know. No one could see the horror that crawled underneath his skin, the shout that was building in his chest. Why had this happened?

Ben felt sick as he skipped down the stairs after Emily. He placed her arm in the crook of his elbow, and they started down the hallway. As Emily pointed to this and that, he used a smile and a chuckle to hide his dreadful discovery.

Locked in Imogene's gaze, Ben had wanted nothing more than to rush across the room, take her into his arms, kiss her until their knees gave way and they tumbled into a pile, and . . . He could take his thoughts no further in that direction—*should* take them no further.

Ben had always appreciated young ladies, been drawn to them, and greatly enjoyed their company. But never had he felt such a mixture of euphoria, excitement, and awe. Never before had he wanted to stay in any one person's company . . . forever.

This was terrible!

IMOGENE WAS QUIET most of that afternoon and well into the evening. No one noticed. Not even Emily—she was too busy staring at Ben.

Perhaps Ben was aware, but he stayed away from Imogene and rarely looked in her direction. If Ernest was puzzled by her lackluster conversation, he said nothing to that effect. Instead, he filled in their discourse with recitations of various poems, snippets of several books he had enjoyed, and descriptions of Musson Hall that he recalled with great affection.

Far from being unwelcome, it was the salve Imogene needed. Not only distracting, but also little effort was required of her. It gave her time to find a pigeonhole in her mind into which she could stuff her confused and confusing feelings about Ben. It gave her time to assess the strange expression she had seen on his face.

It was the face of realization. . . . But of what? Had it anything to do with her? While it made sense—he was staring at her at the time—his thoughts could have gone wandering and hit upon something unsavory. The thought was definitely not of a pleasant nature; Ben had gone rather gray.

The best indication that it might in some way be associated with her was Ben's unexpected new manner. He no longer looked her in the eye, not even in her direction. Whenever they inadvertently stood near each other, Ben moved away. Twice he made as if to pass her something—her fan when it dropped and then a letter that was being shared with the company—changed his mind, and allowed Ernest to do the job in one instance and Emily in the other.

Imogene was terribly confused and, without a doubt, hurt. She had no contagion. Had her father's aversion finally affected Ben's opinion? Did he, too, now find her annoying—like a pestering insect? She thought their rapport had progressed beyond friendship, more like comrades in art, and there was a chance that she would be his sister-in-law one day. And yet, suddenly—for it was very sudden—Ben no longer valued her company. It was devastating, for all that Imogene could ever have of Ben Steeple would be his wit and laughter and his company. The thought of losing even that small allotment was close to tragic.

She didn't know what to do. . . . Well, she did, but she was loath to do it.

They had to talk.

Tired and nervous after a sleepless night, Imogene met Ben in the cellars for their next art lesson—where he could learn how to draw supports, foundations, keystones, and such. Emily had suggested it, and Ben had agreed, though reluctantly.

Emily walked with Imogene into the depths of the manor as the wine cellars formed a complicated labyrinth.

"Just around the corner and then . . . Well, look who is already here." Emily's tone took on a cooing quality.

Imogene could easily guess but didn't bother.

"Oh, the extra candles are a vast improvement. Excellent idea. What do you think, Imogene?"

"Yes indeed, excellent." Imogene avoided meeting Ben's eye. She placed her supplies on the table that had been brought down for them to use and made a great chore out of arranging the materials. She glanced around for something that might be of interest for her to sketch while Ben was busy with his bricks and mortar.

Bottles . . . hmm, more bottles and bottles in a rack. She decided to sketch the chair.

Emily stayed for a quarter hour, trying to engage Ben in conversation, but he kept lapsing into silent concentration. She finally shrugged and headed back upstairs into the warmer environs of the manor. Imogene had brought a serviceable shawl, knowing that it would be cool belowground and not feeling a need to impress with a pretty, summery gown.

The silence of the cellar continued for some moments until Imogene saw an excuse to break into the stifling atmosphere, which had nothing to do with the airless room. "I'm afraid the proportions are off between these two stones. Perhaps if you make this one smaller, then you will . . . Yes, there. I think that works better. . . . Don't you?"

Ben nodded, head still down, graphite pencil still scratching across the surface of the rough paper. "Yes. Indeed."

"Excellent." Imogene took a deep breath, swallowed, and cleared her throat. "And, perhaps, while I have your attention, I might ask what it is that I have done to put you so out of charity?"

Finally, Ben lifted his handsome head, frowning. "Out of charity?"

"You have been behaving in a peculiar manner since yesterday. As if I had been inflicted with smallpox and you were afraid of the contagion."

Ben laughed, but not in his usual casual manner. It was staccato and forced. "Smallpox, indeed. What an idea." He dropped his eyes back to his paper and lifted his stick, focusing on the sketch once again. His easy charm was on hiatus.

Imogene rubbed at her forehead, sighed—as quietly as she could—and settled her nerves again. "Ben?"

"Yes."

"Ben, please look at me. Thank you. Something is wrong, but I can't repair the damage if I know not what has caused the rift. Yes, I know that is a terrible metaphor, but I am vastly uncomfortable, and it's getting worse the longer you stare at me without saying anything, without explaining why I am no longer your friend. Don't insult my intelligence by saying you have no idea of what I speak. You can tell me that my sense of guilt is misplaced, that you are upset about something else, that I am not the cause of your discomfort but merely the benefi-ciary. That I would consider. But an out-and-out denial that anything is wrong . . . well, it will only serve to make me more uncomfortable and not resolve the situation at all."

Imogene took a deep breath, looked down at her shaking hands, and moved them to her lap. She closed her eyes briefly and then lifted her gaze back to Ben. He was still staring. "You are still staring and saying nothing. Time is of the essence; we must resolve our differences before you go. To not do so would be folly . . . for all of us."

She watched him take a deep breath and then swallow visibly, as if he were the nervous one. . . . Which was ridicu-lous, as he was a confident young gentleman from a good family who cared about his welfare. He had no reason to be uncomfortable . . . . Unless . . . With a sudden realization of her own, Imogene was fairly certain she had ferreted out the problem.

"Oh dear. You have decided that I am not worthy of Ernest . . . . And you don't know how to tell me . . . or him."

With a melancholy smile—which is quite a feat—Ben shook his head. "No. That is not it."

"No? Then . . . then, could you please enlighten me? I would not normally utter such a personal query. You must know how difficult it is not to simply hide inside myself and fret in silence. It is a testament to how close we have become that I am comfortable sharing my dreams and . . . now, my distress with you. And I am distressed, Ben. No matter what happens with Ernest, I would like to think of our friendship continuing. You are a kindred spirit. And . . . well . . . I . . ."

"I humbly beg your pardon, Imogene. I was not aware that I was causing you any concern. I am not conscious of behaving abnormally."

"Well, you are."

"Again, I apologize."

His smile lifted, losing its dejected aspect. Sitting up straight, he nodded. "Yes. We are indeed kindred spirits, and I, too, wish our friendship to continue regardless. . . . However, I have come to realize that there will be a significant change in the dynamics of our family should Ernest . . . well, you know. We have been each other's support since we were knee-high to a grasshopper. Circumstances will have to change." He blinked, nodded again, and looked expectant.

"That's it. You treat me like a leper because I am going to change the family?"

"In a delightful way, of course."

"Are you certain?"

"Well, I believe the change will be delightful. Though that remains to be seen, and it would be up to Ernest and yourself—"

"Are you certain that this is the cause of our rift?"

"Yes." Ben looked serious, and his downhearted smile re-appeared. "There are some who find changes challenging."

"I wouldn't have thought *you* to be stymied by change."

"It depends on the significance of that change. This is monumental."

"My joining the Steeple family would be monumental?"

"Yes. I believe it would be." Laughing, Ben reached across the table and tapped Imogene on the hand with his graphite pencil. "Marriage is monumental."

Imogene ignored his words and the slight doleful tone; she instead stared into his eyes. The tenderness of his gaze warmed her from her fingertips to her toes. She knew his excuse to be a bouncer, but the reason no longer mattered as long as they had returned to their easy rapport.

Imogene grinned and grabbed his hand, giving it a little squeeze; he didn't pull away. Yes, the world had righted itself again.

WHILE IMOGENE'S SILENCE but a day earlier had caused little notice and no comment, her affability created a stir. With a smile and a nod, Imogene ignored all remarks on sparkling eyes, queries about bended knees, and covert looks that volleyed back and forth between Ernest and her. The speculation that he had made an offer was rampant. It was fortunate that he was either blissfully unaware or ignoring the wheedling questions.

Ernest was all kindness and consideration, abiding by her request to delay any questions of a matrimonial nature.

Knowing that, he waited for her to signal her preparedness, allowing Imogene the opportunity to settle her anxieties. Father could prod and grumble as much as he liked.

However, the weather was most disobliging the last day of the Steeples' stay at Shackleford Park. Rain, rain, and more rain. A fluctuating combination of persons occupied the various family rooms. While the fathers seemed to prefer the billiard room and the mothers the drawing room, the younger generation meandered between the music room and the library. Private conversations were nigh on impossible. The evening was devoted to cards, and most made an early night of it.

Standing in the shelter of the portico, waving Ben and Ernest away the next morning, Imogene was subjected to an inquiring look from Emily. "Well?" she said, lowering her hand. "You do not have the countenance of a bride-to-be."

"I don't look sanctimonious?"

"Most definitely not."

"Well, I *was* asked a question." Imogene grinned at her friend's sudden intake of breath. "No, no. Not that one." She laughed. "He asked if he might write."

"And you said yes, of course."

"I didn't have the opportunity. Father agreed for me."

"Are we talking of Ernest or Ben?" a voice queried from the shadows of the portico.

"Mr. Tabard, I did not see you there. I thought everyone had gone back inside." Imogene turned a grimace to Emily, sharing a wide-eyed look of embarrassment.

"Don't concern yourself, my dears. I was just trying to understand. The maneuverings of your generation are quite beyond me at times. Clara always kept me straight. It seems as though you are talking of Ernest, and yet I thought it was Ben who was casting calf-eyes at Imogene. No, no, I see that I have it mixed up. Never mind my ramblings."

Mr. Tabard sighed. Shifting his balance from one leg to the other, he squinted toward the drive and the diminishing figures. "There is always a great deal of fuss when strangers are about. Perhaps now the stay will return to ordinary days. More comfort, as Clara used to say, in familiarity."

"You are off on the morrow, Mr. Tabard," Emily reminded him.

"Yes, yes, I know. Well, then perhaps when you come to visit at Greytower. Yes, things will be as they always were at the Hall. Except that Clara . . . of course."

Imogene swallowed against the tightening of her throat and joined Mr. Tabard at the door. "It will not be quite the same, but I'm sure . . ." Her words petered off. It wouldn't be the same without Cousin Clara at all, and to pretend otherwise almost felt disrespectful to her memory.

"Might I ask"—Mr. Tabard turned his watery eyes to Emily—"that you include Jake in your company at Greytower? I know you to have a calming influence on him."

Emily's frown came and went quickly; it was unlikely that Mr. Tabard saw it. But Imogene knew the frown's source. Any influence Emily had on Jake lived solely in the imagination of poor Mr. Tabard. "Of course," Emily said easily. "Though I'm not sure he or Percy will be interested in the same pursuits. They have a tendency toward more energetic jaunts."

Mr. Tabard nodded, but Imogene was fairly certain that though he had heard, he would not heed. Percy and Jake had always treated Imogene and Emily as pestering little sisters with no wit. There was hardly any chance of that changing in the near future.

Looking back over her shoulder, Imogene sighed silently. The drive was empty, the Steeples were gone, and she did not know when she might see them again. The prospect of returning to ordinary days, as Mr. Tabard had called them, held little appeal.

GREYTOWER HALL, DOWERSHAM, KENT—
EARLY AUGUST 1817

EMILY'S BAROUCHE WAS an ideal carriage for a summer drive through the countryside. It provided unobstructed views when the hood was pushed back, and it seated four. There was plenty of room for a close friend and two sisters, but not their governess. Miss Watson complained bitterly; the girls did not.

As they were traveling to Dowersham *en masse*, the Beeswangers arrived from Tishdale in their travel coach, Emily's barouche, and a luggage cart. They added the Chively coach, Percy on horseback, and, of course, their own luggage cart to the convoy. It was just as well that the journey would take only an hour. . . . Perhaps an hour and a half, since there was negligible wind and the pace was slow.

With little privacy, deep matters—such as whether or not

any letters had been received in the past fortnight—were not discussed. Instead, the discourse seemed to center on a new milliner in Tishdale, the Beeswanger cook's attempt at French cuisine, and the spot on Harriet's pretty gown—which may or may not be ruined. Imogene paid scant attention.

For the first time ever, Imogene found that she was not interested in yet another stay. Too much gadding about in her mind, though it was not dissimilar from every other summer of her life. Still, this time the families had spent the spring in London. Perhaps it was the combination of constant upheaval for the better part of two seasons that had given her the unsettled feel. . . . Or it could have something to do with the Steeple brothers and indecision. It would be most inconvenient if that were the case; it would mean her lackluster humor could be laid only at her own door.

Emily said nothing—nor could she with younger ears seated so close—and yet she tossed a fair number of frowning glances her friend's way. Imogene shrugged and smiled, in a most convincing act of nonchalance that didn't fool Emily one iota. They were barely out of the carriage—the girls bounding toward the front door of Greytower while their parents stretched and laughed together as they stepped down onto the gravel—when Emily pulled Imogene aside.

"Has Ernest not written?" Emily asked in a voice ready to be outraged.

"Yes. Yes, indeed," Imogene said quickly, divesting her friend of the idea that Ernest was an inconstant suitor. "Nearly every day. And you? Did Ben write?"

"No, goose. He did not have Papa's permission." She winked. "Though I would not have sent any missives away had he done so. . . . But it is irrelevant as—"

A shout of amusement cut through the air and the company's conversations.

"Jake!" Percy laughed loudly. "What are you about?"

The Tabards had come to greet their guests and stood waiting by the door. With the antiquity of Greytower Hall in the background—its ivy-covered tower entrance with a steep roof and rows of chimney pots peeking over the ridge—the tableau was dramatic and unexpected. Mr. Tabard and Jake were dressed in London fashion. Gone were the country brown coats, plain waistcoats, and buckskins. In their place were black tailcoats, richly patterned waistcoats, pantaloons, and hessians. With shoulders back and chin lifted, Jake looked entirely unlike himself. He bowed to the parents, nodded to Emily and Imogene, called "hullo" to the girls, and then ruined the effect by grinning—and hooting—with Percy.

Imogene had to admit that Jake was imposing; though not handsome in the classic sense, as the glint of mischief in his eyes was still too pronounced by her way of thinking, his toothy grin was infectious—and he was well turned out. It was somewhat of a surprise, as Imogene did not recall Jake being as well attired in London.

"Did you take a detour on your return to Dowersham?" Percy circled his friend. "By way of Town?"

That would have been a significant deviation.

"Indeed. Jonathan Meyer of Conduit Street. Do you like it?"

It was a rhetorical question. It was clear that everyone was duly impressed. "Do I not look the epitome of a gentleman?"

"Your mother would say that a gentleman is not a braggart, Jake." Mr. Tabard gave his son a quick glance and then turned back to the company. "But accommodating . . . accommodating and welcoming. Or was it obliging and hospitable. . . . I can't quite remember."

"Oh. Oh yes." Jake lifted his chin once again. "Welcome to Greytower, one and all. We are so very pleased that you have come to join us. We have excellent entertainments planned, and I'm sure you will have a most excellent stay. . . . Lawks, I believe I used *excellent* twice—let me try again—"

"A gentleman does not—" Mr. Tabard interrupted.

"Repeat himself?" Jake frowned.

Mr. Tabard sighed. "Use vulgar language."

"Oh Lawks, I forgot about that, too."

Mr. Tabard shook his head as the company burst into laughter and made their way into the manor.

Imogene's father patted Jake on the shoulder as he stepped past. "Well done, my boy. You'll get the right of it in no time. Percy, take note."

"Entertainments?" Emily whispered in Imogene's ear. "Since when have we done much more than appreciate the serenity of the Hall's isolation? I have two novels with me."

"There might be time for both."

"Oh, I'm not worried about it overly. The wonderful aspect of books is that they wait for you . . . and are not in the least insulted if you deviate for a bit. It is merely the oddness of the enterprise. Your Cousin Clara thought that enjoyment of nature was as much as anyone needed."

"Yes, but then Jake was not behaving like a buffoon. Perhaps this is meant to keep him out of mischief. Whether it does so remains to be seen."

"Indeed."

The remainder of the afternoon was spent settling in. As the Hall was a rather humble home in its number of bedrooms, Imogene and Emily shared a small room with dark wood paneling and a window that overlooked the formal gardens. In the way of many medieval manors, a small alcove—just large enough for a narrow bed—accommodated Kate.

The evening included an exemplary meal and a pianist—far superior to Miss Watson. . . . But none were unkind enough to say so. Yet perhaps the best entertainment was that of Jake attempting to emulate an erudite country gentleman with the prods and hints of his father. It was rather charming, and Imogene found herself in far better charity with Jake than she had ever been. Percy was not charming in the least. At first, he tried to goad Jake into misbehavior and then chose to sulk. The company did their best to ignore him.

The next morning saw Jake and a prune-faced Percy not up early with the other gentlemen but dawdling with the girls at breakfast midmorning. Emily and Imogene had yet to decide on their plans for the day, but they found the boys expected to be included.

"You do not have to play the host to us, Jake. We will entertain ourselves as we usually do and then meet you at dinner."

"Would that I could, Emily, old girl, but I'm afraid that I have been instructed to see you happy."

"I would be happy to be left alone."

"That won't work. Perhaps I can take you on a tour of the Hall?"

"Why would you do that?"

"For some reason, Father thought you were interested in architecture."

Imogene laughed and shared a significant look with Emily.

"I appreciate the offer, but no." Emily pushed away from the table, glancing out the front window as she did.

Imogene followed her puzzled gaze down the long, tree-lined drive. Two riders were approaching, followed by a cart. They looked very familiar. Imogene gulped, her belly clenched with excitement, and she found it suddenly difficult to breathe. Could it be? No. They weren't invited . . . were they?

"Hold on. What's this?" Jake joined the stare out the window. "It looks like Ernest and Ben. What are they doing here?"

"Father invited them," Percy said airily.

"Pardon?" Jake whirled around and faced his friend.

Percy shrugged. "Yes. I overheard him talking to Mother about it. He sent an invitation a few days ago. And . . ." He jerked his head toward the window. "Apparently they accepted."

chapter 12

In which there are missteps, missed cues, muddles, and mayhem

Stormy skies and a chill breeze provided the appropriate backdrop to Ben and Ernest's reception at Greytower Hall. It certainly did not compare favorably with that of Gracebridge or Shackleford. No members of the family waited by the front door, the grooms were slow to arrive, and a rather frosty butler ushered them into the entrance hall with a sniff of disapproval.

Ben had warned Ernest that the invitation to join the company at Greytower Hall had come from the wrong party—that Mr. Chively had overstepped when he extended an invitation to the *Tabards'* manor. It was high-handed and suspect. The only motive could be that of allowing Ernest the opportunity to propose to Imogene. Mr. Chively was manipulating once again.

Ernest had countered that it was not uncommon for families as close as the Chivelys and Tabards to add other guests to a country visit without the host making a personal solicitation. And while true enough in general, Ben was fairly certain such was not the case here.

Ben had also argued against the idea of hopping into the saddle and heading west once again. He knew that Imogene had asked for a delay and thought it ill-advised for Ernest to hover at her elbow . . . waiting and watching. It was likely to make her nervous; it would make anyone nervous. And thereby do more damage. Ben thought a month or so of eloquent letters would have done his brother greater service—but Ernest would not listen. He had to see her, be with her, look into her lovely eyes, and bask in her smile.

It all made Ben quite green, and he refused to join Ernest in his folly.

There was nothing his brother could say that would entice Ben back into Imogene's presence . . . though he had not worded it quite that way. Bored. Tired of gadding about. Needed to focus on his art. Spend more time at Musson House before returning to Canterbury. He thought up an overabundance of excuses. Ernest shot each and every one down. His brother's ability to debate was remarkable—he should take up politics and stop coercing his younger brother. It was outside of enough!

Then Ernest simply said that he needed Ben's support.

With a heavy sigh—very heavy—Ben relented. He could sustain no justification against that, short of the truth. And Ben had no intention of *ever* telling Ernest why he did not want to be around Imogene. There were not many secrets between them, but this confidence was for *all* time.

And so, here he was once again, smiling and laughing and acting the nonchalance he did not feel as the younger members of the company greeted him with varying degrees of enthusiasm. Parents were conspicuously absent. He was acutely aware of Imogene: her lovely, shy smile; her beguiling fragrance; her tinkling laughter; her intoxicating curves that took his breath away; her swaying walk that made his mouth dry; her enticing . . . With a shake of his head, Ben rubbed at his temple and then acknowledged Jake's imperial greeting.

"Thank you, yes, the journey was not overly taxing. Though it does look like rain. Yes indeed, rain. Gray clouds . . . and all that." Ben studiously ignored Imogene and his brother's quizzical glance at his vacuous speech. He could hardly think straight standing in such close proximity to Imogene.

Returning his gaze to Jake, Ben frowned. There was something odd about him, something that did not quite fit with his character. . . . But Ben was hard-pressed to say exactly what it was. Had Jake styled his hair differently?

"Hospitable, yes, a gentleman is hospitable, right?" Jake turned to look at Emily, who nodded rather vigorously. "Fine. Let me see . . . ah. Well . . . please, join us in the morning room," Jake suggested with a grand sweep of his arm. "I'll ask Mrs. Thompson to make up a room while you wait. You were not expected, you see. Only just learned that Mr. Chively had taken it upon himself to extend an invitation. Well, this is not Gracebridge . . . nor is it Shackleford, for that matter. It is likely that you will have to double up. Best we can do under the circumstances. Puts the numbers off complete—"

"Ahem." Emily cleared her throat, interrupting Jake. She shook her head as well.

Jake scowled. "Lawks, this is not as easy as it looks." His words were thought to be quite humorous by the rest of those standing nearby.

There was no arguing that their arrival was untoward . . . and that this was not Shackleford. Greytower was much older and smaller—perhaps as much as a quarter the size. The entrance hall was dark, paneled, and only one story. Ben could see a dining hall off to his right, but it was near impossible to see into the rooms on either side of the large staircase to his left.

"You speak to Mrs. Thompson," Emily instructed Jake. "We'll return to the morning room." At which point, she pivoted and led the way to the room to the left of the staircase.

Harriet and Pauline followed them in, but an echo reverberating down the staircase brought them to a halt just inside the door. "Girls? Where are you? Lesson time."

Pauline curled up the corner of her mouth, Harriet huffed, and yet they both quickly marched out the door and up the stairs. Unfortunately, that left Percy, Emily, Imogene, Ernest, and Ben to attempt a civil conversation.

"You need not have come, you know." Percy flopped into a chair, leaning back in an excessively casual manner that fooled no one. "Father might have invited you, but . . . well, you are not really welcome."

Apparently civility was hard to come by for some.

"Percy!" Imogene and Emily expressed their horror in the same tone and wide eyes.

"Please ignore any unrefined attitudes that might be floating about." Emily stepped to the sideboard, lifting a silver urn. "Chocolate?"

"Ben prefers coffee," Imogene answered for him. "And I believe Ernest does as well."

Emily nodded, switching pots and pouring. "I, for one, greatly appreciate Mr. Chively's initiative." She offered Ben a come-hither grin with his coffee. "And your perfectly timed arrival, for we were just at the point of deciding on our entertainment for the day."

A loud clap of thunder shook the Hall. The patter of rain on the glass quickly changed from charming to alarming while a blustery wind rattled and pulled at the windows.

"Oh dear, a storm is truly upon us." Emily moved to stare outside. "It's a very good thing you are not still on the road. What a fine mess that would have been. Well, staying indoors seems to be the order of the day. Don't you think, Imogene?"

Imogene nodded, sharing her smile equally among them. . . . Well, not Percy. Her brother received a grimace.

"All set," Jake said from the doorway as he entered. "Mrs. Thompson is airing out the tower room. It's rarely used, being that it is haunted, and you will have to share as I have already said. . . . But I'm sure you will be comfortable." His tone implied that he hoped just the opposite. "I have sent your man up to unpack. *He* will have to stay above the stables."

Ben sipped his coffee, glad of the excuse to delay his reaction. It gave him time to ease down his hackles—after all, Ben had known their welcome was not going to be generous. Mr. Chively had put his interests ahead of those of his friends. . . . And Ernest knew it. They were intruding.

A loud bang drew everyone's attention toward the hall. Unseen, the front door had slammed open. While not visible from inside the morning room, the commotion of the older gentlemen rushing inside out of the rain was loud enough for all to hear.

"Blast the weather. Here, Radley. Take this brace. Better than nothing, I suppose. The hare were plentiful, and we would have had a week's worth if not for the storm." There was no mistaking Mr. Tabard's slow delivery.

"They will wait for us, Tabard. Worry not, we can go out tomorrow," Mr. Beeswanger said.

"It looks to storm a month of Sundays," Mr. Chively said in his typically dreary tone.

"What's that?" The floor squeaked as if Mr. Tabard had turned on a wet tile floor. "Speak up, I can hardly hear you. Who?"

There was an indiscernible mumble through which Jake half smiled at Ernest and Ben and then rolled his eyes for Percy's benefit. They all waited for the inevitable burst of indignation. While Ernest looked uncomfortable, Ben was ambivalent; if they were sent packing, he would not have to suffer the agonies of unrequited lo . . . No, he would not finish that thought.

The reaction, when it came, was not of disgust, nor did it originate from Mr. Tabard.

"Excellent. Yes, indeed. Pardon? Oh, I asked him myself. I knew you would not mind, old man. Shall we do the proper?"

The sound of approaching footsteps echoed even before Mr. Chively had finished his sentence. The thoroughly damp gentleman entered the morning room with great verve and affability. Ben hardly recognized him.

"Ernest, my fine young man. So good that you could make it to Dowersham. I hope you had a pleasant journey despite the weather."

"Oh, indeed, sir. The storm began just after we arrived."

Mr. Chively's face was suddenly excessively still. "We?" He turned to look across his shoulder to where Ben was standing next to the window. "Oh." He scowled and returned his decidedly piqued expression back on Ernest. "It would seem that you did not receive *all* my letter. I believe I explained that Greytower Hall was a small manor with far fewer rooms. That it suited an intimate gathering."

Mr. Tabard, chuntering in the background, momentarily drew the attention from Mr. Chively.

"No insult intended, Tabard. You run a fine establishment. A very pretty estate . . . on a sunny day. I merely wish to help Ben, here, understand why he will be required to take a room at the inn."

"Oh, that's all settled, Mr. Chively," Jake piped in. "I had Mrs. Thompson air out the tower room."

"The tower . . . But Jake, my boy, it's in a deplorable state."

Mr. Tabard was horrified. "Not used in years. Your mother quite despaired of that room."

"Yes," Jake said with more glee than was seemly in a proper gentleman. "Because it is haunted."

"Really, Jake," Imogene huffed. "There are times that I quite despair of *you*. Everyone knows that the ghost gossip is two centuries old. Besides, I don't believe the Steeple brothers are easily dissuaded or liver-hearted." She smiled broadly to Ernest and then winked in Ben's direction.

Ben felt his heart accelerate and decided to label his reaction fear of spirits, not joy at Imogene's attention. The idea of ghosts was far, far more acceptable in his eyes.

Emily, watching the exchange, put paid to the whole episode by offering to show the boys to the tower. There was great consternation that a young lady would suggest such a thing. The footman was quickly called to be their guide. As they were heading out the door, Ben glanced over his shoulder in time to see Emily and Imogene share a look of satisfaction. The outrageous offer had done the trick—circumvented the arguing and established that Ernest and Ben were here for the stay.

Ben followed on Ernest's heels, not entirely certain why he was so pleased. Hadn't he wanted to return to Musson House?

"You know, of course, that Jake is up to mischief. That he made mention of the *haunting* with purpose." Sitting on the brocade settee nestled in the oriel window, Emily straightened her skirts and curled up the corner of her mouth in disgust.

They had adjourned to the drawing room upon the arrival of their mothers, ready to break their fast. The morning room was too small a space to accommodate everyone, so Emily and Imogene had slipped across the threshold while the news of the Steeples' arrival was discussed in both enthusiastic and lifeless tones.

Imogene nodded, looking out the window to the slanting sheets of rain, sighed, and sat beside her friend. "After a lull of two centuries, the ghost of . . . who is it that is supposed to haunt the tower again?"

"Lady Ester—I believe. Jilted by a lover and all that. Threw herself from the window. I believe that's the story."

"Yes, I think you might have the right of it. Though Cousin Clara never believed the drivel. She left the room unused because it is drafty and cramped—no other reason. Still, I am fairly certain there will be a visit from the netherworld tonight."

"Rattling chains?"

"And howls, I would suspect. Jake couldn't have given up mischief entirely—Percy won't let him. They both have much to learn about being true gentlemen."

"Not like Ernest and Ben. They are well versed in the state."

Smiling to herself, Imogene agreed.

"Ah, there you are," Jake interrupted, calling from the doorway as he advanced on them. "Wondered where you had run off to. I have a plan, a great plan. Actually, it was my father's suggestion, but I think it a splendid way to spend a rainy day." He waved a book and several pieces of paper through the air.

"Oh?" Imogene looked up suspiciously. Percy and Jake seemed determined to interrupt their affairs for the purpose of keeping Emily and her occupied. While the concept was gallant, the execution was not. They had never required such attentions before, and they certainly did not now. It was more overbearing than anything else.

"Thank you, no," Emily said, and then turned back to Imogene. "I have a book you might be interested in, called *The Confessional of the Black Penitents*—"

"*A Midsummer Night's Dream* is much more exciting," Jake interrupted yet again.

"So kind of you. But I have already read it." Emily's diction was exceedingly correct, though it was doubtful Jake was aware that he had stepped onto thin ice.

"Yes, but have you performed it?" He passed her a piece of paper. "You would make a most excellent fairy queen."

That caught Emily's attention. "Titania? *What angel wakes me from my flowery bed?*"

"Exactly. We could perform it for the parents."

"Not the entire play, surely. That would take a fortnight of rehearsals."

"No, indeed. What would be the fun in that? No, just the scene where Puck puts the flower juice in Titania's eyes and she awakes to fall in love with Bottom—and his ass's head. Comedy at its finest."

"Let me guess, you would play Bottom. Prancing around, playing the fool."

"I think it appropriate, don't you?"

Emily laughed as she tilted her head to look around Jake. "And you? What part would you choose, Percy?"

"An attendant," he grumbled. "Mustardseed . . . or Cobweb. It matters not, as long as I have little to say."

"Easily done." Jake's voice grew louder with his enthusiasm. "Father chose Puck for you, Percy, but now that Ernest is here, he can play Robin Goodfellow."

"Ernest to play a mischievous fairy? I think that should be Ben's role, don't you, Imogene?" Emily questioned.

"Mayhap a better fit." Imogene grinned; she thought it most appropriate. Warming to this idea of hilarity and high jinks, she sat forward. "Perhaps Quince for Ernest? And me? What role for me?"

"Not to worry, Imogene, we would not ask you to stand in front of company and spout Shakespeare. It would be unkind," Jake said magnanimously.

"Well, no, I think it would be fine." Imogene's sudden enthusiasm ebbed. "A small role?"

Jake shook his head, patted Imogene on the shoulder, and shoved the book in her face. "We need you to give us our lines."

Imogene lifted her cheeks, took the book, and opened it to the marked page. "Act three, scene one," she began, and then looked up. "The wood. Titania lying asleep."

Emily closed her eyes and gracefully collapsed against the back of the settee.

Jake pulled a chair closer, and Percy harrumphed as he dropped into a chair on the other side of the room.

"Speak up," he admonished as he turned his head to stare at the unlit fireplace.

By the time Ben and Ernest returned to their company, the younger generation had removed to the music room for their rehearsal. The parents had come into the drawing room and proceeded to complain of the hubbub. It was too much for those wishing to have a little peace and quiet on a miserable day. Mr. Tabard grinned to see them all so well occupied, taking up his suggestion with great eagerness.

Not surprisingly, Ben was pleased with the idea of putting on a play—even if not thrilled with those in the company. Ernest was less so. As time went on, Imogene became happier with her duties. Rarely did she have the opportunity to tell everyone what to say and do and correct them when they got it wrong—which was fairly often.

Perhaps the most satisfying aspect of directing for Imogene was the ability to stare at Ben without censure or notice. She could watch as he flailed about, attempting to emulate a fairy . . . until Emily suggested swooping gestures were more dignified. She could enjoy his figure and form as he pranced from one side of the room to the other. And she could observe how he avoided speaking directly to Jake—and Percy—until he shook his head at some inner thought and then made an effort to ignore their mockery and jibes.

Within a short space of time, the tension had eased enough that their dealings were reasonably amicable. Missteps, missed cues, muddles, and mayhem provided enough hilarity to distract everyone. Laughter abounded. The atmosphere inside was the antithesis of the storm outside. Even Percy came around when they started discussing props and costumes.

DESPITE THE CONTINUING RAIN, Ben unhooked the window latch and pushed the tower window open. At least the wind was coming from the other direction and not likely, hopefully, to pour into the room. The smell of must was just too strong for them to remain shuttered in the tower all night without some fresh air. The temperature of the gray stone room dropped precipitously, but the blankets on the bed looked ready to remedy any chill.

"Are you sure you will be all right?" Ben asked Matt as he hung up Ernest's coat in the wardrobe. "In the stables?" He looked at the rough carpet in the sparsely furnished room. "I had hoped that there might be a place for you in here . . . but—"

"Not to worry, Mr. Ben. The men's quarters are above the stables—they're not putting me in the hayloft. Sharing with the Beeswangers' valet. Nice fella. I'll be just fine." A slight frown creased across his brow. "I might be better off than you."

Ernest snorted as he pulled off his neck-cloth. "It wouldn't be hard." He glanced at Ben. "Don't you get tired of being right? It must be tedious."

"To which aspect of this fiasco do you refer?" Ben dropped onto the bed to remove his boots; there was no chair beside the washstand . . . not even room for a chair. The mattress was lumpy, and the board beneath squeaked.

"I was speaking of the lack of accommodation—though,

I would not call this a fiasco. Far from it. I grant you the welcome was a little frosty, but I believe we won the day. That was, in fact, the most entertaining evening we have had since we joined this traveling menagerie. A shame that the soprano Mr. Tabard had hired never showed, likely deterred by the storm, but there was enough easy conversation to compensate."

"Humph," Ben offered.

"Even Percy and Jake seemed to come around."

"Yes, well. That was more a lowering of hackles than an out-and-out capitulation. I am not yet ready to let bygones be bygones. They have still to atone for their tomfoolery—that verged on nastiness—but it seemed politic to appear as if matters were resolved. Imogene looked quite anxious until I did."

"Thank you, Ben . . . for putting Imogene's emotional state ahead of your own. I do appreciate it."

Ben winced and looked up at his brother, but Ernest had his head down, shucking off his waistcoat. Ben met Matt's gaze instead. It said nothing and spoke volumes at the same time. Had Matt realized what Ernest had not, that Ben was besotted with Imogene? Ben looked away, not wanting to know the answer to that question.

"Yes, well. I'm not about to call them my friends, but we can certainly keep antagonism at bay . . . for now."

"Excellent."

By the time Matt had finished his duties and taken one of the candles away with him, Ben hunkered under the covers, listening to the rain, trying desperately not to think of Imogene. She had certainly changed from the appallingly shy young lady

he had met in London. He had never seen her look so confident as she had ordering them about, calling out lines and stage
directions. The penetrating stares she had fixed on him had set
his heart to thrumming. . . . No. Stop. He was only making
matters worse. Think of other things.

Emily had been rather charming. Lovely smile, slightly
saucy expression. So different from Imogene. They were quite
opposite in their natures. While Emily was confident, Imogene
was hesitant. Though not as much as she had been. . . . No,
no . . . he had circled back to a certain *someone* yet again.

Constant thoughts of *someone* kept drowsiness at bay. Even
counting sheep did not help; the fence-jumping creatures gained
Imogene-like qualities. A blond sheep here, a sheep smelling of
roses there. Finally, he hit upon a distracting subject. Roof design. Yes, far more interesting than the color of *someone*'s eyes
or hair or her gown or . . .

Gambrel, mansard, Dutch gable . . .

Ben was almost relieved to hear the start of a soft and low
noise, like an echo of whispered indistinguishable words. It grew
into a moan as the volume increased, came to a crescendo, and
then faded, only to start again. It was rhythmic and constant
and diverting. In no time at all, Ben's eyelids became heavy, and
with an amused smile, he drifted off to sleep.

GREYTOWER WAS POSSESSED of a long gallery lined with portraits of Tabard ancestors. It ran the length of the east wall next
to the drawing room and offered a view of the front, side, and

back of the house. It was somewhat chilly at either end due to a lack of proximity to the fireplace and the dampness of another rainy day. However, in the center, cozied up to the coals, the place became a snug little nest—which had nothing to do with Imogene's presence.

"I like this one." Ben passed a sketch to her from his folder. He had spent the entire time at Musson House drawing—to the point that his grandmother had asked him if he was ill; she was not used to such restrained behavior. "But these two . . . no, three. Here. I know something is wrong but not what."

"This one is easy enough. Look at the angle of these two lines; they are supposed to be parallel, and yet—"

"Yes. Excellent, yes. I stared at it forever and a day and didn't see. Thank you."

"My pleasure," Imogene said with a warm smile. She lifted her head to stare back at him, and they continued to do so—locked in each other's gaze—for several moments. While Ben would have been quite content to stay that way for an eternity or two, he could see that Imogene was starting to color up. He winked and lowered his eyes to the papers once again.

"Did you ask?" Emily asked as she walked through the door, directing her query toward Imogene.

"Ask what?" Ben frowned, watching Emily take the chair opposite in a graceful descent.

"Were you haunted last night?" She bounced her brows and grinned.

Snorting a laugh, Ben nodded. "It was a rather pathetic attempt, but it was amusing."

"What was pathetic?"

Looking up at the door again, Ben sighed inwardly. Gone was his quiet time with Imogene. "Your haunting abilities," Ben said to Jake . . . and Percy, who was at his side.

Moving to stand in front of the fire, Jake rubbed his hands. "Wasn't me." He chuckled and then looked over his shoulder at Percy. "We decided to wait. Give it a day or two." Then turning toward Ben: "It seemed too obvious to try to scare you the very first day you took up residence."

"Too obvious by far," Ben agreed.

"It wasn't me," Percy said as he draped himself over the back of Imogene's wingback chair. "Thought it best to regale you with a ghoulish tale or two first—a dismembered body hidden under the floorboards or some such. Build it up, lots of drama . . . and then scare the pants off you."

Ben frowned. "Really?"

"Yes, really." Jake looked over Ben's head. "You know, I believe this to be a better setting for our play. Yes, indeed. We could put chairs at that end, with the stage at the other. I think I have hit upon a most splendid idea. What think you, Imogene? Wouldn't this work better than the music room?"

"Far better." Clearly pleased at being consulted, Imogene stood with a smile, placing Ben's sketches on the seat behind her. "I think the other way around might work better, though, as the door would be a perfect way for the actors to enter and exit the stage." Leaving Ben still sitting, she wandered the room with Jake and Percy, discussing the ramifications of the setting.

"Is anything amiss?" Emily stared at him with a puckered brow.

"Do you believe Jake and Percy, in regard to haunting the tower room?"

"There was an odd tone of sincerity to their denials. Something I seldom hear."

"Hmmm. I thought so, too." He turned his gaze to the glowing embers of the fire.

"Why is that a problem?"

"Well, someone tried to scare us. Moaning and howling for several hours. And if it wasn't Jake or Percy, who was it?"

"The ghost?" Emily said with a laugh.

"Since I don't believe in its existence, I am going to have to look a little further."

"To where?"

"That, my dear Emily, is the cause of my consternation. I know not." Looking up from the fire, Ben noticed that Emily was reddening like a beet. "Are you well?" he asked.

"Yes, of course." She swallowed. "I . . . I . . . I think I will ask Imogene if she has any ideas about our culprit." And so saying, Emily stood, leaving Ben staring at the fire once again.

chapter 13

*In which lamenting, ethereal creatures
add to the mystery*

"Excuse me, Jake, might I take Imogene away for a moment? We will be right back." Emily held her hand out toward Imogene, taking her elbow.

Pulling Emily close, Imogene leaned toward her friend's ear. "What—"

"Right back," Emily called to the room, interrupting Imogene and pulling her through the door and into the corridor. She made a beeline for the large window seat on the stair landing between the ground and first floors, hauling Imogene behind her. Settling her Paris green skirts in an artful display, Emily pointed to the bench beside her.

Sitting as directed, Imogene bided her time—while her curiosity grew large.

"I am thrilled to pieces, Imogene." Emily said in a whisper, glancing up and down the staircase. "I am having the hardest time not dancing a jig right here and now. Most unseemly, I know, but . . . but . . . well, I can hardly believe it. I have imagined it for so long, waited for a sign, and now . . . at last—"

Laughing softly, Imogene lifted her finger to her mouth. "Shhh. Calm, my friend. Breathe. Excellent. Now, tell me. Only slowly this time."

"Oh, Imogene, Ben just gave me an indication of his feelings, his attachment to me. He called me his *dear Emily*."

"*Dear Emily?*" Imogene blinked, remembering the warm look she and Ben had shared moments earlier. How was it possible? She swallowed, briefly closed her eyes, and lifted her cheeks into an inane smile—countermanded by a sharp shake of her head. The incongruity was lost on Emily, who had turned her gaze to the carpet.

Imogene was both baffled and frustrated. It would appear that she was entirely inept at understanding the meaning of a young gentleman's glance. . . . But words, well, there was no misunderstanding them. "Ben said—"

"*Dear Emily. Yes, my dear Emily*." Clasping her hands to her bodice, Emily lifted her eyes to the ceiling. "At last."

"That is wonderful, Emily." Imogene heard the waver in her voice and glanced over at her friend. Emily had not noticed.

"I know. We will be sisters after all!"

Imogene closed her eyes and felt the slow blanket of misery swaddle her entire body. "I don't believe we will," she said. "I know Ernest to be an admirable person, but alas, my heart is not affected. My appreciation for him is that of a friend, and no matter how I try to see him otherwise, I see only a friend." The realization was as new to her as it was to Emily, but it felt right, true.

Imogene opened her eyes to find Emily staring at her.

"Oh, Imogene, I am sorry."

"Strangely enough, so am I. Ernest is such a kind person; the very sort of husband I should be happy to call my own. And now . . . well, now I must disappoint him terribly."

"When will you tell him?" There was an unnatural stillness to Emily's shoulders.

"As soon as possible. It is not fair to string him along. Poor Ernest has been at my beck and call for long enough."

"Could you wait, Imogene? Please?"

With a deeply entrenched brow, Imogene tipped her head, trying to understand.

"If you tell Ernest right away, they will leave. Ben will go. And . . . and he has only just come to realize . . . Please, Imogene, can you delay? Just for a day or two."

"But, Emily, that's not fair to Ernest."

"Yes, it is true. . . . But . . . might you not use the time to prepare him? Hint to him that your attachment might not be what he had hoped for . . . make the blow a little softer by . . ."

"Preparing him?"

"Yes, exactly." Emily beamed, not hearing the repetition of her own words. She reached over to hug Imogene.

Behind Emily's back, Imogene swallowed and fought back tears. She didn't know if the excessive emotion was the result of losing Ben or the thought of hurting Ernest. It hardly mattered.

AFTER HAVING HEARD Jake and Percy discuss at length how they might change a cold, somewhat drafty gallery into an enchanted forest, Ben considered taking his art lesson elsewhere. After all, he had lost his teacher. Scrubbing at his face and wishing himself back in Musson House, away from all intoxicating, lingering scents, Ben collected his papers and stuffed them back into his folder.

"Ready?"

Ben looked up to find Ernest staring down at him. "Ready for what?"

"To rehearse, of course. I was in the library when these fine ladies came to get me." He smiled rather broadly and then stepped aside to allow Ben the sight of the bright, open expression of Emily and the serious countenance of Imogene. The second was rather worrisome, for Imogene's seriousness held more than a hint of melancholy.

"Is all well?" he asked, and was reassured with a false smile and overly cheerful tone that it was.

Ben spent the hours before luncheon observing Imogene, trying to discern the reason for her disquiet. There was no outward show of bashfulness, and she did not refrain from expressing her opinion or calling out cues in regard to the play, but it was with a most lackluster timbre. She did stare and converse with Ernest far more than was her norm, but without any pleasure. Yes, that was the missing ingredient. There was absolutely no gladness in her—as if she were defeated, dejected, and beaten down.

No one seemed to notice.

Several times, he pointed out as much to Emily, who apparently needed to be at his elbow the entire rehearsal, and yet she merely laughed and said Imogene was tired.

With a quick luncheon, the afternoon was spent the same as the morning. The rehearsal went well; so much so that it was thought the performance could take place in another day, perhaps two. Of all the actors, Ernest had the most difficulty with his lines, which was not to be wondered at. His brother had never aspired to the stage. The jibes from Percy were now few and seemed more rote than venomous. Jake desisted completely. And yet the hilarity was not as unfettered as it had been.

At dinner, Ben watched Imogene offer Ernest far more attention than she had previously. Any passing comment that might be considered critical to his person would see Imogene leap to his defense, invariably followed by a wistful smile.

Ben pondered a tragic possibility. Had Imogene capitulated to her father's demands without returning Ernest's regard? If that were the case, it would be a misfortune for them both— for them all. Her melancholy ate at Ben. His belly churned. Even the lemon ices held no appeal.

"I HAVE WON the day," Ernest said, puffing up his chest, standing akimbo in the center of the tower room. "Imogene will soon give me leave to make my offer—perhaps as early as tomorrow. Did you see how she hung on my every word?" He reached over to Ben, slapping him on the shoulder. "It was worth the journey and the awkward greeting. All will be well. . . . All will be *better* than well."

With a great grin that served only to increase Ben's queasiness, Ernest turned to Matt. "There is no longer any doubt of her attachment."

Looking nonplussed, Matt blinked. "Excellent, sir. Very glad to hear it." He stood before the wardrobe hesitant, as if unsure of his role in this atmosphere of conflicting emotions. He had just raised his hand to take their coats when a knock sounded at the door.

Percy and Jake stood in the narrow corridor, gasping.

"Lud, that was a climb and a half." Percy clutched at his neck-cloth dramatically. "Forget the ghost. No one should use this room on account of the stairs." He tried to look around Matt, his head bobbing from side to side.

"Yes," Matt said in a tone emulating the frostiest of butlers.

"Call off your man, Ernest," came Jake's disembodied voice.

"Thank you, Matt," Ernest said, switching places with their valet. "To what do we owe this honor?"

Ben could hear the distrust in his brother's voice, and, apparently, so could they.

"Well, we're here to show you that while we might like a bit of fun . . ." Percy's braying laugh delayed the rest of his explanation. "We are not liars. Wouldn't care—or give you the time of day ordinarily—but it turns out that you are good company after all. So we are here to divest you of the suspicion that we were up haunting last night."

"Haunting is the least of it."

"Yes, yes, I know. The burr. We can say 'not us' only so many times. Perhaps if you accept our word about the haunting, you might be less inclined to lay blame over the burr."

"There is no logic in that."

Ben heard Jake huff. "Fine. Come, Percy, they don't want to be convinced. Still see us as villains. Their loss."

Ben chuckled. "Was that an attempt at acting or manipulation, Jake? Either way, it was poorly done."

Jake's head appeared over the shoulders of the two blocking the doorway. He grinned. "Can't blame me for trying," he called.

"May as well invite them in, Ernest. See what they have to say for themselves." Ben took a few steps back so he could lean casually against the wall while providing more space for the intruders—now, their guests.

As the two young men crossed into the room, Ben told Matt to head to his own bed. The valet was not best pleased with the idea of leaving without fulfilling his duties. However, he allowed that he could iron out the wrinkles of their coats in the morning . . . because it was most likely that the coats would be hung incorrectly and be in need of care.

Ben just nodded; it was easier that way.

"Lawks, this *is* a small room." Jake glanced around. "Don't know if our plan will work."

"What plan is that?" Ernest asked, taking up a position by the head of the bed.

Percy reached into his coat pocket and pulled out a deck of cards. "Whist."

"Whist can prove that you are not behind the moaning and groaning?" Ben said, his words full of skepticism. "How?"

"Simple. We play until the ghost appears, and then you know we are not responsible."

"And if the ghost does not appear?"

Jake shrugged. "Well, then it is just a full night of whist. Wouldn't be my first."

In the end, Ben and Ernest sat on the bed; Jake leaned against the washstand while Percy leaned against the window-sill. It was rather cramped, and as the time ticked slowly by, rather pointless—for the ghost was in *absentia*.

"You realize that your guilt is still in question—if not more so, now." Ernest collected the cards and began to shuffle. And yet, despite saying so, he looked relaxed.

Jake grinned. "Most erratic creatures, the tormented spirits—" He paused, tilted his head, lifted one side of his mouth in a lopsided smile. "There."

Sitting and standing, almost not breathing, the four of them waited and listened—with eyes widening.

Softly, as it had begun the night before, a voice whispered, growing louder and changing into a moan, only to drop into a whisper once more.

"There," Jake said again. "Now we know *you* weren't lying."
He glanced at Percy. "We thought it a bag of moonshine."

Ben snorted a laugh. "That makes better sense."

"It lasted near on two hours," Ben told Imogene and Emily the next day as he stifled a yawn. They were sitting at the table in the morning room breaking their fast. Not many were up and about as yet, the sideboard still laden with foodstuffs. It was as if the damp had drained the company of their humors.

"We traipsed up and down the stairs trying to find the source to no avail. Percy thought the sound might be coming from the roof; Jake thought the room below. But we checked, and nothing."

"So it truly is a ghost," Emily said in a voice filled with awe.

Imogene watched Ben blink, lean forward as if unsure that he had heard correctly, and then sit back and rub at his temple. "Ah, no. I don't believe so. We have just not caught the culprit as yet. Or it might be something as innocuous as a whistling breeze through the halls."

Pursing her lips together, Emily waited a moment before speaking. "Oh dear," she said, her eyes sparkling with mischief. "I did so want to meet a wandering spirit."

"I believe Ben is too tired to recognize funning, Emily." Imogene picked up her bread to add a scraping of strawberry jam. It was a pretext—she couldn't eat. She glanced over at Ernest, seated sedately beside his brother, sipping his coffee . . . and staring at her over his cup.

"Yes, of course you were." Ben shook his head as if to clear it.

"If Percy and Jake were with you, then who can be party to this latest attempt to cause trouble?" Imogene paused. "We have always assumed that they were the guilty ones . . . that it was their insatiable need for mischief that has been the purpose of these incidents. Must we now rethink that premise?"

"Absolutely." Emily nodded. "Though the waters are quite murky, if we have to look beyond tomfoolery . . . it takes on a rather baffling aspect."

"Indeed. The reason all but disappears." Imogene bit at her lip, frowned, and glanced back across the table at the tired faces—staring back, blankly. "Yes, well, too tired to discern teasing likely means too tired to unravel a puzzle."

Ernest nodded his agreement; Ben just yawned.

Imogene turned back to Emily. "If we filter out the mischief—ignore teasing the dogs, dousing Pauline, and over-turning the boat—we are left with the topaz necklace, tying up Jasper, the burr, and the ghost." Imogene was not about to mention the letter—it didn't *need* to be discussed. "Had my necklace been found where it lay, Ben and I would have suf-fered the worst consequences, though Ernest, too, would have been affected. But it might simply have been the work of a thief." She frowned and then added, half to herself, "an inept and inconstant thief . . . as nothing else that I know about has gone missing."

She dropped the unappealing toast on her plate and wiped the crumbs from her fingers. "As to the night of the storm, the men working on the ruins claim not to have tied up Jasper, but not all the same men were there when I asked. . . . And enticing a rescuer across a floor ready to collapse could have been an accident."

"The burr was not an accident," Emily interposed.

"No, that certainly appears to have been deliberate, and Ben could have been terribly injured." Imogene shook her head in frustration and then heard the echo of her words. "And the haunting was meant to scare Ernest and Ben away." When listed, there was a common thread. "Ben."

"Hmm?" His eyes were open, but was he awake?

"Why would . . . did you have a disagreement . . . ?" Imogene could hardly articulate her question; it felt too intrusive, almost rude. She thought of a way to rephrase her query. "Can you think of any person who might wish you ill? Ill enough to follow you about from one manor to the next trying to cause harm?"

"Someone who could enter a house at will and sneak into the stables without causing alarm?"

"Yes, indeed. Ludicrous. We cannot blame a stranger. More's the pity."

"Or I am not the intended target." Ben shrugged.

Imogene shook her head. "I *might* agree if it were not for the burr."

Ernest cleared his throat. "I prefer the idea that these are separate incidents—that there is no one underlying purpose, no *one* intended victim. Accidents."

Emily frowned. "It would certainly be easier to sleep at night. I'm not at ease with the idea that someone under this roof has some sort of sinister intent. That is something that happens only in novels, not in reality. Besides, between staff, guests, and family, there are near on thirty people to consider. No, no: mischief. Simply mischief. Perhaps not Percy's or Jake's, but someone else's naughtiness."

"Accidents," Ernest repeated, sounding almost certain.

Imogene stared across at Ernest, surprised. There was no foundation for this belief. The thought of someone setting out to intentionally harm his brother would be very disconcerting, but burying his head in the sand was not the wisest of approaches. As she continued to stare, she realized that Ernest was staring back . . . and that he might infer the wrong reason for this overly long look. She gulped, blinked, and turned her eyes toward Ben . . . who was also staring at her. With a sharp shake of her head, Imogene dropped her eyes to her plate, picked up her cold toast, and added another layer of jam.

"Just as I had hoped," Mrs. Beeswanger said as she entered the room in a soft lavender gown festooned with ruffles along the hem. Mr. Beeswanger and Mr. Tabard followed on her heels, looking smart in their country casual. "We caught you before you set off on your day's adventure." She walked over to the sideboard, lifted a plate, and waved it absentmindedly in the air as she talked. "The weather has cleared—and so we thought we might away to Taverock Castle. An alfresco luncheon, perhaps. What say you? The girls have always enjoyed the castle," she said, pointedly talking to Ernest. "Might you take a break from *A Midsummer Night's Dream*?"

Looking over at Emily, Imogene felt a stirring of enthusiasm. The castle was a wonderfully picturesque ruin, excellent sketching fodder, with nooks and crannies aplenty. Perhaps there she might begin a conversation with Ernest—about the value of friendship.

"Most accommodating, Mrs. Beeswanger. I think it a capital idea." Ernest looked expectantly at Imogene.

"We can sketch." Imogene lifted her cheeks, uncomfortable with his scrutiny.

"Where are the boys?" Mr. Tabard asked, frowning while he waited behind Mrs. Beeswanger to choose her breakfast. "Slugabeds?" He snorted with disgust. "At their age, I was out riding every morning just after the sun came up." He turned toward Mr. Beeswanger, who had snorted a laugh. "Yes, well, perhaps a little later than that."

"Percy and Jake were up very late with Ernest and Ben, Mr. Tabard," Emily explained. "Chasing ghosts."

Mr. Tabard started. "Ghosts? Spirits? Ethereal creatures wandering the land of the living lamenting their loss of . . . whatever they have lost? Nonsense. Utter nonsense. Clara would stand none of it. No, no. No ghosts at Greytower." He turned back to Ben. "Did you catch it?"

Stifling another yawn, Ben shook his head. "No, sir, I'm afraid not." He stood, pushing back his chair. "Think I need to clear my head. A brisk walk might do the job."

Mr. Beeswanger leaned around Mr. Tabard. "Plenty of time, plenty of time. We won't be going immediately, young man."

Ben nodded and lifted his hand in a haphazard wave. "Excellent."

"Might I join you, Benjamin? I would enjoy the fresh air as well." Emily stood, not waiting for the reply. "I'll just run upstairs for my bonnet."

Imogene watched the Beeswangers share knowing looks and matching smiles as Ben and Emily left arm in arm.

TAVEROCK CASTLE WAS an odd, triangular fortress of red stone surrounded by a wide but shallow moat, which was now predominantly water lilies. It had undergone many alterations in its golden era but had been a ruin for the better part of fifty years. Time had taken its toll on the six-hundred-year-old building; crumbling, it was now half covered in ivy, home to countless birds and rodents and a bat or two. The grounds were rough from neglect but added to the charm. Far from possessing an atmosphere of desolation, this castle was now a destination for many a summer visitor in the northern part of Kent.

With the sea visible but not too close, the breezes were warm and the ambiance festive. At least it was festive for those who were not vastly uncomfortable walking beside a young gentleman with love and hope in his eyes, when said person would have to tell this kind gentleman that his patience was for naught. And yet said person was obligated to say nothing for at least a day or two—which she thought terribly unfair for all parties involved, and she was not sure she was going to be able to—

"I am going to invite everyone to Musson House," Ernest declared, interrupting Imogene's agonizing pangs of guilt.

She tipped her parasol to the side so that she might see him better. He was grinning; Imogene's roiling insides did an extra tumble. "That is very kind of you but unnecessary."

"Oh, I do not agree. I have been welcomed at Gracebridge, Shackleford . . . and Greytower, and I want to reciprocate the generosity."

Imogene noticed the hesitation and thought Ernest's attitude admirable considering the *rude* welcome he had received at Greytower.

"I spoke to Grandmother before we left, and she thought it a perfectly equitable idea. Besides,"—he cast her a come-hither look—"it is the perfect setting for any questions or offers that might be upcoming." He pushed the hair out of his eyes and bobbed his brows.

"Please, Ernest, I would like to talk to you about friendship and the marvels of that institution."

"Worry not, Imogene. I am not pressing you. I simply believe that your understanding of who I am might be better brought about when you see where I call home . . . and you might one day, too."

Shaking her head, Imogene dropped the side of her parasol, cowardly hiding from his cheerful expression. "Ernest, I believe we—"

"I shall wait until dinner and speak to everyone all at once. Don't want to ruffle any feathers about who was asked first."

Most people would not care when an invitation was issued; however, her mother and father were not most people. Ernest was being observant and considerate again. Bother! "Ernest, my father might have given you the impression that I do not have a mind of my own."

"Well, he tried. But I have—happily—learned better." Taking her hand, he placed it on his arm.

Imogene tipped her parasol once more to accommodate the closer proximity and tried to broach the subject again. She had to divest him of this false euphoria, or her refusal was going to hit him all the harder. "Ernest, you seem expectant. I know I asked for time—" She frowned as he raised his other hand and waved.

Glancing over her shoulder, she saw that Pauline and Harriet were wandering through the grass just off the path. They waved back, and while Pauline continued to smile at them, Harriet's head was once again bowed.

"What are you doing?" Imogene called across the lea.

"Looking for lady beetles," Harriet said without looking up. "You know, those spotted red ones."

Imogene laughed. "I do indeed."

"You have to see this." A new voice caught Imogene's attention, and she turned toward it; it was a lively voice, full of amusement and no longer yawning. "Come, I'll show you." Ben grabbed her hand from Ernest's arm and then made a show of looking at her from side to side. "Did you not bring your sketching paper?" He puckered his mouth in mock disapproval. "Left it with the food baskets? Shortsighted, my dear girl. Very shortsighted. No matter, I have mine."

Imogene started and glanced at Emily's grinning countenance; her friend was apparently unaware that Ben had just used the same endearment that had set her all atwitter the day before. It appeared to be a habit, not a declaration—but Imogene was not about to say so.

"We have to go inside," Ben said, leading her across the narrow wooden bridge. "The tower staircase is tilted, and there has been erosion."

Emily, now behind Imogene, chuckled. "Such an *exciting* discovery."

Ben pulled Imogene under the pointed arch of the entrance and across the courtyard to the rear roofless building. In the corner, a tower lay half exposed to the elements.

Glancing around at the curious faces, Imogene nodded to a woman and her two small sons, who were leaning over the edge, staring into the moat. Well, they had been staring until Ben had rushed in. They were now staring at him with great curiosity.

Naturally, the mother admonished them for such rudeness while commenting on the strange proclivities of overexcitable persons, something that she hoped her children would *never* try to emulate. The mother shepherded them to the far side.

Oblivious of the disapproval, Ben dropped Imogene's hand and pointed. She wasn't entirely sure at what he was pointing; the lovely ivy climbing up the wall and draping down into the water, perhaps the large, somewhat disconcerting, wasps' nest clinging to the arch, or the crenellations encrusted with bird droppings. Remembering Ben's affinity toward foundations, Imogene lowered her gaze and saw that erosion had exposed the supporting structures of the stair treads.

"Wonderful," she said, surprised that she actually meant it. Ben's excitement was contagious.

In short order, Ben set up near the stairs, paper and board propped up on what was left of a wall. Using it as a seat rather than a table, Imogene settled beside him half turned so that she might look over his shoulder. Without her own drawing supplies at hand, she concentrated on her role as teacher and simply enjoyed Ben's proximity. Ernest had, at first, stayed with them, but boredom and the call of his book had won the day. He and Emily had headed back to join the rest of their group to laze about and wait until Ben had perfected his sketch . . . or two.

Twirling the handle of her parasol, tapping her heel against the wall, Imogene closed her eyes and imagined another time, another place, and for a moment reveled in happiness born from a vision of life with Ben. A buzzing insect pulled her from her reverie, and she opened her eyes to swat at it. . . . A wasp. Lazily flicking her hand, Imogene hit two more and frowned.

A rock skittering across the old ruins floor on the other side of the wall caught her attention, and she stared as another followed in its wake. A hollow *thunk* brought her eyes up, and Imogene watched in horror as the wasps' nest above their heads broke free from the arch and dropped.

"Bees!" Imogene screamed as the nest landed next to them. "Look out!"

Within seconds, a loud hum accompanied the mass exodus of wasps from the nest. They were furious, and they were going to take their wrath out on anything in their proximity.

chapter 14

In which an ordinary parasol bestows both protection and privacy

Throwing her hands up, Imogene frantically swatted at the wasps charging down on her. They swarmed around and in her bonnet, some trapped by the brim. The noise was horrendous. She felt a sharp prick on her neck, and then on her cheek. She shook her head wildly, sending them spinning, but only for a moment.

A sharp gasp brought her attention to Ben. With no hat and gloves off, the wasps were crawling and stinging at will. Protecting his face with his hands, he was forced to blindly endure the insects' rage.

Flailing, Imogene sent clouds of wasps flying. She felt a puncture as her unprotected wrist connected with an angry insect, but she kept swinging madly at those around her, at those around Ben.

But there were too many. Too many! She had to do something. Something else. Desperate, Imogene tore off her bonnet.

"Into the moat, Ben! Drop!" She swung her feet to the other side of the wall and jumped into the cold, waist-deep water, parasol in hand. A great splash next to her announced Ben's arrival. The spongy bottom sucked at her feet as she fought to close the gap between them.

"Get under," she yelled, lifting the parasol. She dropped it as soon as he obeyed and pulled him down into a crouch, with their heads at water level. Swatting one-handed, Imogene chased the remaining wasps around the canopy to no avail. "Duck," she said when she realized they had no other option.

Imogene squeezed her eyes shut as she plunged beneath the water. The moat was murky and silent, otherworldly. Strangely calm. If only she could see Ben . . . but she knew he was there because he reached out and touched her arm. Not surprisingly, Imogene's air was the first to run out. She surfaced with the parasol mere inches above her head and the edges still in the water to prevent any new arrivals. She hunkered and waited for Ben to appear.

When he slowly rose out of the water, her relief was extreme . . . for a moment.

Telltale marks dotted his forehead. Oh yes, and there, near his eye. Those rotten little beasts!

Glancing around with caution before opening his mouth, Ben grabbed a lung full of air. She could feel his breath on her cheek. "Lud! My hands hurt like the devil." He lifted them out of the water to examine, clicking his tongue in disgust. "Could have been worse, I suppose."

It was hard to see how; his fingers could hardly bend. *They* had received the brunt of the attack. Wincing, he frowned and then glanced at Imogene. "And you . . . Oh, my poor dearest girl, one stung your cheek. I can see the mark even in this half light."

He huffed a heavy sigh and shook his head slightly. It was a small move, necessitated by the tight conditions, very tight. While it was not one of her smallest parasols, neither was it one of her widest. They were practically on top of each other. If they shifted at all, and perhaps leaned a bit more, their lips could brush at the edges. The corners perhaps . . .

So tempting, so very appealing, so warm.

Imogene's heart began to race, and even though she felt breathless, she gulped at the air—quietly and in time to Ben's breathing, for he, too, was gulping.

Her whole person thrummed—from her toes to every hair on her head. She wanted to sing of glory and to praise the heavens for the day that Ben Steeple had walked into her life. There was nowhere she wanted to be more than in this lost world, where only the two of them existed. Nothing—just the two of them, for eternity.

Ben leaned closer, just ever so slightly. It was no longer the warm glow of his skin but his lips—soft, so very wonderfully soft and gentle and exciting and intoxicating—that lay against the corner of her mouth.

Imogene was in an agonizing heaven. She had never considered what it would be like to be kissed, and suddenly it was all she could think about. Ben's lips became Imogene's entire world. A kiss, yes . . . what she wanted, needed more than anything, more than breathing. Staring into his eyes, Imogene saw an echoing smolder. His lips curled up, and his eyes asked a question.

Imogene nodded. His eyes widened and then flew to her mouth. Imogene knew his desire was as strong as—

"Imogene!" Emily screamed from a distance.

Imogene blinked, instantly pulled from the strange netherworld she had entered. She watched as Ben shook the ardor from his eyes, too. They glanced at the parasol's buzzing canopy and realized that their lapse had been but a moment.

Sharing a baffled look, Imogene wondered if Ben ached of loss as much as she did. Was her smile as wistful as his?

"Just stay down," Ernest ordered, the anxiety evident in his voice. "They are still swarming."

Imogene, most inappropriately, giggled; Ben joined her with a chuckle.

"I don't think we were planning on going anywhere as yet," Ben whispered, his words stirring the strands of hair hanging across her face. "Besides, I'm quite comfortable as I am."

"Standing in a moat, hunkered under a parasol?"

"Yes, a mite chilly but rather cozy. Must be the company."

Imogene grinned. "Why, thank you, kind sir. There is no one I would rather be with when threatened by wasps."

While her words were meant to add levity to the moment, Ben's expression turned serious. "Indeed? No one?"

In the awkward silence, Imogene swallowed. "No one," she

said, and then forced a laugh, trying to make light of the conversation. "Had there been more of us, we would not have fit under the parasol."

"Imogene!" Emily screamed again.

"I'm fine, Emily," she shouted back. "We are fine!"

"We are?" Ben asked, glancing purposefully at her cheek and then his hands, which looked terrible.

"As there is nothing we can do but wait until the beasts fly away, I think it best not to encourage Emily or Ernest to approach . . . which they would try to do if we say anything other than we are fine."

Staring at Imogene, Ben shouted. "Just fine and dandy. How are you?"

Ernest's snort was loud enough to be heard over the buzz of the wasps.

Ben dropped his voice again. "You know you shouted bees when they attacked. These are, in fact, wasps."

"Yes, but shouting *wasps* is more of a hiss than a shout."

"Ah, yes. Quick thinking." He nodded with dramatic approval.

The buzz beyond the parasol continued for a good quarter hour—tenacious, nasty creatures. By the time they could wade out of the moat safely, Ben's hands were horribly swollen. He held them awkwardly, while the baskets, blankets, and persons were quickly loaded into the carriages for their immediate return to Greytower. Mr. Beeswanger covered a shivering Imogene with his coat, while Ernest did likewise for his brother.

Unable to hold his reins, Ben sat with Emily and Imogene in the barouche, Lancelot tied to the back. Emily cooed in great sympathy, and Ben said very little—gritting his teeth and wincing whenever the uneven road required that he use his hands to right his balance.

Imogene hardly spoke. She was thinking about the rocks skittering across the stone floor just before the wasps' nest came down. Someone had been throwing rocks. Someone had meant for the wasps to attack, to swarm. The question was, as always, who?

ERNEST WAS WALKING toward the front door when Imogene finally stepped down into the entrance hall. She had spent nearly an hour under the kind administrations of Mrs. Beeswanger, seeing to her stings. There weren't that many, really, in comparison with Ben. Mother had thought it not worth the fuss, but Mrs. Beeswanger was a motherly sort and not happy until the stings were cleaned, iced, and dotted with onion juice.

"Ernest, might I talk to you?" Imogene called just as he was about to step over the threshold.

He pivoted straightaway. "Oh, Imogene. There you are. I am so very glad that I got a chance to see you before we left. How are you?"

"I'm well. . . . Well enough. Are you going somewhere?"

"Oh, indeed. Ben is quite miserable. And there is nothing that anyone wants more than to be at home when they are feeling out-of-sorts. I've put him in the cart with Matt, and if we set off now, we will be at Musson House before dark. But worry not; I apologized to one and all and have spoken to the fathers about coming to Musson. They have all agreed. Strangely, your father was the most enthused." He winked, bowed, and turned back toward the door. "We will put on our little play there. Grandmother and Grandfather will quite enjoy the novelty."

Putting her hand on his arm, Imogene brought his attention back to her. "Ernest, I think we should talk before you go."

"Time is of the essence, I'm afraid. Can it not wait a few days? I'm sure it can."

"Ernest, I believe someone threw a rock at the wasps' nest to bring it down."

His expression turned grave. "You think it was no accident."

"Yes."

With a nod, he patted her arm. "If so, it was likely one of the young boys running about the place who thought it a great lark."

"Would that it were true, Ernest, but as it is only one of many incidents, I think we are going to have to face the fact that someone intends Ben harm."

"Yes, yes. Well, let us argue about it at Musson. I must be off."

And with a wave, he went, leaving Imogene entirely dissatisfied with their conversation. Nothing had been resolved in regard to Ben; she had been given no opportunity to offer friendship in place of matrimony; and now, they were all off to Chotsdown, where Ernest and his family would host a houseful of guests for the sole purpose of accommodating a betrothal that was not going to happen.

Or would it? Was she going to be coerced and ignored until she cried stop on the steps of the church?

Imogene closed her eyes for a moment and took a deep breath. Feeling helpless in the face of such determination was not a new sentiment; she had been dealing with the iron will of her father for eighteen years. It had been easier to capitulate. Life was difficult when Father was crossed, and this would be a most significant revolt.

There was a chance, a very good chance, that Father would refuse to have anything to do with her after he learned how Imogene felt about marrying Ernest. . . . Mother would follow suit—she always did. Percy wouldn't care. And so, there she was, either being ignored by her nearest and dearest or looking for room in the stables to bed down at night.

Perhaps that was doing it much too brown, but there seemed to be no happy consequence to thwarting a determined parent.

Undulating misery washed over Imogene as she allowed melodrama to grab hold of her imagination. A vision of the noisy, unfriendly streets of London came to mind, where she walked all alone with a small bag containing her worldly possessions. Sick, cold, and starving.

Imogene snorted in a most unladylike manner. It was a highly improbable scenario. Being in possession of many friends and relatives, the likelihood of ending up on the streets was quite ridiculous even if her father did something as shocking as wash his hands of her. Though being sent to live with a maiden great-aunt in the moors of North Devon was not beyond the realm of possibility.

Strangely enough, it was not the thought of being isolated that brought back that horrid thread of misery that seemed to imbue her every waking moment—for the moors and the west coast would make excellent subjects for painting. It was the knowledge that Ben would be on the opposite side of the country.

The possibility of securing a position as an art teacher offered a ray of hope and a life more suited to her character. It was not a pipe dream; she had a worthy portfolio. Eventually, if she was permitted a flight of fancy, she could secure a patron and set up a teaching studio or art academy of her own. If the Fates were very kind, she could settle in the charming, pictur-esque city of Canterbury. Yes, she would know people there, charming people . . . if Ben could be called people.

And so her thoughts had once again circled back to Ben. With a shake of her head in self-disgust, Imogene resolved to speak to Emily right away. They were going to see Ben again within a seven-night, and they had to be certain they were not bringing danger with them. They had to try to understand who might be behind these incidents, or if they truly were accidents and a very long run of atrocious luck.

Yes. Imogene needed to talk to Emily.

Looking up, for it seemed that at some point during her con-templation Imogene had begun to stare at the tiles, she met the quizzical gaze of the Tabards' butler.

"Ah, Radley, just the person I need."

The pinch-faced man stepped forward. "Indeed, miss."

"Might you know where I could find Emily?"

"Miss Beeswanger has gone for a walk." Sniffing sharply, the man turned as if to go about his immensely important duties.

"Along the road? Down the drive?"

With a sharp pivot, Radley turned back as if being greatly put-upon. He stared.

It was quite a talent—the ability to make you squirm without saying a word.

"Do you not know, Radley?" Imogene refused to be intimidated.

"In the garden. I believe she and Mr. Jake are strolling among the roses. I'm sure they will be returning to the Hall presently."

"Excellent. Thank you. I can find them on my own. The rose garden is on the west side of the Hall?"

"East, miss."

Nodding her thanks, Imogene entered the dining room and exited through the doors at the far end. She followed the path through the formal gardens, barely aware of the profusion of color as she passed. However, upon gaining the rose garden, she was stymied—no Emily and no Jake. As she scanned the greenery, she saw Percy two flower beds over, seated on a stone bench, flicking playing cards into his upturned hat.

"Well, that looks entertaining," Imogene said as she got closer. Her brother exuded boredom.

"Yes. Indeed."

"Have you seen Emily?"

Percy paused, holding the three of clubs between his fingers.

"Going to drag her away from Jake?" His voice sounded hopeful.

"Well, I want to talk to her."

With a smile, Percy grabbed his hat, dumped the cards into his hand, and jumped up from his seat. "At last. A reprieve." He bobbed his head in approval. "I'll show you where they are." He started off down a gravel path, leading to the west side of the gardens.

"Why a reprieve?" Imogene asked as she hastened to keep up with him.

"Dictates. Mr. Tabard is suddenly full of them. Seems to think Jake is running wild. Accused me of the same. Can you imagine? Father would be the one to rein me in if it were necessary. First Mr. Beeswanger, and now Mr. Tabard quoting Cousin Clara against us! I don't ever recall her saying 'kindness is the cornerstone of a gentleman's behavior.' I'm starting to think he is making it up. Really, we are being hounded for no purpose, no purpose at all."

Imogene kept her mouth firmly closed.

"Emily looked troubled when we all got back from . . . oh yes." Percy glanced over his shoulder. "How are you feeling? You look fine. . . . Well, no. You look idiotic. What *is* that on your face?"

"Onion juice."

"It doesn't do you any favors."

"Thank you ever so. Could we get back to Emily?"

"Oh yes. Emily was rather disturbed. Mr. Tabard thought Jake should keep her company until . . . well, until you were ready to face the world again. There you have it, and there they are." As they crossed the grass, he waved at the couple standing in the shade of a tall elm. "Jake, I have come to rescue you," Percy called.

It was no great surprise that upon seeing Imogene, Jake took his leave. Though that he did so with a gallant bow to Emily and a polite comment to Imogene was quite startling.

"Who was that?" Imogene asked after the boys had walked beyond earshot. "I don't believe we have met *him* before."

Laughing distractedly, Emily glanced around.

"Are you missing something?"

"Missing? Oh no. I was looking for a place to sit. Ah, there. That will do." She led them over to the stone fence that marked the end of the gardens, choosing a spot out of the sun. Dropping her parasol, Emily untied her bonnet ribbons, pushed her hat back on her head, and exposed her damp curls. "You were wise not to wear your bonnet. It's much too hot. Dinner is going to be delayed because of it. No one is hungry. . . . Although that might be as much the consequences of a topsy-turvy day as the temperature."

"I wish I could claim wisdom. But I wasn't thinking of the heat when I ventured out of doors."

Emily snapped her fan open, wafting the air toward her face. "If I could hazard a guess, I would probably say that you were worried that the bees' nest was another *incident*. Another—I beg your pardon? Oh, you are quite right. Wasps' nest." With a huff, Emily tore off her bonnet, dropping it onto the grass. "Ah, that is much better."

"I know you think me to be tilting at windmills, Emily, but if we are going to spend any more time with the Steeples—and it would seem that we are—then I think we should know and understand what is going on. Ben's safety is threatened."

"I quite agree."

With her mouth open, Imogene turned toward her friend, paused, and then frowned. "You do?"

"Yes, absolutely. One incident too many. No one can be that unfortunate."

"That is tremendous. . . . Not the unfortunate aspect, but the not-having-to-persuade-you-that-it-is-serious aspect."

Emily just nodded and turned her eyes to stare at Greytower Hall, looming large and . . . gray in the near distance. It had a formidable facade that Cousin Clara had softened with ivy and abundant gardens, but it would always exude a fortresslike character.

"I'm quite concerned, now that I have to admit that there is a problem."

"Oh, Emily, so am I. We have to discover who is behind this and stop them . . . him . . . whoever it is! Can we say *suspect*? No. That smacks of melodrama. Perhaps *dubious character*."

"Not certain that *dubious character* is any better. Let's just say *someone with questionable behavior*. . . . After all, we are talking about people we know."

"Too true. Unfortunately." Imogene sighed very heavily. "We must consider everyone . . . at first. Though, the field of who might possess this questionable behavior was narrowed by today's incident. Not everyone was with us at Taverock Castle, and only a smattering of servants. Right away, we can rule out Miss Watson. She stayed behind."

"And her ability to throw a rock that high is doubtful. I know I couldn't."

Imogene nodded. "In that respect, I think Pauline and Harriet can be discounted as well. I have seen them toss a ball back and forth. Now let us cross off those who never entered the castle—"

"What if this person of dubious character paid one of the boys in the area to do the job?"

"Oh dear, that is a possibility, too."

"Still, I believe we can eliminate my mother . . . and yours. They were quite content to sit and chat to each other all afternoon, watching the rest of us adventure forward. I didn't see them talk to anyone outside our group." Emily changed her fan to her other hand.

"Agreed."

"That leaves five gentlemen, two footmen, and three drivers."

"That's still quite a lot, but the footmen and coachmen stayed by the road. We would have noticed had any of them entered the castle. Their livery would have been quite obvious."

"Yes. So, if one of the servants is involved, he would have had to get a proxy to do the job."

Imogene shook her head. "Yes, but this is not the only incident—what about the necklace? A coachman would not have been able to wander the house without being seen. Nor would he have known the location of . . . oh, and I don't believe you brought your footmen to Gracebridge."

"No, there was no need. Excellent, Bernie and Charles are off the list as well as the drivers."

"Not excellent. Our list is shorter but more disconcerting. We are left five—five members of family and friends. Though it has been only Percy, Jake, and my father who have at times been at odds with Ben."

Emily clicked her tongue softly. "Oh dear. Oh dear, dear, dear."

Imogene turned toward her friend. "Emily? What is amiss?"

"We have not been considering someone. There are actually six gentlemen we should be taking into account."

Motionless, staring at each other, Imogene's eyes grew large. "No. It couldn't be. Ernest?"

"It makes sense. He can walk about without notice, inside and out. He knew where Ben's room was."

"And he would only need to ask to find mine. A little search and voilà—my topaz in hand."

"Collecting Jasper and tying him in place after the laborers had—no, that wouldn't work. He returned to Gracebridge with us."

"But he could easily have placed the burr under Ben's saddle pad." Imogene chewed at her lip.

"Though he was with Ben, Jake, and Percy when they heard the ghost. So he did not have a hand in the haunting."

Mulling over the many possibilities, Imogene shook her head. "It's too much; there has to be something that ties it all together. We just can't see it."

"Perhaps we need to focus on *why*—why would someone want to hurt Ben?"

"Father does not think well of Ben, but would he lower himself to throw rocks or sneak into Ben's room with my necklace in hand? I cannot think so poorly of him. I am certain he would do no such thing."

"As much could be said about Papa and Mr. Tabard. Are we back to Percy and Jake again? That can't be right."

"And Ernest," Imogene whispered. "I don't want to think this; I greatly esteem Ernest. . . . But he is the most logical candidate. Perhaps he had nothing to do with tying up Jasper or the haunting, but the burr, my necklace, and . . . oh, wait. Ernest was with you at the castle. Oh, I am so relieved. It could not be him. We do not need to see a reason why he might want to hurt his brother."

"I wish that I could be as pleased, Imogene, but I can't. Ernest and I left to join the others, but he turned back. Said he had forgotten to ask Ben a question. I only rushed into the castle when I saw a woman and her sons running through the gate. Ernest was standing in the yard when I got there, watching."

"Oh dear heaven. I can't think it of him. Why would he do such a thing? No, Emily, it makes no sense."

"Jealousy?"

Imogene stilled, breathing heavily through her nose. No. It was impossible. Ernest could not know how she felt about Ben. Ernest had not said anything—anything at all. She brought her eyes up and met those of Emily. Did Emily know how

237

Imogene felt? They stared at each other for several minutes until Imogene vigorously shook her head and jumped to the ground. "No," she said, far louder than she meant. She began to pace, staring at the grass, the path, a rock, the grass, the path, a rock.

"Yes, I'm afraid so. Jealousy. It's obvious. Despite being the firstborn, the heir to the heir, Ernest does not have the charm and easy way that Ben has. Ernest sits quietly reading while watching his younger brother dally with young ladies, laugh with the company, and share witty banter. It must be very difficult."

"Jealous of his brother." Imogene scratched at her forehead. "Then why would Ernest travel with Ben? Why not leave him in Chotsdown?"

"Perhaps their grandparents asked it of him or Ben did. There can be any number of reasons. . . . But, Imogene, this theory fits the most. It makes the most sense."

"No, Emily. It cannot be Ernest. He wants to marry me."

"And that is relevant how?"

"Not relevant, I suppose. No, it's not."

"I think we will have to watch Ernest very carefully at Musson House. I am so very glad that you have decided that you do not suit. It would have been a horrible shock to learn that your betrothed was capable of such duplicity."

"I'm still not convinced, Emily."

"I know." Emily sighed sadly, pushing away from the stone fence, as well, and picking up her bonnet and parasol. "I hope I'm wrong. . . . There is no win in this situation. We will just have to do our best to keep Ben safe."

chapter 15

*In which Ben would rather commune with
a tiger than have a private talk with Imogene*

Musson House, Chotsdown, Kent—
August 1817

Ben stood in line with his grandparents and brother on the balcony of the horseshoe staircase outside the great edifice of Musson House. On each side, one to a tread, a uniformed servant waited with them. The entire household was present, right down to the scullery maid and boot boy. Grandmother was trying to impress.

And what an impression it would be, coming straight up the gravel drive past pristine lawns toward the large foursquare manor. Three stories above a raised rustic, huge Corinthian pilasters framing generous windows and capped with a pediment filled with stone swags and the Steeple coat of arms. There was no doubt of grandeur.

One of the footmen had been positioned in the observatory with spyglass in hand. As soon as the coach had been spotted, the call had gone out, and there had been a great rush to get into place—chests heaving at first, calming as the coach sedately made its way to the front door.

Ben did not want to be there. Anywhere else would have suited him just fine. Anywhere Miss Imogene Chively was not. However, Grandmother would not be persuaded. Even the suggestion of returning to Canterbury early to reestablish himself before Lord Penton mustered his troops fell fallow. Grandmother wanted a show of support for Ernest. Besides, Ben was needed to help entertain—a duty that Grandmother deferred to him because of her age and vacillating health.

There was nothing wrong, in fact, with Grandmother's well-being other than possessing a character somewhat like Ernest's: a preference for little company and a pile of books by her elbow. Grandfather was just as bad—his greatest amusement was a nap in his chair midafternoon. The family pretended not to notice his snoring.

And so it was that company depended on Ben's chatter and easy manner to be comfortable. It was all very taxing..... Though it wasn't usually. No, it was more common for Ben to be eager to have others about, laughing and regaling them with fantastical stories of one sort or another, and then listening to their offerings. His reluctance for the arrival of the Chivelys was solely his lack of enthusiasm to see Imogene.

No, that wasn't right, either.

Ben ached to see Imogene. Every night, hers was the face that saw him into his dreams, and recollection of her laughter brought him awake in the morning. He thought about her constantly, always knowing, always aware that she was not for him. That he could never court her. That if she ever agreed to marry a Steeple boy, it would be Ernest meeting her at the altar, not Ben. That thought alone crushed his heart.

And then there was the guilt. He was extremely mindful of his breach under her parasol. If Emily had not called out when she had, Ben would have kissed her—Imogene . . . Ernest's soon-to-be-intended. There was no doubt that he would have to apologize and forget the look of mutual longing that he thought he had seen on Imogene's face. He had been mistaken—his error was mired in his own desire, not hers. He would have to beg Imogene not to tell Ernest of this terrible near blunder and then walk away.

No, Ben was *not* looking forward to the arrival of the Chivelys. And to make matters worse, the Beeswangers and the Tabards were not to arrive until tomorrow. A full afternoon and evening with no other focus—no one, like Emily, to provide a distraction. Perhaps he'd chat with Percy—pull him out of his sulks, engage him in a rousing game of billiards, or something of that sort.

Grandmother sensed a problem, but Ben refused to speak of it. He claimed his lackluster sensibilities were a result of his sore hands. In truth, they had stopped hurting, but as he had been stung only six days ago, he could get away with a little prevarication. He would have to look for another excuse soon.

"Chest up, Sir Andrew," Grandmother instructed as the coach came to a stop below them.

Looking across to where his grandfather stood, Ben chuckled.

Grandfather had a generous belly, and this order had to do with the protrusion of his gut more than the straightening of his shoulders.

"Doing my best, Lady Margaret, but it seems to be quite content where it is."

Catching Ernest's glance, they shared their amusement by way of a silent grin. Ben was pleased to see that Ernest was all anticipation. He hoped and prayed that he had not ruined his brother's chances by gawking at a beautiful young lady under her parasol and looking at her luscious, delectable . . .

"There she is," Grandmother said under her breath.

As Imogene stepped down from the coach, she released her hold on the footman's supporting hand and placed it, instead, on the back of her bonnet in order to look up. Up, up, and up, until she saw the line of people waiting on the balcony. Her eyes grew wide, flew to Ben, and then immediately back to the ground.

"She's lovely, Ernest," Grandmother continued to whisper.

But his brother heard and beamed. "Yes, I think so, too."

"I should hope so," Grandfather added, offering Ben a wink.

Once everyone had been handed down, Mrs. Chively picked up the skirts of her ochre gown and led the family up the stairs in a procession that left Imogene at the end. Ernest conducted the introductions, following the expected protocols. While once again Imogene was the last to be presented, Ernest made it very clear that she was not the least. His tone and broad smile hinted at a welcome and pride that made Ben swallow in discomfort.

It was the oddest of positions to be in—everything was

contrary. He didn't want to see Imogene but longed for her company. He was pleased to see Ernest happy and yet wished that *he* could wear that smile, hold her elbow, and stand close. He was filled with guilt over a nonexistent kiss when all he could think of was how it would have felt had it occurred.

"Ah, Miss Chively, I am so very happy to meet you," Grandmother said, taking Imogene's hand in between her own and giving it a little squeeze. "I know you young people have decided to use given names, but I hope you will forgive me if I don't. I'm an old woman not used to these modern ways."

"Of course, Lady Steeple, I quite understand." Imogene blushed prettily and tried to pull her hand away, but Grandmother resisted.

"I am so looking forward to meeting all your friends; it has been many years since we had a houseful of guests. Yes, indeed. What a lovely gown, my dear."

"Thank you, Lady Steeple." She swallowed in discomfort as Grandmother continued to converse about trivialities while still in possession of Imogene's hand.

Somewhere around the third compliment, Ben looked up to see that rather than rescuing Imogene from her discomfort, Ernest was watching the exchange with a ridiculous grin.

Ben sauntered over to his brother and jabbed his elbow into Ernest's side. "Ernest! Free her. What are you thinking? Imogene is going to pass out from embarrassment if Grandmother does not let go of her soon."

"What? Oh yes." Ernest blinked stupidly. "Shall we go in?" he asked the company at large.

Ben was relieved to see Grandmother drop Imogene's hand and nod in agreement. With a hearty laugh about nothing at all, Grandfather gestured toward the arched French doors leading into the vestibule. As the rest of the group traipsed into the manor, Imogene turned.

"How are your hands?" she asked Ben's feet.

"Much better, thank you."

The bonnet nodded, so it was obvious that she had heard him. . . . And yet he had still not seen her eyes.

"Is all well, Imogene?"

"Of course. Why do you ask?"

"Perhaps because you seem more fascinated by the floor than the company."

The bonnet instantly tipped back, and Ben could see Imogene's beautiful face. Her beautiful blond hair framed her face . . . beautifully, and her beautiful eyes sparkled beautifully. Ah . . . no. They were not sparkling in the least. Grandmother must have frightened her far more than he realized. She looked quite forlorn. Though, on Imogene, it only served to make her look even more appealing. He almost sighed like a lovesick calf. *Almost.*

As they stared at each other, voices drifted out from inside the vestibule.

"Do you take snuff, Sir Steeple?"

"Yes, indeed. An excellent pastime, though Lady Margaret is less than happy with it. Says it makes me sneeze excessively."

"Excellent, I have brought you a gift. A snuffbox that I acquired from France just before the war."

Mr. Chively's voice grew faint as he moved to the back of the vestibule and toward the cavernous hall enclosing the grand staircase, and yet Ben and Imogene continued to stare at each other.

"Come along, my dear." Grandmother stepped back across the threshold, frowned slightly, and then regained Imogene's hand. "Let me take you up to your room. We have given you one of the nicest of our guest rooms in the southwest corner of the manor. I'm sure it will suit you well. It's been decorated in the softest green chintz. Overlooks the front drive—a view not unlike that of Ben's. So relaxing."

And as she continued to talk, Grandmother led Imogene away from Ben, who stood outside for some minutes . . . wishing he were somewhere else.

As the day progressed, Ben found that he could avoid Imogene almost entirely by way of playing the host. Since it was the role to which Grandmother had assigned him, he did so with aplomb. He took it upon himself to see everyone seated at luncheon, with Imogene as far from him as possible. There was no snub, for Ernest was right there beside her—staring at her, so absorbed with *looking* at her he failed to *see* her, failed to see how uncomfortable he was making her.

Ben knew that Ernest was rehearsing in his mind. They had talked at length of where and when he would propose—in the folly overlooking the channel, three days hence, was the final decision—and how he would react to her acceptance. Ben had tried to instill some sense into his brother, mentioning several times that his offer might not be accepted. Ernest had laughed, waving his hand around.

"After seeing all this, I think not. What young lady would not want to call such a place home?"

"Yes, but do you want someone who wants you for yourself or your inheritance?"

"You are being naive, Ben. They are tied together. You can no more take Musson House out of me than you can take architecture out of you."

It was true enough.

After luncheon, Grandmother took Mrs. Chively for a lovely little chat in the drawing room, while Ben suggested a game of billiards in the hunting room for Mr. Chively and Percy. Grandfather looked wistfully at the ladies—no doubt preferring his favorite chair and occupation—but did his duty, following them into the long room where the paneled walls were covered by sets of trophy antlers. Ernest took Imogene on a tour of the house, which was to be followed by a tour of the gardens. Ben watched them walk away arm in arm, frowning at Imogene's awkward gait. It almost appeared as if she was leaning away from his brother.

The game was not as successful as it might have been had any of the players actually wished to be knocking a ball around a felt-covered table. Grandfather fell asleep while waiting his turn, and Mr. Chively proceeded to complain about not being able to concentrate in such a noisy environment. Grandfather's naps involved snuffles and snorts as well as the usual sawing breath. Eventually they scattered. Percy to see the stables, Mr. Chively to join the ladies, and Ben to the library, where he thought no one would look for him. Grandfather didn't notice their departure.

Ben spent a good half hour doing nothing other than staring at the tree outside the library window. It really wasn't that fascinating, and yet he couldn't concentrate on anything else. . . . So it served.

"There you are," Ernest said as he entered, cutting up Ben's hard-earned peace entirely. "I have been looking for you everywhere. Had Stanford not seen you sneak in here, I would not have come in. Didn't think you even knew this room existed."

"That's rich, brother dear. Where do you think the best architecture books are stored?"

"Oh yes, true enough, I suppose." Flopping down in the wingback chair opposite, Ernest scrubbed at his eyes and then raked his hair back. "Ben, I need your help."

Ben said nothing. The purpose of this conversation would be apparent soon enough. He knew he did not need to contribute yet.

"Something is wrong with Imogene. I don't understand it. She is acting like a skittish colt again. I thought we had gotten over all that. Moved past her bashfulness. She knows me now; we have had many delightful conversations. . . . And yet she looked as uncomfortable as the day I first met her. Unless I understand what is amiss, there will be no point in asking her anything. She would not consent to be my wife if she remains in this state."

Ben frowned and moved his eyes to stare once again at the tree. This was a puzzler. Something had changed since . . . hunkering under a parasol . . . looking deep into each other's eyes. With a churning gut, Ben swallowed in anxiety. "Did she say? Did you . . . ask? Does it have anything to do with the day at the castle when the wasps attacked?"

Furthering Ben's uneasiness, Ernest nodded. "I think it does."

Ben took a sharp, though silent, breath. "Oh?"

"I think . . . I hate to say this, Ben. But I believe Imogene is easily upset. Worries needlessly."

"What do you mean?"

"She is talking about the *incidents* again. Saying that they could not be accidents. That the wasps' nest was knocked down by a rock. That you are in danger. That someone is *orchestrating* these disasters. She is worried about your safety. Stop smiling, Ben, I am being sincere. It's a little troubling—that she cannot take these happenstances in stride without seeing a villain in our midst. You need to talk to her."

Blinking, Ben looked back at his brother. "What, me?" he said with great intelligence.

"Yes. Could you? I don't know what to say, but as it is you who seems to be suffering the brunt of these *incidents*, perhaps you can explain to her, explain that they are only accidents and that we must move past them . . . look forward to other events."

"Such as a proposal in the folly."

"Yes, exactly. See, I knew you would understand."

"Understand, yes. But can I assist? I doubt it, Ernest. Imogene has a strong mind and her own opinions."

"We see her so differently."

Ben nodded. "There now, with that I will agree."

"But will you?"

"Will I what?"

"Speak to her, Ben. That's what we are talking about."

"But I don't think . . ."

"Please, Ben."

Ben closed his eyes and pursed his lips for a moment before answering. A private talk with Imogene was *not* on his list of agreeable pursuits. He would rather commune with a bear . . . perhaps a tiger. "Where is she?" he asked instead.

"Thank you. I knew you would. I left her in the garden, sketching the fountain."

Pushing himself to his feet, Ben offered his brother a long-suffering look. Ernest just laughed.

IMOGENE WAS INDEED sketching by the fountain. It was a shame, for if she had moved at all, even to a neighboring flower bed, Ben would have rushed back to Ernest claiming that he knew not where she had gone. But no, there she sat, a vision of loveliness and tranquillity. She wore a light rose-colored spencer atop a cream gown accented with lace, matching bonnet sitting on the bench beside her; the sun kissed her golden tresses with great affection. . . . No. He should not use the word kiss to describe anything about Imogene Chively; it was too . . . fraught with peril.

"Hello, Ben," she said without looking. Quite the feat when he was standing off to the side.

"I did not mean to intrude." If Imogene sent him away, then that, too, could be an excuse, a reason to return to Ernest with the quest unfulfilled.

"No, not at all." She turned her head and smiled— ruefully . . . wistfully? Something was indeed wrong. But did he want to know what that was? "Did you wish to sketch as well?" she asked. "I have an extra piece of paper and can break my graphite pencil should you—"

"No. No, thank you. I have drawn this fountain seven times to Sunday, though better success with it of late."

"Of course." She returned her gaze to her paper and continued her rendering.

Silence hung in the air as Imogene sketched and Ben stood off to the side, glued to the gravel, wishing himself a hundred miles away and sitting next to her at the same time. That would have been quite the feat, too.

"You have improved greatly, Ben," she said, misinterpreting his inability to speak. "I think you can be comfortable returning to Lord Penton."

"Would that I could, but my sketches are of small matters, pieces. I have yet to draw a full door let alone a building."

Smiling, though still looking back and forth between the fountain and her paper, Imogene laughed . . . with little amusement. "Try a window first. Then a door. Then a window and a door. Build it up, Ben, as you would erect a building, layer by layer."

Giving up his position of strength and distance, Ben sighed and joined Imogene on the bench. She moved her bonnet, hanging it from the back of the bench to accommodate, and then she returned to her sketch. It was a great distraction, making it easier for Ben to concentrate when her eyes were elsewhere.

"It will be a fair number of years before I have the ability to render what I have in my head—my own designs." He winced, for even in his ears that sounded as if he was ungrateful for all that she had done.

"Not necessarily," she said, as if unaware of his churlishness. "You could form a partnership with a fellow architect or find an artist who understands your vision." Turning finally toward him, she lifted the corners of her mouth in a semblance of a smile. "A flexible artist, a conduit for your ideas."

Ben swallowed and tried not to look at Imogene's mouth. "Someone well versed in straight lines." He added a chuckle to make it seem as if he was not preoccupied.

"And perspective."

"Indeed," he said, and then made the mistake of lifting his eyes to hers. And there he was, lost for a moment or an hour; it was hard to know which. His heart hammered; his fingers itched to reach out and touch the contours of her face. He wanted to pull her hair free from its constraints and nibble at her neck. Watch her back arch; feel her body pressed to his and ease her furrowed brow.

Furrowed brow?

With a sharp intake of breath, Ben looked away. Why had Imogene been frowning? "Is something amiss, Imogene?" He studiously watched the water fall from the center of the fountain and into the collecting pool. Dripping. Droplets. Ripples. Tiny rainbows.

"Yes," she said in a doleful tone.

That was the wrong answer. If she had said no, he could have excused himself and run back . . . sauntered back . . . to his brother with no news.

Fearing the worst, he took a gulp and asked *the* question. "Does it have to do with the day at the castle? The day the wasps attacked?"

"Yes."

Again the wrong answer.

"I would like to apologize."

"For what?"

Ben turned, surprised by the seemingly genuine puzzlement in her voice. "For being so bold . . . under your parasol. For—"

"I'm not distressed about that, Ben. In fact, I would rather not talk about . . . that. Ever. Nothing happened. It was just an odd moment where our emotions nearly got the better of us."

If Ben was not mistaken, Imogene was talking about *that*, despite professing an absolute preference not to do so.

"It didn't mean anything. We were simply in a heightened state, a state of anxiety and intimacy. You would not have kis—No. I really don't want to discuss something that didn't happen. That is not my difficulty."

Shaking his head in confusion, a deeply entrenched frown

taking up residence now on *his* brow, Ben waited for an explanation. "What is, then? Of what are we talking?" he finally asked when none was forthcoming. Imogene's swallow of discomposure did nothing to sooth his qualms.

"I don't believe that these incidents are accidents, Ben. I believe someone intends you harm, and you need to be careful, watchful—vigilant."

"You have postulated the same before. This is no great revelation. Not worthy of a new set of worries."

She sighed. "Ben, is it possible . . . You and Ernest seem to be on the best of terms. But is that so?"

Ben bristled and sat up straighter. "What kind of a question is that? Are you going to try to lay blame on my brother?" Fury replaced indignation, and Ben rounded on her. "My brother? Do you realize what you are asking? What you are implying? How could you? How can you come into our home—Ernest's home—and ask such a question?"

Ben was so angry he could hardly think straight. "Ernest would never do anything to hurt anyone, me least of all. And if you knew my brother well enough to consider marrying him, then you should know his integrity." Shaking his head in disbelief, Ben jumped to his feet.

"Shame on you, Imogene. I will not tell my brother of what you suspect. It would crush him to know you think so little of him."

And with that, Ben stalked off, disregarding Imogene's openly shocked expression and the little voice in his head that warned him that he was being unfair. That he had jumped too quickly, flying at her for a simple question. That he should be asking Imogene why she inquired about their brotherly relationship. That she had not accused Ernest of anything. That he had taken umbrage and run with it because it was far easier to be around Imogene and not want to take her into his arms if he was angry with her.

He ignored the little voice and slammed the door behind him.

chapter 16

*In which Imogene weighs the merits of living atop
a mountain with no one around for miles*

I mogene found that she could smile, make light conversation, and look up from her lap occasionally while dying inside. It was not a new trick, but one that had never covered such total despair before. She was in shock—still hurting, feeling battered and bruised by Ben's outrage. She had asked a simple question. He had not given her the opportunity to explain whence came the query. He had not refuted or debated, as she had expected . . . or even reassured.

No. Ben had shown a side of himself that Imogene hoped never to see again—an angry, unreasonable side. Still, she prayed that this horrible aspect of his nature would not interfere with his ability to think clearly—that he would be watchful, aware of anyone intending harm. Be it his brother or not.

Ernest seemed aware that a barrier had formed—a wall of

hostility—but other than look apologetic at both parties and talk far more than was his norm, Ernest was of little help. It was fortunate that Imogene's shy and quiet nature was expected to resurface with a change of surroundings; the dinner and evening conversations went on around her without causing any insult or concern. The occasional comment was tossed her way, and then attention returned to those actually participating in the discourse. While nothing was said directly, Father and Lady Steeple constantly inferred that Ernest's and Imogene's futures were entwined.

It was not a comfortable meal.

The night was long. Though the bed was comfortable, the unusual squeaks and thumps of a foreign household kept Imogene awake. It had nothing to do with a broken heart and wishing herself a hundred miles away. Her only reprieve was in knowing that Emily would arrive on the morrow and with her a conversation that might help shed light on what had happened. A different perspective might be of benefit. . . . Might.

As Musson House did not keep town hours, Imogene arrived the next morning to a bustling dining room. Mother and Lady Steeple were in deep conversation about the importance of lace while finishing their toast and jam. They looked up, made a smiling comment about the tardiness of the young, and returned to their conversation. Had Ernest truly been her heart's desire, Imogene would have been pleased to see how well the two ladies related to each other. As it was, it only added another crack to the floor eroding under her feet.

Sir Steeple sat at the opposite end of the table with Father,

Ernest, and Ben. Percy was nowhere to be seen. At least she was not the last one down. The gentlemen's conversation seemed to be about a beach and the wonders of rock collecting. They offered her more than the ladies had done, a cheerful "hallo" and an inquiry if she had slept well. Imogene assured Sir Steeple that she had, hoping he did not notice the dark circles under her eyes that proved her words to be a lie.

Sitting with the ladies, Imogene found she was much more interested in the conversation at the other end of the table. When Ernest mentioned a ruin, curiosity overcame her wretchedness.

"Is it far?" Imogene asked, raising her voice slightly to be heard. She didn't have to shout; the room was generous, accommodating a table that seated twenty or more, but it had been well designed—sound carried. A fleeting thought that Ben might add such a room to his designs was summarily dismissed as unwanted. She kept her eyes on Ernest, not allowing them to wander about on their own.

"Not far in distance," Ernest explained. "But requiring the use of a boat. You can see it from the beach, but only the tip of the tower peeks above the trees. If it is something you wish to sketch, we can make arrangements to visit. I know ruins are one of your favorite subjects."

"Yes, that would be wonderful." Imogene smiled sincerely for the first time in many, many hours. Drawing a ruin would be a great distraction; she could lose herself in a sketch. It would give her aching heart a much-needed respite and ease her troubled thoughts away from Ben.

"It is a favorite haunt of Ben's, too. Perhaps Emily would be interested, and we can make a day of it. Four can easily fit in the skiff with a food basket."

Imogene's smile remained in place but lost its luster. Not away from Ben, then. She stifled a sigh.

"Seas might be a bit rough today." Sir Steeple glanced toward the tall windows despite their view of the gardens and not the nearby channel. "Winds are up, means the waves will be high. Best wait for a day when the clouds aren't as low, too. Don't want to be marooned on a foggy island."

"No, indeed," Ernest agreed, looking at Imogene with what appeared to be a twinkle in his eye. "It would be a disaster. Marooned on an island with two lovely ladies. Who would wish *that* upon us?"

Ben snorted in derision. Imogene kept her gaze firmly on Ernest.

꩜

At the back of the manor, collected in an elegant room of blues and yellows on the second floor, the company was deaf to any sounds of arriving guests. Imogene had no knowledge that the Tabards had made an appearance until Jake walked under the gilt transom of the drawing room door. Percy, too, was in ignorance, because his greeting was louder and higher pitched than was his usual.

Once again, Jake outshone the company. Though wearing countrified fashion this time, there was no doubt that his coat was of a fine quality and expertly tailored. Even his father, following on Jake's heels, did not cut the same figure as his son.

Wrinkled in face and coat, Mr. Tabard made up for it with his smooth smile.

"Well met," he said as Lady and Sir Steeple stepped forward to offer an effusive welcome.

There was far less pomp and ceremony than there had been the day before. Recognizing why that would be, Imogene turned back to her book with an uncomfortable churn in her belly . . . and then, after having read the same passage twice without comprehension, she stared out the window. She caught Ernest watching her from the corner of her eye but did not turn; she couldn't give him the reassuring smile he wanted. She did not have the fortitude.

Sometime later the scene was replayed. Only this time it was Imogene who squealed with delight at the new arrivals. The Beeswangers *sans* Pauline, Harriet, and Miss Watson had found their way to Chotsdown. Imogene stood to greet Emily after the Steeples had done so, but she was stymied in the intent to pull her friend into her corner. Someone else leaped into the fray. Someone else took Emily's hands and declared her arrival to be the most wondrous of all possible happenings. Someone else made it perfectly clear that Emily needed to sit right beside him.

Emily shared a look with Imogene that spoke of excitement and anticipation as she joined Ben near the ornate chimneypiece on the opposite side of the sizable room. They would have to catch up later.

Imogene turned back to the window. A light rain drizzled against the glass panes, trickling down to the sill in long streaks; they put her in mind of tears.

"WHAT HAS HAPPENED?" Emily whispered a few hours later as they climbed the stairs to the third-floor gallery. They were about to tour the collection of marvels that Ben and Ernest's parents had sent back from Italy. It had been Sir Steeple's suggestion; Ben had argued that the viewing could be saved for another day, but Ernest had sided with his grandfather, and up they had gone. Ben, despite his initial disagreement, had led the way, followed by Ernest, allowing Emily and Imogene to slow their steps for a private, though brief, conversation.

"Ben was not at all pleased when I asked him about Ernest in regard to the incidents. In fact, he was furious."

"Oh dear."

"He was so affronted that he gave me *no* time to explain that it was only speculation. And now he will not talk to me at all. I am miserable, Emily. I do not want to be here. If I could, I would pack up immediately and head home. Please give me leave to talk to Ernest. As soon as I have broken his heart, I can rush home to be harangued by my family."

Emily frowned. "Gracious, I don't believe I have ever seen you this distraught before."

"It is likely a first. I am as wretched a creature as can walk this earth. I am about to break the heart of a fine young man—who, in fact, I *don't* believe had anything to do with these incidents. And now his brother thinks very, very poorly of me because I suggested something I don't credit."

"It is my mistake, Imogene. I was the one to speculate that

Ernest might be involved. Dear, dear. I have made a mull of everything."

"No, Emily. It is not—"

"I hope you will agree that the collection is worth the effort," Ernest said with a smile, watching Imogene and Emily climb to the top stair. The excitement in his voice was a clear indication that he expected no argument.

"I'm sure we will. Though, for the record, a flight of steps is hardly an effort."

While Imogene could hear a hint of irritation in Emily's rejoinder, she hoped that Ernest could not. It stemmed from their broken conversation, not Ernest's comment. Really! There were times the idea of living atop a mountain with no one around for miles was quite appealing.

And then Imogene lifted her eyes and tripped to a standstill. She ceased moving, thinking, and breathing. She merely absorbed the glory, the mastery, the beauty that was this room. For an eon of minutes, Imogene beheld a sight that she had not expected.

The Musson House gallery was a wonder of wonders. Stretching the length of the manor, with large, arched windows at either end, the walls had been painted an unobtrusive green, the planked floor was stained pale gray. They were a quiet background for the riot within the room; the wall space was entirely covered in gold-framed masterpieces: still lifes, landscapes, seascapes, triptychs, portraits, and mythic representations. Some were hung in stacks of three; the larger paintings stood alone.

Running down the center, on white pedestals, were marble

statues of such artistry they made Imogene want to bow in awe at the sculptor's talent. Separate and yet part of the whole, carved stone in stark white, they were a perfect antithesis to the burst of color on the walls. Here was a place she could stay forever. Stare and absorb and try to understand how such marvels were achieved, day after day, month after month . . . yes, forever. This was a haven far better than a mountaintop.

Without thought, Imogene turned to the one person who would recognize her stupor. The one who would know that bliss had escaped her heart and was racing through her veins. She turned to Ben.

He was watching. He knew; he understood. His mouth quirked up into a one-sided smile. They stood by the stairs, locked in each other's gaze for what seemed like hours until something moved behind her and Ben blinked. His eyes clouded, his smile disappeared, and indifference replaced it. Bliss slowed to a trot. When he turned, bliss walked away with him.

"This is beautiful, Benjamin," Emily said in a bright voice, clearly enthralled. "Are they all Italian?"

"No, not all. My parents began their Grand Tour in the Low Countries. These two are Van Eyck and this is a Rubens. When they passed through France on their way to Italy, they sent home a Chardin still life."

Rather than follow Emily as she wandered down the length of the gallery, Imogene stopped in front of one particularly poignant painting. It was of a young girl in what seemed to be a Bavarian costume; her mother, behind her, was placing a wreath of flowers on her head. A Maypole and dancers could be seen in the background. A rite of spring. A jubilant painting, one of revelry and merriment.

Imogene tried to let it seep into her listless heart.

"I knew you would like it," Ernest said, coming to stand next to her. It was likely a reference to the gallery in its entirety rather than this one painting. "It is a shame that my parents cannot be here to enjoy their own collection."

Imogene nodded. "Still searching for more? Looking to expand the gallery?"

"Always."

Perpetually composed, Ernest said the word in a tone that Imogene could have mistaken for resentment had she thought about it overly, which she chose not to do. There was a possibility of invading his privacy had she done so—Ernest might not have realized how much his voice had revealed.

"They have been gone close to five years now." And then he added, as if compelled, "Their letters say little, though it is clear that they are utterly caught up in their Tuscan life, where they have taken a villa. It must suit their needs, for there is no talk of returning anytime soon."

Lifting her eyes away from the expertly rendered cloth, Imogene was surprised to note Ernest's brooding expression. Aware of her scrutiny, he turned to offer her a mollifying wink. "Perhaps a wedding will do the trick."

Taken aback by the sudden change of subject and mood, Imogene opened her mouth to deny that possibility when she overheard Emily's words from the other side of the room.

"Benjamin, I believe we have to discuss these incidents you keep experiencing. Imogene and I have been talking—"

"No, no we don't. It is not a subject in which I am interested." Ben's tone was forbidding. "Accidents and incidentals all. There is no need to let them ruin a perfectly equitable rainy afternoon. Come, I must show you this Francesco Guardi painting."

Realizing that Ernest was still locked in her gaze, Imogene blinked. His next words made plain that they had both been guilty of eavesdropping. "A subject not worthy of our time or concern, Imogene. All is well. Fear not, worry not. Nothing is amiss."

Imogene did not appreciate the slight patronizing tone of this denial of reality and thought it foolhardy in the extreme. It was disturbing as much for the fact that Ben was having a perilous summer as it was that if they never discussed the reasons or culprit of these *accidents*, then the misunderstanding between them could not be put to rights.

IT SEEMED CLEAR to Imogene that Ben and Ernest had made some sort of pact. Any time Emily or Imogene approached the subject of a dubious character who might be party to the odd happenings, one or the other interrupted and changed the subject. Finally, Emily shrugged her submission to Imogene and gave up the attempt. Upon returning to the drawing room, Emily whispered that she would stay close to Benjamin's side . . .

in the interest of his safety, of course. She would be his guardian. Imogene didn't think Emily would find it a hardship.

It also suited Ben's mood, as he seemed quite determined to lavish Emily with attention, ignoring Imogene. Their camaraderie was gone. She didn't even have the opportunity of an art lesson to make amends for—forgetting that he had demanded secrecy at the onset of their classes—Ben declared before all that Imogene was such an accomplished teacher that he was now capable of guiding his own path. There would be no quiet *tête-à-tête* to smooth over the whole.

Probably just as well.

Better to think of him as an unreasonable, self-centered sot with a terrible temper who jumped to conclusions rather than a kindred spirit who, under different circumstances, would have made an excellent companion through life. Not to mention the possessor of expressive eyes, a physique that made her mouth dry, and a mouth that looked to fit hers perfectly.

No, best *not* turn her thoughts in that direction at all. As soon as she turned down his brother's offer of marriage, Ben would be exceptionally happy to see the back of her. The holiday would be cut short, and she would never see either of the Steeple boys again . . . unless Emily and Ben . . . No, it didn't bear thinking about, either.

Dinner did not prove to be the ordeal that Imogene expected. With a full table, it was easy enough to look elsewhere. Her eyes settled on Ben only every few minutes, and he spent the entire time entertaining the group at large—studiously looking around her. His family smiled indulgently, and only Percy glanced her way from time to time with a frown of confusion.

One of the topics that received a fair amount of attention was that of rock collecting . . . again. It would seem that while Sir Steeple was now unable to walk the beaches in search of treasures himself, he thought that those in the company would find it immensely entertaining. It was not hard to see whence came the obsession to collect.

And so it was decided that, should the weather cooperate, an excursion would be planned for the next day. There was general assent, but Imogene saw the look that passed between Percy and Jake and was fairly certain that rock collecting was not high on their list of amusements. *A Midsummer Night's Dream* proved to be more to their taste. They were both greatly enthused when Ernest suggested another rehearsal, and Lady Steeple thought the ballroom might be just the place to do it.

Emily and Imogene smiled at each other—cleverly done. The adults now had the drawing room to themselves, including Sir Steeple's favorite chair, and the younger generation could be lively without censure. Had Imogene not been carrying around a heavy weight of anxiety and guilt, she might have enjoyed the process.

And so it was that the company made it through another day with no disaster and no threat to Ben's person. Imogene thought it unwise to let their guard down, and Emily agreed. And yet it was hard to see danger in an elegant ballroom, in a gracious manor where all is calm and full of laughter. Perhaps this being Ben's home meant that the peril and the perpetrator were no longer in their midst. It was a comforting theory that saw Imogene into her dreams.

IT WAS NOT to be wondered that, when the beach walk was organized, several previously enthused guests were no longer inspired to partake in the grand excursion.

"A little too damp for my taste," Mother complained at breakfast.

"I'm sure the mists will clear, Olivia," Mrs. Beeswanger said. She had expressed a continuing interest in stepping out and letting the wind blow out her cobwebs. Mr. Beeswanger quite agreed.

"Count us out," Jake called from what had now become the gentlemen's side of the breakfast table. "Percy and I are going to fish in . . . what did you say the name was?"

"Duff Lake. More of a pond, really, but a reasonable place to wet a line," Ernest said.

"It wouldn't hurt you to accompany us and lend an arm to the young ladies, Jake." Mr. Tabard looked across his raised cup at his son. "Beaches are notorious for uneven ground. We wouldn't want a twisted ankle for want of a sensible young man."

"Not to worry, Mr. Tabard." Ben laughed. "Ernest and I will be there. No need to press Percy and Jake to join us if it is not what they wish."

"Capital," Jake said. "In that case, we will go fishing. And hope that the mists *don't* clear."

Mr. Tabard did not look mollified. Imogene suspected the excursion was meant to provide more gentlemanly lessons—Jake had knowingly escaped.

And so it was that just after luncheon, when the sun *had* burned away the last vestiges of the morning mist, a much smaller party of walkers and beachcombers emerged from a side door in the rustic. They numbered only eight—the Beeswangers, Mr. Tabard, Imogene's father, the Steeple brothers, and two fast friends.

Though not visible from the house—protected from the wind by a stand of larch—the coast was not distant enough to warrant ordering the carriages. It was, in fact, faster to traverse the winding lane to the cliffs and then along the ledge to a dip that brought the path and the beach together. A bit steep in parts, the adults had already decided to let the younger members of the group climb down, while they would enjoy the vista, the breezes, and steadier footing along the cliff's edge.

"Careful of the erosion," Lady Steeple warned as she waved them away.

After five minutes or so of an easy walk, they stepped out from behind the trees and were greatly rewarded with sweeping views of the channel. It was breathtaking, and Imogene instantly and instinctively turned to Ben . . . who was watching Emily. Casting her eyes at Ernest, she saw him frown. He had noticed that her first glance had been toward his brother.

Imogene lifted her cheeks and gestured toward the channel.

"It would make a marvelous painting." It was an explanation, of sorts.

Ernest nodded. His expression of bewilderment faded, and Imogene felt the joys of the view succumb to her worries once again. She turned back to the vista, trying to shunt all but the glory of the moment aside.

A meandering path topped the hilly grass cliffs, and beyond that the gray-blue of the water and the cornflower blue of the sky. Fingers of rock formations stretched into the water, creating rugged coves and reaching toward an island not far from shore. Visible above the foliage, the top of a crenellated tower offered a hint of the ruin below. Turning back to Ernest, *not* Ben, Imogene pointed toward the tower. He nodded again, this time with a grin.

"Oh, Benjamin, look!" Emily shouted against the wind. "The tower. We shall have to go tomorrow." She skipped closer, taking Ben's arm and leaning into him. She had left her parasol behind, opting for a wide-brimmed, well-secured bonnet in its stead—as had all the ladies. A parasol was impractical in the gusting wind. Better yet, a bonnet allowed for closer proximity.

Glancing over her shoulder toward the Beeswangers, Imogene was relieved to see that Emily's parents wore agreeable expressions. Far from being uncomfortable with Emily's behavior, they were pleased. Beyond them, her father's glare told Imogene she should be doing the same with Ernest, and Mr. Tabard looked oblivious, staring at the view. Imogene returned her gaze to the path.

As planned, the younger members of the party left the adults just up the trail. Ernest helped Imogene down to the beach, and he would have retained her hand had she not demurred, saying that the terrain was not conducive to intimacy. The rocks—for it was not a sandy beach—made footing and balance a challenge. The shrug she received might have meant that he was hurt, or insulted, or in agreement.

Imogene shook her head in self-castigation—she was being overly sensitive on everyone's behalf. Emily offered her a look of sympathy and then went back to exclaiming over each rock or stone that Ben pointed out to her. They were soon dropping their treasures with a regular plunk and plop into the bucket Ben carried.

Imogene found that she was not really interested in rocks, even the striped ones with golden flecks that Emily seemed to think superior to all others. No, Imogene found a small piece of shell, and as she admired the shiny pearl casing, Ernest handed her another larger piece. It was suffused with shades of pink.

"It's lovely," Imogene said, turning it this way and that, watching the light reflect and change color. It was really very pretty.

"I'll find you another," he said in a muffled voice. His head was already down as he was doing just that.

Staring at the top of Ernest's hat, Imogene sighed, trying to understand why her pulse did not race when he looked at her. Why she didn't want to fling herself into his arms. Why thoughts of a future with Ernest felt stifling. He was such a good person, and he cared greatly for her. Was that not enough? And then she heard Ben laugh . . . and knew that it wasn't.

"Come see this, Benjamin," Emily called sometime later from farther up the beach. She had skipped ahead and was pointing to some object that had captured her attention. "It's too big to lift, but the layers appear to be folded."

"Be right there," Ben said as he sidled up to the cliff, reaching toward a spot a few feet above the beach floor.

A skitter of stones from overhead dropped at his feet. Imogene looked up with him in time to see the ground above start to shake.

"Ben!" she screamed. "The ledge is coming down!"

Grabbing her skirts to her knees, Imogene ran. But she wouldn't reach him in time. She was too far away.

chapter 17

In which Ben spends a fair amount of time <u>not</u> noticing Imogene

Jumping back, Ben lost his balance and fell hard, still under the path of the falling rocks. Someone grabbed his collar and hauled him back—half choking, half lifting. Hat knocked one way, bucket flung another, Ben braced his feet and pushed away from the cliff just as the ledge gave way. A shower of dirt and rocks, large and small, piled onto the very spot Ben had been standing moments earlier.

Senselessly, Ben leaned back farther, only to encounter a wall. A wall sitting on the ground behind him, feet extended. A familiar wall, who had lost his balance and fallen, too, in the rush to pull his brother out from under the rockslide.

As the screams faded, Ben realized there had been three sources, not two. One had come from overhead, from where the eroded ledge had given way. Gasping for breath, he looked over his shoulder to see Emily rushing toward him and heard Imogene behind, doing the same. Ernest patted Ben's shoulder while gulping at the air.

Scrambling to his feet, Ben dusted off his hands, his posterior, and his hat, and puzzled about the scream from above. Imogene and Emily fluttered about, touching Ben's arms and exclaiming excitedly, while Ernest got to his feet and proceeded to dust *himself* off. All seemed unaware that there was an unidentified party in this mishap.

"Oh Lordy, that was close, Ben." Ernest shook his head and laughed weakly—still wheezing from panic. "You have become quite accident-prone."

"Indeed," Ben said with a final glance at the top of the cliff. He turned his gaze toward Imogene. "Ernest, my brother, has saved me from certain death. My brother. Saved me." He repeated, refraining from adding: This proves how wrong you were.

"Certain death? Might be doing it up a little brown, Ben." Ernest bent to retrieve his hat.

"Halloo," a voice called from above. "Is everyone all right down there?"

Startled, Ben pivoted to stare at the head peeking over the top some thirty feet or so above them. It was Mr. Beeswanger.

"I say, is everyone all right?"

"We are all fine, Papa," Emily called up, hands cupping her mouth so that her words would carry.

"Oh thank heaven. So glad to know. Your mama almost landed at your feet, dearest Emily. That would have been a terrible tumble." He laughed in an affable manner, but there was a telltale shake to his voice. "Weren't paying attention, I'm afraid. Standing too close to the edge. Tabard grabbed your mama just as it gave way. Quite the scare, yes . . . quite. Well, not to worry, she's a bit mussed but otherwise fine." A murmur behind him could be heard, but not the words. "What's that?" Mr. Beeswanger turned. "Oh. Very good, then." He turned his head toward them once again. "Been told," he said, chuckling, "to get away from the edge. Very well. We'll see you back at the house. Your mama wants to clean up a bit. . . . I think she looks lovely. . . . But, well, there you have it. Cheers."

And so saying, the head of Mr. Beeswanger disappeared.

With a most unladylike snort, Emily pivoted to face the group. "Yes, well, humble apologies, everyone. Apparently my mama wanted to add a little excitement to our day."

They all smiled, as they were meant to, and then set about picking up the bucket and all the treasure that had been spilled. Within a quarter hour, they were meandering around the beach again—well away from the overhang.

CAREFUL MANEUVERING SAW Ben sit down to dinner between Emily and Jake. He would have preferred to be at the other end of the table, well away from Imogene, but this would do. When he looked up, it was to see Ernest, and he could ignore the lovely young lady beside his brother—in a soft sage green gown cut to a neat fit around her tantalizing figure with an enticing décolleté . . . with ten . . . no, twelve pearls sparkling in her golden upsweep. Yes, he could ignore her completely.

He hardly noticed when Imogene gave Grandmother the cockleshell she had found and exclaimed over on the beach. Ernest must have mentioned that Lady Margaret was partial to shells. It was certainly *not* impressive that Imogene had given the treasure away to someone who would enjoy it equally.

And Ben certainly did not notice that Imogene ate little—pushing her food around the plate. Was she paler than usual? Were those dark circles under her eyes? How could he notice any of those things when he was not paying the least attention? Besides, why should he care? He was angry. Still angry. Nothing had been resolved. He had merely pointed out that Ernest could hardly be considered a villain when he had pulled Ben out of harm's way.

The speed with which she agreed was inconsequential. He was angry. Still. And he would hold on to that rage—yes, it was rage, fury, and all other descriptors of being incensed that he could think of. He had to hold on to all those emotions that would push Miss Imogene Chively from his heart.

And just as important, he would disregard the look of bafflement that Grandmother was sending in his direction. A look that seemed to volley back and forth between Imogene and him. Him and . . .

Imogene.

"Imogene is really looking forward to sketching at the ruin. Do you think we will be able to go tomorrow?" Emily asked, breaking into his effort of not noticing Imogene.

"Yes, of course," he said with a nod and a ghost of a smile. It meant another day of studiously not noticing Imogene. "As long as the weather holds. We keep a skiff on the beach for that very purpose."

"It's only a short row over," Ernest added. "We can bring a basket and have an alfresco lunch in the shade."

"That sounds promising," Jake said from Ben's other side. "Might we join you?" He glanced across the table to Percy and then back to Ben.

"Six? No, no, I think not." Grandfather raised his voice to join the conversation from the head of the table. "Too many. The boat can take five at the very most . . . but six . . . Hmm, I think not. We could ask Lord Brennan if he might lend us his dory later in the week. Takes eight, I believe. Though you might need an oarsman, as the darn thing is heavy and a bit unwieldy."

"Might Jake go in Ben's stead?" Mr. Tabard asked. "After all, Ben knows the ruin, and yet Jake . . . well—" The surprised expressions brought Mr. Tabard's reasoning to an abrupt halt. "Oh, that wasn't well done," he said as if talking to himself. "I beg your pardon."

"Not at all, Mr. Tabard," Grandmother said with an indulgent smile. "I'm sure Ben would be more than happy to offer his seat to Jake."

"Yes, of course—" Ben nodded without any hesitation.

"No, no, thank you but no. Percy and I will find some

mischief or another, not to worry. It was just a passing thought, not a great ambition. Definitely not worth ousting Ben or disturbing your neighbor."

"If you are certain." Ben sighed. It would have given him an excellent excuse to avoid Imogene's company for the better part of the day.

"Oh, absolutely certain."

Ben sighed yet again and studiously ignored Imogene's forlorn smile. He hoped his brother had noticed—perhaps Ernest could put everything to rights.

THAT EVENING SAW Imogene laughing and smiling with the best of them, to Ben's great relief—not that he noticed. The youngest members of the house finally attempted, stress the word *attempted*, to put on act three, scene one from *A Midsummer Night's Dream*.

Percy and Jake had returned from fishing earlier than the beachcombers had returned from collecting, and in the interim they decorated the ballroom. With Grandmother's approval, huge vases had been filled with flowers from the garden and placed strategically around one end of the room. A settee had been brought in for Titania to use as her resting place—so that Emily would not be required to recline on the floor. And the chairs had been brought away from the walls into the center of the room. A very basic theater, there was no doubt, but with imagination—a great deal of imagination—one could envision a deep forest glen and home of the woodland fairies.

Percy and Jake had brought a few props with them to add to the atmosphere, the best of which was the head of a hobby-horse that Jake, playing Bottom, used as the ass's head. Many lines were forgotten, forcing Imogene to call them out from the sidelines, and comedy abounded—though much of the jocularity could not be attributed to Shakespeare.

When all was said and done, the audience was duly impressed. And the actors had had a great time. The night ended with smiles and "good evenings"—though Grandfather had to be awoken so he, too, might retire to his bed.

THE NEXT DAY dawned into a disobligingly sunny day with little wind and few clouds. Most people would call it an excellent day—but Ben was in no mood for excellent. The excursion was to go ahead as planned. Hours in Imogene's exclusive company did not bode well for his patience. There was a danger that he would fly at her for something inconsequential or find her adorable and forget his anger—neither was in the least appealing.

Cook had prepared a delicious alfresco meal, full of fruit and tarts, cheeses and breads of all sorts, and divided it into two baskets for Emily and Imogene to carry in one hand, a bailing bucket and blanket in the other. Ernest and Ben heaved a set of oars, each on their shoulders, and they set off. Emily and Ernest chatted as they strolled down the lane toward the cliffs, seemingly oblivious of the heavy silence of Imogene . . . and yes, Ben as well.

Once on the beach, they set off in the opposite direction

from the day before toward the overturned skiff sitting six or seven feet from the water. Neap tide was within the hour, so they would not have to haul the skiff far. With a practiced move, Ben and Ernest overturned the small wooden boat, untied it from the post embedded in the rock, and dragged it to the water one foot at a time. Once the back end was floating, they set the oars and food inside—and then helped Imogene and Emily aboard. Taking off his coat, Ben draped it atop Ernest's in the bow.

"I don't believe I have ever been out on the ocean before," Emily said with excitement as she lost her balance in the dip and lift of the waves. She landed with a thump on the center seat and giggled.

Imogene smiled as she took Ernest's hand and shifted to the stern seat. He had to slosh through the water to deliver Imogene to the back, but he did not appear to mind. Emily clung to the oarsman seat for a moment and then dove for the back . . . nearly upsetting the whole. She dropped down beside Imogene and giggled again—in a thin and forced manner.

"Don't think I would make a good sailor." Emily glanced at Imogene as if expecting a reflection of her discomfort in her friend's eyes.

"I imagine it is the same as anything—you would get used to it."

Emily nodded without conviction and then turned to glance over her shoulder. "How long did you say it takes to row to the island?"

"Just fifteen or so minutes. Not long," Ben answered.

"Not long," Emily repeated, and then turned back to sit ramrod straight—eyes glued to some midway point on the beach. "Not long."

Pushing the boat into the water a little farther, Ernest then lifted his leg, stepping over the gunwales, dripping water everywhere as he did. Ben pushed off as soon as Ernest had the oars locked in place and jumped into the skiff, trying, unsuccessfully, not to drag his feet in the water. Apparently, there would be two with sodden feet for most of the day.

Using the retreating wave to pull them deeper, Ernest hauled on the oars and turned them about in jig time. Ben was soon settled on his bench, gripping his oar handles. After watching Ernest's rhythm for a moment, he matched his pace. Soon they were away from the beach and past the most treacherous of rocks—Ben had not mentioned them to Emily, though he saw Imogene looking into the water with wide eyes.

As the beach receded, Ben glanced over his shoulder to sight the island. When he turned back, his gaze fell on Emily, who was no longer gripping her seat with a white-knuckled grasp. "Better?" he asked, impressed. Bravery was not about being nonchalant in a dangerous situation; bravery was doing something despite being terrified. Emily was being extremely brave.

"Yes, thank you. It seemed as if we were about to tip, and I cannot swim."

The swell of the waves provided a gentle roll as they pushed past the halfway point. Imogene swiveled her head from side to side, smiling at the view, while Emily stared straight ahead at—Ben assumed—the nearing island.

"Most. Ladies. Can't," Ernest said, talking in time to his exertion.

Ben couldn't see his brother, because he was facing stern as well, but Imogene was watching him, and something on his face made her smile. "A necessity for those living by the sea, perhaps?" she asked.

"Indeed."

Looking up, Imogene caught Ben staring. He flushed, swallowed, and glanced back over his shoulder to gauge their progress. The rocky shore was visible now, odd boulders peeking out of the water, offering a hazardous maze. The best landing spot was a cove around the point near the ruins. Ben directed his brother to pull to the right.

"Almost there, ladies—"

"Benjamin?" Emily sounded anxious again.

"No concern, Emily. This beach is on the lee side of the island. Far fewer waves. It will be easier to disembark. Let us do the work—"

"Ben!" This time it was Imogene who spoke, and she sounded as anxious as Emily.

"Not to worry," he started to repeat, but glanced her way as he did so and saw that Imogene was pointing to the bottom of the boat. Water was seeping up through the floorboards—far more than could be accounted for by wet boots—and the line was rising. "Bail, Imogene!" Ben shouted. "Grab the bucket! Anything! Ernest, hard left, we have to go in double time."

"But the rocks!" Ernest shouted, even as he set the boat on the new course and picked up the pace.

"Better hung up on a rock than swamped." Looking past his brother, Ben could see the girls bailing. They had flung off their bonnets and were throwing water out of the boat as fast as their bucket . . . and fruitless bowl . . . could manage. But they were not getting ahead of it.

For several eons, Ben and Ernest raced time until they rammed into a rock and it bounced them sideways. Dropping his oars, Ben turned. He flung himself across the front and stared into the water, shouting instructions at Ernest. Terra firma was still a good hundred or so feet away, and the skiff was getting lower in the water. It was harder to maneuver. "Hold on to the boat, Imogene, if it swamps completely. Do you hear me, Emily? It's a wooden boat; it will float. Right, Ernest! No, the other right! There. Straight on. Give 'er a strong pull and then left."

Glancing over his shoulder, Ben could see that the water was still only halfway to the gunwales. There was a good chance they were going to make it.

Then a wave dipped into a trough, exposing a rock directly ahead of them. "Left! Left!" Ben shouted as the skiff jerked sideways, glancing off the rock—directly into the path of another boulder. "Right!"

This time a cresting wave took the skiff up and over with a screech and groan of splintering wood. They were thirty feet from shore, but it was a shore strewn with obstacles, and they had two ladies who could not swim.

"I'm going in," Ben shouted, jumping to his feet. He grabbed the mooring rope. "I'll guide. Don't pull against me, Ernest."

"But—"

Ben didn't let his brother continue. He slung one leg over the side and then stretched across the gunwale. Shifting his weight, he pulled his other leg over and dropped into the cold, brackish water. It wasn't as far down as it should have been. Kicking out, his boot slammed into an unseen rock; Ben used it as leverage—pushing away, taking the skiff with him. The rope ran through his hands, burning, as the boat fought, pushed in the wrong direction by the waves. Scraping across another rock, the skiff ground to a halt. It shifted slightly with the next wave but only to hang up further. Pull as he might, Ben could not get it off the rock. It would not budge.

Sputtering as the waves crested and splashed into his face, Ben swam to the other side only to see that the rock had staved in the planking below Ernest's oarlock. Not a hole . . . yet. Looking over the gunwale, he saw Imogene's anxious face looking down at him.

"I'm afraid you are going to have to get wet," he said, shaking the water out of his eyes as another wave crashed against the side of the boat.

Imogene smiled, though it was a weak attempt. "We are already wet," she said.

"There are too many rocks to get the skiff any closer, but that means there are enough to cling to—"

A rogue wave startled Ben, lifting him up higher than he expected. He was almost nose to nose with Imogene, but only for a second. As soon as it crested, the wave rushed back out to the channel, dropping Ben into its deep trough. He slammed into the rocks below. He kicked, trying to push his head above water, but his foot caught in a crevasse, and there it remained.

With waves crashing over his head, Ben gulped at what little air he could and then bent down into the swirling water. He gripped his boot and pulled—to no avail. He tugged and tugged until his breath ran out and he was forced to straighten. Only then did he realize the cresting waves were above his head. Stretching his chin up and his mouth as high as possible, he was able to breathe when the waves rolled out—occasionally. Worse still, the tide had not yet reached its peak. Soon there would be no air for Ben at all.

Salt stinging his eyes, Ben watched Imogene through the murky haze of the foaming water and saw the horrified comprehension on her face. She opened her mouth. Ben thought she might be screaming, but his ears were filled with water—all he could hear were the muffled roar of the waves and the thud of the skiff on the rock.

chapter 18

In which a crumbling ruin offers the perfect
backdrop for abject misery

errified, Imogene watched Ben struggle. His head wasn't above the water; he couldn't breathe. "Ernest!" Imogene screamed, reaching out, trying to get hold of him. "Something's wrong! Ben needs help!"

She couldn't touch him; he was too far. Without considering, Imogene stretched across the gunwales and rolled over the side of the boat and into the water. Gasping with the cold, she ran her hands down the side of the boat until she was as close as she could get without letting go.

There, she held onto the boat and flapped her other hand toward Ben. Her fingers touched flesh, and she lunged, closing her hand around his wrist. She pulled, but he didn't budge, didn't move. She tried again, but it was as if he were resisting.

"Ben!" she screamed senselessly.

He thrashed and gulped a breath. "Foot!" But the effort had cost him. He had gulped down water in the attempt to speak. Flailing, as he tried to get his head above water, he coughed and spewed water twice before he gasped air and then was back under.

A splash by the front of the boat told Imogene that Ernest was on his way. But would he be in time?

Grabbing a deep breath, Imogene ducked her head under the water. Between the waves and Ben kicking up algae, the water was too cloudy to see anything. She would have to get closer; she would have to let go. And so she did.

Pushing away, Imogene crossed the huge distance of a few inches and sunk. She knew she would. She was ready; she kept her eyes open, grabbed Ben's arm, and used it to propel herself down. She clutched at his vest, his pantaloons, his thigh and then found his foot—jammed in between two rocks. Braced on either side, she hauled up. After two useless tries, Imogene ran out of air. Pushing away from the rock, she surfaced, grabbed a breath and allowed the momentum to take her down again.

This time when she got to Ben's leg, there was an extra pair of hands. Ernest. He was braced as she had been, pulling at Ben's boot. Imogene grabbed Ben's leg instead. They pulled and tugged, and just as she ran out of air again, Ben's foot shifted. Only a fraction, but it was enough for Imogene to ignore the pain in her lungs and pull with every last ounce of strength. And with that, his foot slipped free. Free of the rocks. Free of his boot.

All three shot to the surface. Grabbing a breath, Imogene expected to sink again, but Ben reached out and seized her about the waist, even as he was gulping at the air. For several minutes, they gasped, choked, and wheezed, and Ben held her tight.

Leaning her head back against the cap of Ben's shoulder, Imogene stared skyward. . . . Or at least she tried; there was something in the way. "Emily? Are you all right?" she asked. Emily was leaning over the boat, looking down at them. Her hair was a tangle, hanging over her shoulders, her face red as if she had been crying and yet . . . she was laughing.

"Couldn't be better." Emily's voice was scratchy, as if strained. Her gaze shifted to something over Imogene's shoulder. "I thought I was going to lose you—lose all of you. What's being marooned compared with that?" She laughed again, even as the tears streamed down her face.

GETTING TO SHORE was miserable but not treacherous. There were rocks aplenty. Ben scouted out the best route, while Imogene and then Emily followed. It had taken a fair amount of convincing, but Emily had eventually dropped over the side and into the cold, crashing waves. Hence the misery. They were soaked and shivering, covered in algae and grit, with rescue a good many hours away. They wouldn't be missed until dinner.

Once onshore, Imogene and Emily huddled on a downed tree and watched the boys swim back out to the boat and collect their belongings. Other than the fruit, the lunch was a soggy, inedible mess. Her sketching paper was pulp. Bonnets, coats, and blankets all ruined, only the bucket and oars were fine.

Dropping onto the ground in front of the girls, Ben sat with his knees bent, leaning against the tree. He had flopped quite close to Imogene, and she lifted her hand, laying it on his shoulder in reassurance, in camaraderie, in empathy . . . and in love. But he was not to know the last.

"Well, that was an adventure I might have done better without," he said. "Another accident . . . and yet, Josh checked the boat yesterday in preparation." He sighed and shook his head.

"Not an accident," Imogene said, watching his beloved profile. He was safe; he was alive. It had been so terribly close.

Ben nodded, staring at the water. "No, not an accident."

"There are times I do not like to be right. This is one of them." Although her being right had somehow dissipated Ben's anger. . . . Or had nearly dying done it? Mattered not, they were friends again.

Imogene smiled, wishing she could kiss his cheek. Just a chaste kiss, nothing provocative. A sign of her affection and relief. Though, if he turned at the right moment . . . No, best not think it. Emily was sitting beside them a scant two feet away. It was a disloyal thought. She squeezed his shoulder instead.

Pursing his lips for a moment, Ben huffed a sigh and then stilled. "Thank you," he said finally. "You jumped into the water with no thought of your own safety."

"It was but a moment." Imogene laughed. "I wasn't thinking very clearly."

"Imogene?" Ernest's voice was clipped. "What are you doing?"

Imogene blinked, realizing that her hand was still on Ben's shoulder and that she had been staring at him overlong. She pulled her hand away and sat back.

Ernest stood at the water's edge, dripping, holding Ben's errant boot. His head was tipped slightly, as if he was trying to see her from a different angle, and his brow was furrowed very deeply.

Lifting her cheeks into the semblance of a smile, Imogene met his gaze. "Agreeing that this was no accident." She could see Ben bobbing his head in front of her.

"Yes, I think we will have to come to terms with the fact that someone has ill-intent, Ernest. I think Imogene has had the right of it all along."

"I have been saying much the same," Emily added, her voice having gained strength. Her pallor was going.

"Yes." Ernest continued to frown, staring at Imogene for a long minute and then turning to Ben. "Your boot," he said, coming forward. He dropped it at his brother's feet, looked meaningfully at Imogene, and turned away, stalking down the shore toward the point.

Imogene stilled; she hardly drew a breath. And yet her mind roared. He knew! Ernest had seen something in her expression. Something that had told him Ben had won her heart. Her throat tightened, and tears threatened to spill. She gulped silently and closed her eyes for a moment before rising. She had to talk to him. This was not going to be an easy conversation.

Glancing at Emily, Imogene gestured toward the point. "I think I'll join Ernest."

Emily's understanding smile almost undid her.

It took some effort to catch up to Ernest. He had made good time . . . rushing to nowhere. Imogene had lifted her wet skirts above her ankles, trotting after him. He must have heard her pursuit, but he did not slow down until she called his name.

Even then, he stood where he was, not turning around. Motionless, looking out at the channel. Had he gone another thirty feet or so, he would have been forced to halt. He had reached the end of the point.

"Ernest, we have to talk," she said to his back. He neither turned nor answered. She circled around, standing in front of him.

With a clenched jaw, Ernest stared over Imogene's right shoulder. She had never seen a living, breathing human being look more like a statue. A cold, lifeless statue. Not made of stone—but glass. Fragile. Ready to shatter. Even before she spoke, Imogene felt the trickle of a tear on her cheek.

"I am so sorry, Ernest."

"You *are* in love. But not with me."

"I am so *very* sorry," she said again.

"When were you going to tell me? Going to keep stringing me along—spending time with Ben? Asking me to wait. Bah! There was no chance, was there?"

"I didn't know for certain. I have never been in love before—"

"It's hard to mistake."

"Perhaps for you. I wasn't sure if what I felt for Ben was fleeting. My experience is small, Ernest. I hold you in great affection. Admire you. Respect you and enjoy your company. I thought these, too, could be the beginnings of love. I asked you to wait because I didn't want to make a mistake." Imogene swallowed with difficulty. "I tried to say something at Greytower, but you were rushing Ben off—bringing him to Musson."

"Six days before you got here. You could have written."

"That would have been cold and cruel—"

"*Crueler* than keeping me hoping . . . planning a future for *us*? All the while you were pining for my brother. There is no hope for you there, you know. He has no thoughts of marriage. He will be apprenticing for another two or three years . . . at least!"

"I know, Ernest. I don't expect my feelings to be reciprocated, and please . . ." She reached out and touched his arm. At last he turned his chiseled face toward her. "Please, you must promise not to say anything. He would feel terrible."

Ernest leaned in closer. "And so he should," he barked.

Without flinching, Imogene smiled. "Should he? Ben did no wrong. He is who he is."

"He stole you from me."

"I was never yours to steal."

Ernest shifted so that he could see beyond her again. "You

have to go. I don't want you at Musson. Don't want you charming Grandmother anymore. Don't want your scent greeting me in every room. You have to go."

"I will speak to Father as soon as we get back. We will leave tomorrow."

"Today. There is half the day left."

"Yes, but Ernest, we are marooned on an island. I can hardly walk across the water because you no longer wish my company."

He blinked, as if weighing the veracity of her words—as if there was anything to weigh. Without speaking, he pivoted and stalked back down the shore, marching past Emily and Ben. They watched him go and then stared at Imogene with open curiosity. They would not have heard the conversation, but there was no mistaking Ernest's thunderous expression.

Imogene closed her eyes and rubbed at the bridge of her nose. She was not ready to answer questions—not Emily's, not Ben's. She, too, needed to be alone. Opening her eyes, she glanced around and saw what she was looking for. The path up to the tower ruins. There would be shade and privacy . . . and better yet, somewhere to sit and cry.

EMILY FOUND HER not a half hour later, leaning against the outer wall of the medieval tower. She had meant to go through the doorway, find a hidden corner, and sob to her heart's content; the building was roofless, but three walls still stood . . . of a sort. Crumbled and cracked by vegetation, a musty smell in the air, the ruin offered the perfect backdrop for abject misery.

As she had approached the tower, Imogene had observed the many aspects worthy of sketching. It was a habit and her solace. Unfortunately, those thoughts had led her to recollections of drawing with Ben, and quickly on their heels, Imogene lost the ability to hold herself upright. Her knees buckled, and she would have tumbled into an undignified sprawl had the wall not been near enough to grab.

And so she stayed. Using the hem of her soiled gown to wipe her nose and cheeks. She didn't care if the algae-covered muslin left streaks of green and brown down the side of her face. She didn't care about much. She wasn't sure which component of her conversation with Ernest distressed her the most—it was irrelevant. It was all a terrible mess.

Ernest was in pain—pain that she had caused. She hadn't handled it well, not well at all. There should have been a way to temper the hurt—remain friends, still enjoy each other's company. But no, she had bungled it completely. Ernest did not want to be anywhere near her now. She had lost the good opinion of a very kind young man. He hadn't deserved her rejection—if Ernest had not had a charming, handsome, devil-may-care brother, Imogene might have succumbed to his quiet, easy manners. She might have found excitement in his dance steps and poetry. Might. Might. It was all moot.

Ernest did have a brother—a like-minded brother who would want to see the back of her, too. Yes, as soon as Ben learned that Imogene had not accepted Ernest's offer, he would not give her the time of day. Once through the Musson House gates, Imogene would never see Ben again—ever. The looming moors of Devon seemed appealing—the idea of not ever encountering Ben or Ernest again was relieving.

"How are you?" Emily asked.

Imogene didn't look up. *Miserable* was on the tip of her tongue, but civility won the day. "I'm not really in the mood for company, Emily."

"I know that might be true, dearest friend, but, unfortunately, company has found us. Well, actually, in my eyes, it is fortunate. We are about to be rescued."

Imogene lifted her gaze. "Rescued? So soon?"

Emily nodded and then opened her arms, offering Imogene a comforting embrace. "There is a boat nearing the island. Something called a dory, I believe Ben said. Lots of space. Better yet, it floats."

Imogene muffled a chuckle into Emily's shoulder. "Floating is good."

"Ben has gone to find Ernest; I came for you. And the boat is coming round the point to land in the cove. It will be here soon." Emily lifted the hem of her gown, picked the cleanest spot, and used it to wipe away Imogene's newly formed tears.

"Oh, Emily, I have made a mess of everything."

"Perhaps not everything. But I think we need to talk about it later—after we have survived this next ocean voyage."

"Hardly an ocean voyage." Imogene laughed, somewhat

weakly, and then she saw Emily's grimace. "A short trip, Emily. And once we are back, you can stay on terra firma."

"Permanently!"

"Indeed," Imogene said. "Here, take my arm." She offered Emily her elbow. "I'll steady you; you steady me."

"Always," Emily said as she swallowed visibly before setting a slow gait back to the cove. While it was evident she wanted off the island, it was equally evident Emily did not want to get on another boat.

By the time Imogene and Emily emerged from the shrubbery, the dory had landed. Ernest and Ben greeted the four men who jumped onshore wearing jerseys and grins. All were lean and muscled, with the sun-darkened skin of outdoorsmen.

"Heard you got yerselves in a bit a trouble," the shortest and oldest man said with a snicker.

"Yes, I would say a swamped boat would fall into that category." Ernest's voice was unnaturally raspy. "Good to see you, Thirsty. How have you been?"

"Dicked in the nob, young sir, as always. Haven't seen you in a month a Sundays." The older man produced a harsh and phlegmy laugh, this time openmouthed, showing a maw of rotting teeth.

"Been busy," Ernest said simply.

"So I heard. So I heard." Thirsty's gaze lifted, fixing on Imogene and Emily.

Imogene squirmed . . . until Emily squeezed her arm.

"How did you know to come looking for us?" Ben asked.

"All a bit of a rush, young sir. Got word from the big house. Feller came riding down to the port all in a lather. Seems someone saw yer boat go down. Thought we might be too late." Then he laughed again. "Kinda glad we weren't."

Ben laughed, too. "So are we."

THE JOURNEY BACK to the mainland was blissfully uneventful. Emily and Ernest sat with their eyes closed the entire trip—though for very different reasons. Were Imogene to guess: Emily was holding on to every ounce of willpower needed to see her across the water, and Ernest did not wish to inadvertently look at Imogene.

Uneventful, yes, but also uncomfortable.

Ben glanced her way several times, but when she met his gaze, he looked away immediately. Yes, very uncomfortable.

Thirsty and his crew deposited them and their goods back on the beach where they had departed just an hour and a quarter earlier. It had been the longest hour and a quarter of Imogene's life—Emily might have said the same if Imogene had asked . . . which she didn't.

A crowd met them—the Beeswangers, Mr. Tabard, Jake, and Percy. They clapped and grinned and generally acted as if a miracle had occurred. Or a party was required. When Imogene considered the condition of the skiff, it probably was.

A hatless Mr. Tabard rushed into the water as they approached, his hair wild and flying about in the breeze. His gaze was fixed on Emily. "Oh, my dear, my dear. Are you all right?" Grabbing the side of the boat, he helped haul it farther onto the beach, with Jake and Percy opposite. The crew seemed somewhat amused by the attention.

Lifting Emily over the gunwales, Mr. Tabard tried to carry her up the beach, but Jake had to come to his father's aid. They shared Emily's weight, making a chair, of sorts, joining their hands. All rather pointless, because Emily was still wet from slogging through the water at the island, but it was meant as a kindness.

Mr. Beeswanger did the same for Imogene, lifting her from the boat and, without any help, set her beside Emily, away from the water. Tut-tutting, but looking pleased, Mrs. Beeswanger declared their gowns only worthy of the dustheap. She pushed the hair off Emily's face and tucked Imogene's behind her ears in signs of affection and relief.

After expressions of gratitude were doled out liberally to Thirsty and his crew, the company headed down the beach. Jake and Percy led the way, carrying the skiff's oars.

"You gave us quite the scare," Mrs. Beeswanger said with a broad grin as she walked between her daughter and Imogene. "You have Mr. Tabard to thank for your rescue. He was watching through a spyglass and saw your boat get lower and lower in the water."

Looking over her shoulder toward Mr. Tabard, Imogene saw that the old gentleman was frowning and shaking his head while staring at Emily as they walked. And he seemed to be muttering. He did not look jubilant, like a man proud of his role in their rescue; he looked haggard. "Are you well, Mr. Tabard?" Imogene asked.

"So very sorry, my dear." Mr. Tabard was still watching Emily.

Emily shook her head, looking so much more herself now that they were back on dry land. "It is not your doing, Mr. Tabard. You did not swamp our boat. In fact, you saved us from many cold, damp hours of waiting."

"But I did, I did. I am so sorry. I thought it would sink right away. As soon as it was put in the water. Boom, gone. You're wading back up the beach. Disgruntled but fine. I didn't think you would be able to get into it and row to the island. Most of the way, that is. I didn't know. I'm not a sailor. I know nothing of boats. So you see, it is mostly my fault, but not entirely."

Imogene started. Did she hear correctly? She stopped in her tracks, Ben bumping into her as he, too, stared at Mr. Tabard with a slack jaw. "What are you saying? Did you put a hole in the skiff?"

Putting his hand to his temple, Mr. Tabard finally looked at Imogene. "A hole? No, of course not. What kind of monster would put a hole in a boat? That would be dangerous. No, indeed, not a hole. . . . I chipped out some of the caulking."

"What?" Imogene grabbed Ben's arm as he lunged at Mr. Tabard. "You tried to kill us!" he shouted.

Mr. Tabard looked stupefied. "No need to be rude, young man," he said, looking affronted. "After all, if it weren't for you, none of this would have happened!" Shaking his head vehemently, he took several backward steps until Ernest blocked his retreat. "Clara would be most insulted by your accusation. Really. Tried to kill you . . . No, indeed! I tried to get you away from Emily is what I did. But you are a leech . . . a leech, I say." He curled his mouth in disgust and shook his head.

By this time the company had halted. Percy and Jake, after having dropped the oars, had run back to investigate the commotion and joined the circle around Mr. Tabard. Pivoting, his gaze going from person to person, Mr. Tabard looked disoriented. Finally, his eyes lit on Jake, now standing between Ben and Ernest.

"How could you expect to secure Emily with one such as him around?" Mr. Tabard said heatedly, jerking his head in Ben's direction. "You couldn't. *He* is winning the war. Battle after battle, Emily is being charmed. He is nothing if not persistent. He will not *stop* enchanting her!"

"Emily?" Jake looked perplexed. "Why would it matter?"

"Jake, Jake, my son, it was your mother's dearest wish to see you and Emily united. She could talk of little else as she lay dying. Imagining your children. Seeing them running down the halls of Greytower—a happy place. It was a wonderful vision."

"It was a fiction, Father, a lovely apparition, but no more than that. Emily is a sister to me. I have no more intention of asking her to marry me than I have of asking Imogene." Jake glanced at Percy and then back to his father. "Please tell me you did not nearly drown four people in an effort to prevent Ben and Emily from spending time together. It is not your affair."

"No, it is yours. You have done nothing toward securing her favor—"

"Nor will I. Father, listen and listen well. I am not going to marry Emily."

"Please, Jake—"

"No. I will hear no more." Jake lifted his chin and glanced at those around him until his eyes settled on Ben. "I humbly beg your pardon," he said, looking more the gentleman than Imogene had ever seen him before. "It would seem that my father, in misapprehension, has done you great wrong. There is little restitution that I can offer. But perhaps you will know that I feel the weight of it by saying that I can do nothing else other than break with him—"

"No, Jake." Mr. Tabard reached out toward his son, even as those around him gasped.

"It is not necessary," Ben said, looking vastly uncomfortable. "No true harm was done. What is a skiff, after all?"

"Or being stung by bees, or thrown from your horse . . ." Jake turned back to his father. "Father? Should I continue?"

"No. I . . . I was not thinking clearly." Mr. Tabard stared at his son with welling eyes. "I could hear Clara . . . your mother . . . lamenting. She wants to see you happy."

"And I will be happy. But not with Emily at my side." He glanced at her. "No insult intended."

"None taken," Emily said quietly.

"I will make amends." Mr. Tabard started to shake; he turned toward Ben, weeping openly. "Ask anything, anything."

"It is not necessary," Ben said again.

"But I will. I will. There, see, Jake. All is well, my boy. Where are you going? No. Jake? Jake!"

As a flailing Mr. Tabard ran up the beach after his son, those that remained stood in shocked silence for some moments. Eventually, Percy cleared his throat. "If you will excuse me. I believe I have to see to Jake." He bowed formally and followed at a sedate and dignified pace.

"Well," Mr. Beeswanger said, staring at the ground.

"Well," Mrs. Beeswanger said, staring at Emily.

"I don't understand." Emily frowned and blinked and turned a flaming shade of crimson. "Jake and I have never meant anything to each other. There have been summers that we have not even exchanged a single word. How could Mr. Tabard possibly believe that we would make a match? How could Cousin Clara?" She looked past Imogene. "I apologize, Benjamin. I had no idea that our friendship was the cause of all your trials . . . perils. All those incidents that we knew were not accidents. Mr. Tabard put you in danger, no matter his intent."

"I am sorry, too, if I have given the impression of a greater regard than is seemly."

Emily blanched.

"You haven't, my boy." Mr. Beeswanger came forward and clapped Ben on the back. "You have had no hand in Mr. Tabard's delusion. I'm afraid it was all in the mind of a grieving husband." He turned with Ben and Ernest, and the three headed toward the path off the beach, talking quietly. Mr. Beeswanger's reassuring tone dominated.

Emily stared at Imogene in terrible distress—tears on the verge of spilling.

What a ghastly, dreadful day. In his attempt to clarify, Ben had made it all too clear that he did *not* favor Emily—that the special relationship that she thought was seeded and beginning to bloom was no more real than the one Mr. Tabard had imagined between her and Jake. Ben Steeple was not in love with Emily.

Imogene reached for Emily's hand and gave it a squeeze. Wordless, but in sympathy, they followed Mrs. Beeswanger up the slope toward Musson House, where the fun of the day would continue. She was now about to face her father, and not only tell him that Ernest Steeple was not to be her husband, but that they were to leave immediately.

Yes, a lovely day.

chapter 19

In which Imogene's world tips on its axis

Sound didn't usually carry through the halls of Musson House, but the raised voice in the library was so loud that the echo made its way up to the third floor, where Ben finally found Ernest.

Ignoring Mr. Chively's shouting, Ben sighed with relief. "There you are." He had been fairly certain that his brother would not do himself an injury in his melancholy—but a niggling doubt had eaten at Ben while he changed and then searched the manor.

Standing before the windows at the far end of the gallery, clothed impeccably once again, Ernest stared at the sky as if unaware of his brother's presence.

"I am here to offer what solace I can. Ask anything of me.

I will fetch your favorite book, discuss Byron's poetry, or let you borrow my black hessians. Anything, anything at all."

Ernest had said little when Ben had caught up to him on the island other than to state that Imogene had declined his offer to make an offer.

"She might change her mind, you know. It was a harrowing day, and it might have affected her more than it appeared." Ben didn't believe his own words, but he was desperate to see his brother's heartache expunged—even at his own expense.

Ben was confused, very confused. On one hand, he wanted to shake Imogene for not seeing the value of Ernest's love. . . . And on the other hand, he was relieved beyond measure. And the guilt that came with that thought was extreme. It was made worse by the next thought. Could he and Imogene now have a future together? She had broken with Ernest. Where did they go from there?

"I'm fine," Ernest said in a voice that made a lie of his words.

Ben came to stand beside Ernest. "Her father is wringing a fine peal over her even as we speak. . . . There is still hope."

"I think not."

"Can I do anything to help?"

"You have done enough." Ernest's tone was razor sharp.

"I beg your pardon?"

A heavy silence engulfed them for several minutes. The longer it lasted the more difficult it was to break. Ben turned his frown toward his brother.

"You have done enough," Ernest eventually repeated. This time his tone was softer, but his words were still enigmatic.

"I don't understand."

"Yes, I know." Ernest shifted, just slightly, but he made a wall with his shoulder. "Could you say my farewells? I'm not up to it right now."

"Farewells? Is Imogene going somewhere?" Ben's belly roiled. He needed time, needed the next few days to allow things to settle. . . . Then he could see how the wind blew. Then he could see if Imogene might be interested in the heart of another Steeple.

"I asked her to go."

Ben straightened, surprised. It was unlike his brother. Ernest might not be an affable host, but this bordered on boorish—no, in truth, this stepped right past it. "When is she leaving?"

"Immediately—well, as soon as they are packed."

It took great quantities of resolve and clenched muscles for Ben *not* to rush from the gallery, calling Imogene's name. He needed to see her. He needed permission to write. He needed leave from her father to visit Gracebridge Manor. Without establishing some sort of connection, her family could keep her from him. He might never see her again. Never.

A shout formed in his throat, but he swallowed against it. Immediately was not immediate. Preparing the horses would take time, not to mention the process of gathering belongings and persons. And Imogene would not be going alone. All the Chivelys had to be organized. He had time. . . . He could appear nonchalant.

"Tabard will be off as well, I imagine," Ben said, taking a deep breath. Trying to calm his racing heart.

"Yes."

"To think that it was he all along—"

"Perhaps we might discuss our villain some other time. At least you need not be leery anymore."

"I was never leery."

"Indeed."

Ernest lapsed into silence again, and after staring out at the sky with his brother for several minutes more without additional discourse, Ben quietly slipped back down the stairs.

He had to find Imogene . . . immediately.

IMOGENE WAS IN the library. She, too, was staring at nothing. With her eyes turned toward the unlit fireplace, she sat on the edge of the wingback chair as if about to rise—which she did when Ben entered the room.

"Ah, there you are," she said, as if it had been she who had been searching. Now clothed in a soft teal traveling dress, with a freshly scrubbed face and neatly coifed hair, Imogene's skin was still pasty white. "I have made my apologies to your grandparents about our hasty departure. They quite understand and are the kindest of souls. You have truly been blessed with your family, Ben."

The implication, of course, was that hers were far less obliging.

"Ernest wishes us away as soon as possible, and I have set everything onto that path. Mr. Tabard has already departed—without Jake, who refuses to talk to him." She shook her head.

"I am still in shock . . . never would have imagined that such a quiet man could be so wrongheaded. I am very sorry that we brought danger to your door. One can never tell about people, can one?"

Ben opened his mouth to agree with this rather ambiguous statement, but she carried on.

"I don't know if you have heard; the Beeswangers will be leaving as well. So in one fell swoop, your company will be gone. They have agreed to take me with them to Shackleford Park as my parents' carriage will be full, what with Jake joining them to stay at Gracebridge for a time, and there was only room for me beside the driver, and Mrs. Beeswanger thought I need not ride so rough, and Mother thought it best if I visited Shackleford any- way for a few days . . . weeks . . . or perhaps longer." She stopped and gulped at the air, her nervousness clearly running away with her tongue.

"Oh, Imogene, has your father broken with you . . . over your refusal to entertain an offer from Ernest?"

"Well, yes, actually—" She swallowed. "He feels I am un- grateful and not worthy of time, money, or effort. I am very lucky to have such good friends in the Beeswangers. They have made me feel quite welcome, and Emily thinks I will be a great distraction." She cleared her throat as if halting a thought and setting her mind in a different direction. "Thank you, Ben. I greatly enjoyed getting to know you, teaching you where your artistic talent lies, and, as much as he might not like to hear it now, spending time with your brother. It is a summer that I will always remember fondly."

"That sounds like good-bye."

Imogene laughed lightly, but there was no humor in her eyes. "It is good-bye, Ben."

"Could I not come to visit you? At Shackleford Park?"

Smiling sadly, she shook her head. "I don't think so. . . . You are soon to Canterbury. Your mind will be full of rococo ceilings and stonework," she said with a forced laugh. "It is as it should be."

"But—"

"Good luck with your studies. . . . And if ever you need any assistance of an artistic nature, I would be happy to help."

There. Ben let go of the breath he had been holding. Yes, *there* was his opening—his way back into Imogene's company. He didn't know if she meant to provide the means of rekindling their friendship or not, but he had every intention of using her invitation in such a manner.

"STRANGE," EMILY SAID after several hours of riding in silence. "I am starting to feel much more myself the closer we get to Shackleford Park. I don't believe ocean air is as beneficial for the health as it is touted."

Imogene pulled her gaze from the coach window, catching Mrs. Beeswanger's nod as Imogene turned toward Emily. She reached out and patted her friend on the knee. "Very glad to hear it. I am certain that you will be feeling quite the thing within a week."

"You think so?" Emily sounded wistful.

"Yes, absolutely. Time will be your comrade." They both knew they were not talking about health.

"Perhaps the seaside is not for you, dearest Emily," Mrs. Beeswanger joined the conversation. "But there are some that benefited from the salt breezes. Some that will be harder hit by its absence."

A frown flashed across Imogene's brow, and she turned to see Mrs. Beeswanger pointedly staring at her with an expression of deep sympathy. Imogene swallowed and would have burst into tears had she not glanced at Mr. Beeswanger. He was watching as well, but where Mrs. Beeswanger's compassion threatened to break her resolve, Mr. Beeswanger's buck-up-all-will-be-well look served to strengthen it.

"Yes." Imogene offered a weak smile as a thank-you to them both. "But there is nothing to be done." Not in regard to Ben. Not in regard to her father.

Still . . . all was not lost. In fact, might this be the moment to step onto a different path? Seize the day, as the Romans said. Could the rending from her family—and Ben—have purpose? Could she forge her own future, one that might be difficult but bring with it a different sort of contentment? Yes, indeed, might she now find the means to fulfill a dream?

"Mr. Beeswanger, could I meet with you sometime soon to discuss a business possibility?"

"Of course, my dear." His countenance was suffused with curiosity, but he said nothing more.

Imogene nodded as much to herself as to anyone in the carriage. Her rebellion, as her father had termed her refusal of Ernest, had brought with it irrevocable changes—changes that she had both feared and anticipated. She could now step away from convention—the expectations of society—and champion her own wants and needs. But security was no longer certain; she would need advice—good, solid business advice. Mr. Beeswanger was an amply suitable gentleman for the job. He might even be interested in being a mentor, better yet a patron, of a teaching art studio.

A pervasive calm suddenly blanketed Imogene, and she smiled. It was no longer a weak imitation of cheerfulness but a true display of serenity. The future had changed, but it was not bleak. She would forge her own path. . . . And eventually she would no longer wish that Ben walked beside her.

SHACKLEFORD PARK WAS such a familiar environment that Imogene felt at home almost immediately. Well, perhaps not quite like home. There was no tippy-toeing around the manor while trying to judge the mood of the master of the house. There was no haranguing brother, indifferent mother, and snide remarks from all the above.

Still, Imogene was rather dismayed when a fortnight or so after joining the Beeswanger family in Tishdale, a cart arrived with an excited dog, clothes, painting supplies, and a note in her mother's hand.

Dear Imogene,

I thought Mrs. Beeswanger was not mistaken in
her suggestion that a few of your warmer gowns
would be of use for the cooler nights that are now
threatening. I have taken the liberty of including
all your autumn accessories—shawls, coats, bonnets,
and such. One never knows how quickly the cooler
weather will descend, nor do we know how long
your father will remain out of sorts in your regard.
If need be, I will send over your winter clothes.
Mrs. Beeswanger assures me that she quite thinks of
you as one of her own and is more than happy to
have you there.

    I have also included your art supplies, which
I am sure you sorely miss. Percy and Jake took a
liking to your grandmother's studio, setting it up as
a theater. Costumes and props at one end, a stage of
sorts at the other. They have even hung up a
curtain and invited several other young gentlemen
in the area to join their Thespian Society. They
are entertaining themselves nicely. We have
already had a scene from <u>Much Ado About
Nothing</u>. Quite hilarious. Jake is fitting in nicely.

Kind Regards,
Mother

PS: Jasper is being a nuisance; he got into the henhouse yesterday. I'm sure he will be happier with you.

When Imogene rushed to the stables, Jasper's happiness was not in doubt. As soon as he saw Imogene, he put on such a display of enthusiasm that it outshone all his other greetings. Never had she seen him jump so high or wag his tail with such abandon. Eventually he calmed . . . until he saw Emily and repeated his demonstration of undying affection.

After much laughter and excitement, the practicalities of their reunion had to be addressed—the most significant being the question of where Jasper was to be housed. The stable hands were quite taken with him and allowed that they could keep an eye on the dog if need be, but Mrs. Beeswanger had another suggestion.

"There is no need to relegate your companion to the outdoors. Bring him inside. I'm sure he will be more content following you around the manor."

"Pardon? Inside? You will allow Jasper to stay with me?" Imogene could hardly believe her ears. Her mother would never consider such a thing.

"Of course, my dear," Mrs. Beeswanger said with a gasp as two proper young ladies threw themselves into her arms. "All I ask is that he not be underfoot in the dining room."

Of course Imogene readily agreed.

SITTING ON THE side of the bed only half listening to Kate exclaim about this item or that as she pulled them out of the trunk and put them in the wardrobe, Imogene stared out the window, distracted by thoughts that had nothing to do with her self-absorbed family. She missed Ben terribly.

She reached down to the floor where Jasper had curled up at . . . well, actually, *on* . . . her feet. Scratching him behind his ears in an absentminded fashion, she sighed.

Scene after scene ran through her mind: snippets of conversations, recrimination, and self-castigation followed quickly and then a sense of embarrassment. There was much she wished she had said, and much she wished she could unsay. Should she have been brazen and told him that she held him in great affection, or had she saved herself from mortification by offering a casual good-bye? How much of his interest had been in her imagination? How much had been real? Queries . . . many queries, but there would be no answers . . . just time to help her forget.

"Good news, Imogene," Emily said, bursting into the room. "There are two spaces that Mama and Papa think might suit for your temporary studio. Both are in the attics just like the one you had at Gracebridge. One is a tad small, next to the female staff bedrooms, but it does have good light and is easily accessed from the main staircase. The other is on the opposite side—Imogene? Are you not pleased?"

Imogene blinked, realizing that she was still staring at Jasper. She lifted her eyes and then her cheeks. "Oh yes. Certainly. That is wonderful. Your parents are most generous."

Generous was such a mild description of the Beeswangers' support. They were unreservedly behind Imogene's enterprise—the eventual forming of an art academy. They had discussed the project every which way to Sunday. It had been her salvation—her distraction from the pain of losing Ben.

It was not going to be the work of a minute; it would take years of careful, patient labor. She would start with a teaching studio at Shackleford while they sought out a more strategic location. The funds from her grandmother would help defray supply costs, but were it not for Mr. Beeswanger's agreement to act as an advisor and patron, Imogene's dreams would not be realized until far in the future. Yes, *generous* was too small a word.

Emily joined her on the bed, bouncing Imogene gently as she sat down. "Oh, Imogene, I am so sorry about your family—they are the ones to miss out . . . being without your company. You know that Mama and Papa would be quite pleased to have you stay indefinitely."

Nodding, Imogene patted Emily's lower limb. "Yes. They have said as much, and I believe they mean it." She smiled but, unfortunately, sighed at the same time.

"Then what is wrong? What can I do? Say? I am desperate to see you happy."

"Broken hearts take time to heal, Miss Emily," Kate said as she folded a cream-and-apricot scarf. "Everyone is different."

"Mine mended easily enough. I can only think I wasn't as deeply in love as I thought. I am quite up to scratch again. And yours will . . . ? No, that's not it. You turned down Ernest."

"Not Mr. Ernest, miss." Kate glanced over her shoulder. "Mr. Ben. Though, being that he was over the moon about you, Miss Imogene, I don't understand why it didn't work out . . . if you'll excuse me for saying so."

Imogene stilled. She lifted her chin and offered a frown to Emily before addressing Kate. "What do you mean, Kate? Why would you say that about Ben?"

"At Musson, Matt told me he were certain Mr. Ben cared for you, Miss Imogene. Had Mr. Ernest not been so distracted, he woulda seen it, too."

"Who is Matt?" Emily asked; her color was getting higher.

"The Steeple valet." Kate lifted one corner of her mouth. "Quite a nice fella." She turned back, dipping into the trunk for another piece of clothing. "There was no mistaking it, he said."

Imogene closed her eyes and swallowed, breathing in a gulp. "It wasn't my imagination," she whispered with a half smile. "And I told him *not* to call." She hung her head and closed her eyes.

"Clearly, I have missed something." Emily's voice was clipped. "Might I get you to come back in a bit, Kate?"

"Certainly, Miss Emily."

The door closed, and silence took over—a pulsing, oppressive manifestation.

Imogene listened to the small mantel clock tick away the seconds, and then minutes, and still Emily did not speak. Finally, Imogene lifted her head to find her closest friend staring with an unreadable expression. Perhaps that was a good omen, for Imogene had expected anger or hurt. "Emily?"

"Yes."

"There was nothing between Ben and me. Nothing. A few heated looks not unlike those *you* shared with him. He is an incorrigible flirt, remember? Please do not be angry with me. I did not mean to fall in love with him. I thought of him as your beau and behaved accordingly."

"The heated looks that Benjamin and I shared disappeared under examination. Our relationship was friendly and boisterous, with a great deal of camaraderie, but, in truth, he did nothing to entice me. It was all on my shoulders. He is charming—and he cannot behave otherwise."

"So you say, and yet you are still distressed with me. I am not a pea-brain, thinking that your upset is directed elsewhere."

"Of course I'm distressed. I told you Benjamin looked on me with interest and you said nothing of your own sentiments. Nothing of *your* heated looks."

"All my life I have doubted myself, Emily, my actions, my thoughts, my judgment. You talked of your conviction that Ben was smitten, and I didn't know you had doubts. More important, I would never interfere with your growing affection even if I thought there was a chance that Ben would look my way. I would not do that to you. I would never hurt you."

Emily's expression softened. "I know you wouldn't. . . . But you forgot something in all this conjecture. You forgot to give me the chance to do the same. Had I known that you, too, had feelings for Benjamin, I would have looked for signs. We could have approached the puzzle of Mr. Benjamin Steeple together."

Imogene stared at Emily, tears welling. "I beg your pardon, Emily. You are right, I should have told you."

With a sad smile, Emily nodded. "Now that we agree, tell me what you meant when you said that you told him not to call."

"The day we left Musson House, he asked if he might call. . . . But I said that he would be too busy. Implied he should not visit."

"Why?"

"Oh, Emily! I did not know he cared. I thought it was only my heart. . . . I . . . Why did I think he was just being gentle-manly? What was I thinking?" Covering her face with her hands, Imogene leaned against Emily. "Oh, Emily, I didn't even give him a chance. He must have been waiting until I broke with his brother . . . waiting to see how I felt. And I turned him away. This is a disaster."

"No. Not a disaster. It's just a setback." She pulled Imogene's hands from her face. "So, what are you going to do?"

Imogene sat up straight, squared her shoulders, and glanced out the window. "What can I do?" she asked the ether, thought for a moment . . . thought about all that had happened that fate-ful day—the break with Ernest, Mr. Tabard's guilt, her father's rage, turning down Ben . . . and then the salvation of being offered a home and a future—and all the pieces tumbled together.

She turned back to Emily, who had been watching her closely. "Restitution. Mr. Tabard promised Ben restitution. And your father suggested that our art school would be better situated in a town or city . . . such as Canterbury. Even if we find a suitable townhouse, it will likely need to be renovated. Might the two not go together?"

Emily stilled, considered for some moments, and then blinked and smiled. "Yes, Mr. Tabard should be prevailed upon to provide a monetary restitution. He should hire Lord Penton on the strength of his apprentice's excellent reputation to oversee the project."

"Yes," Imogene grinned. "And I am fairly certain that I would need to meet with Lord Penton's apprentice regularly to discuss the plans."

NOT A WEEK LATER, as Imogene was setting up her new teaching studio in the Shackleford attic, Emily entered the narrow room with an excited aspect in her bearing.

"Imogene," Emily called needlessly from the doorway, as they had already spied each other. "You have a caller."

"A caller?" Imogene stood from where she had been rooting through her art trunk. "Should I come down to the drawing room?"

"I brought him up here, being that he is no stranger to art studios."

Emily stepped out of the way to reveal Ben Steeple, looking more handsome than ever. He had his hat in hand and kept turning it as he stared across the room. Imogene had never seen such a beautiful sight.

Jasper must have agreed, as the dog awoke and leaped to his

feet in the same instant. He raced toward the door and greeted Ben with great bounces, tongue lolling, and adoration on his face.

"I apologize for disturbing you." Ben calmed Jasper with inattentive pats and an unusually reserved manner. "I thought that I might write first . . . but then decided to ride over. I have a proposition—an offer, a business scheme—that I thought you might . . . that I might . . . Well, I'm sure you understand."

Imogene could hardly hear his halting words over the clamor in her ears. Her heart was trying to beat out of her chest. Her breath seemed to have left her lungs, and yet she was filled with joy. . . . And she did not understand anything that he was saying. But did it matter?

"No, no, that's fine. Please come in. It's lovely to see you." She turned toward Emily, who was making odd faces behind his back, and waved at her to go away.

"I think I will leave the two of you for a bit. I have to . . . check . . . yes, I have to check. Nice to see you again, Benjamin. I hope to see you more often."

Imogene lifted her cheeks at her friend and flicked her hand in a *be-gone* movement. Emily winked at Imogene as she turned to go, taking Jasper with her.

Stepping forward, Imogene paused, blinking stupidly at her hand full of brushes—wondering how they had come to be there. She dropped them on a nearby table. "A business scheme? But my letter went out only a week ago," she said, swaying her hips as she sashayed toward him.

Ben met her in the middle of the room. They were now only

feet apart. She could almost touch him, and she was desperate to do so. There was no doubt that he had the most appealing gaze; his eyes were like liquid warmth, even when they were frowning. . . . which they were doing now.

"Letter? To me?"

"No, Mr. Tabard. Oh." Imogene frowned. "You are not here about the school?" She tipped her head—and watched him watch her. "Well, yes, I thought it too soon. To what business scheme are you referring, then?"

Upon closer inspection, Imogene decided that she had never seen Ben look so edgy, almost nervous. His engaging smile was gone entirely, and he looked uncomfortable. It was almost as if they had reversed their characters, for she was the far more tranquil of the two, conversing easily.

Ben gave his head a short shake, continuing to frown. He turned his hat again. "I have come to ask if . . . if you might . . . will consent to be my artist."

Imogene giggled—yes, an unintentional giggle, not a good sign. Well, not a bad sign, either—just a sign. "Your artist?" She was feeling rather light-headed. Probably best if she started to breathe again.

"Yes, I spoke to Lord Penton. Told him that I had been less than truthful about my drawing abilities . . . but that I had worked on it over the summer and better still knew an artist who was excellent at rendering buildings and detail and who might be willing to work with me on future projects. He was quite relieved—said he had seen quite clearly that I could not draw and thought that collaborating with an artist was an excellent suggestion. So there you have it, would you, please, consider a collaboration . . . with me?"

Imogene grinned. "I think it a most estimable idea." She offered her hand, as a gentleman might do upon the conclusion of a business deal.

But rather than take it as he ought, Ben dropped his hat and, using both hands, encased hers. "That, my dear Imogene, is the best news I have had in some time. It would require regular visits . . . to discuss various projects and . . . why did you think I was here because of Mr. Tabard?"

Imogene stared hypnotically at their joined hands. Propriety dictated that she pull her hand away—break the bond—but she was too content to give propriety any heed. "I wrote to Mr. Tabard suggesting that he might make amends to you financially. That he should secure Lord Penton and his highly recommended apprentice, Mr. Benjamin Steeple, for a long-term project . . . that of building or renovating a studio, a teaching art studio."

"A teaching studio? Would that be your art school?"

She grinned. "Eventually. A teaching studio at first, growing into a school and then, if all goes well, an academy."

"Oh, that is too splendid, absolutely the best news ever. Imogene, I am so very pleased for you."

"Thank you. It is not the work of a minute. There is a significant amount of planning, but with Mr. Beeswanger's guidance, I'm sure it will come about. Something I never thought possible before." Reluctantly, she freed her hand but did not step back. They were standing very close—almost under-the-parasol close.

"You are a marvelous teacher, Imogene. I know the school will be a great success."

"Thank you. I have high hopes."

A slight fold formed above the bridge of his nose and then disappeared. "Designing, settling on plans, and then executing them would place us in each other's company a fair amount over several months."

"I assumed as much." She laughed at his surprised and then brightening expression. "I have missed our time together . . . our lessons, of course."

"Have you? But when we last spoke, you did not seem at all eager to continue our acquaintance."

A cloud formed in Imogene's eyes. "It was a terrible day, Ben. I was not thinking clearly. I had just devastated your brother, broken with my father. . . . How is Ernest?"

This time, Ben's frown stayed. "Not as well as I would like, I must admit. But his letters are becoming frequent and no longer filled with doom and gloom. Still, it has been only a few weeks—time is his best ally."

"I did not mean to hurt him. I hoped we might be friends; I did so like his company. He has such wit and gentleness."

"Yes, well, he might not thank you for friendship right now. He avoids the topic of you almost entirely. He only mentions Miss Chively—yes, I'm afraid your given name has disappeared—he only mentions you as a necessary evil when haranguing me to pay a social call on the Beeswangers. In that, he was rather emphatic—relentlessly insistent, in fact."

"Oh?"

"Yes. And he urged me to approach you with the idea of rendering my designs. He thought you would be highly amenable. That was how he put it, *highly amenable.*"

"Really. Ernest sent you to . . . me." Imogene swallowed and blinked rapidly for a moment.

"Yes. Why does that thought upset you, my dove? I thought it a kindness." He wiped away a tear that had escaped and was sliding down her cheek.

"Yes, it is a great kindness. A very great kindness." She took a calming breath and reached out to touch Ben's hand. She did not have to stretch; he was still standing much too close for proper modesty. It was marvelous. "Did Ernest tell you why I was not favorable to his suit?"

"No. I thought your tastes were . . . that your interests . . . No. He didn't say."

Imogene stared at Ben, reveling in the sight, finding ecstasy in the warmth of his hands and the heat of his gaze. Could she tell him that she loved him? Could she be the one to take the first step? Would she die of mortification if she had misread his fixed gaze? Was Matt wrong? Did it matter?

No. Love was a gift, a compliment. It might not be reciprocated—but what if it was and Ben was simply waiting for a sign from her? After all, she had mistakenly asked him *not* to call. And if he did not feel the same . . . ? Well . . . she would survive—not happily, but she would survive. Better to know one way or the other.

Stepping infinitesimally closer, Imogene took a deep breath, clasped both his hands, and opened her heart. "I have never been more terrified in my life than when you were trapped under the water. The thought of losing you was unbearable; I would have gladly traded places. I could hardly contain my joy when you were safe and sound once more. . . . Ernest realized . . . he knew . . . I am in love with *you*."

Six words. Imogene had spoken the six words that would change her world—tip it over. She had taken her destiny in hand. For good or ill, the die was cast.

Ben stilled. Imogene wasn't sure if he was breathing. And then, finally, he spoke. "Indeed?"

It was more of a croak.

"Beyond a shadow of a doubt," Imogene said, reveling in the freedom wrought by exposing her feelings. She lifted her hand, touching his lips lightly for a moment. They were soft and inviting, and she could think of nothing else other than how it might feel to press his lips to hers. So tantalizingly soft. They lured her closer.

But Ben had not spoken further. She waited for an eon of seconds.

He did not lean away; he did not back away; he did not run from the room screaming. All was well. . . . Better than well, for the look of astonishment had changed. There was something compelling about the way his eyes dropped to her mouth. Something that made her heart beat at an impossible rate, made her want to wrap her arms around him.

Then he smiled.

And the world righted on its axis.

Leaning toward her, with his eyes glued to her mouth, Ben

paused. Imogene could feel his breath on her face; they were within kissing distance . . . but not touching. She ached with anticipation. Why was he waiting?

"I love you, too," he said, finally placing his mouth on hers.

Fire shot through Imogene's veins, and she wrapped her arms around Ben's neck, standing on her toes, pressing every part of her body against his. His kiss deepened, and the world disappeared. All that existed was the ecstasy of their entangled hearts, minds, and bodies. She hummed in pleasure as Ben kissed his way down her neck and then back up to her mouth.

All too soon, he pulled away, but not far. She was still in his arms, his mouth ready to continue its exploration.

"Should I ask your father or Mr. Beeswanger for your hand in marriage?"

Imogene grinned. "Perhaps you should ask me?"

With a quiet chuckle, Ben shifted his gaze to her eyes. "Imogene, my dove, will you—"

"Yes." Imogene smothered his words with her mouth. There would be time for talking later.

Glossary

COVERLET: bedcover, such as a bedspread or blanket

HESSIANS: popular style of boot in the nineteenth century, with military origins

MANSARD ROOF: a four-sided roof that has two slopes, the lower slope being much steeper than the upper one

MORTAR: bonding material for bricks or stones, grout

MULLION: a vertical support that forms a division on a door or window

OAST HOUSE: building designed for drying hops, an ingredient used in brewing beer

ORIEL WINDOW: a form of bay window that projects from a building but does not reach the ground

PILASTER: a rectangular column, often projecting from the wall

SNUFFBOX: pocket-size decorated box used to store snuff (finely ground tobacco)

TABLEAU: an artistic grouping or scene

TO NO AVAIL: with little success

TRUANT: absentee, away without permission or explanation

VISAGE: a person's face

WOO: to try to gain the love of someone, usually with the intent to marry

Acknowledgments

Under the "no man is an island" category, I would like to express my great appreciation to the many people who helped me take a blank page and turn it into a complete novel.

Thank you to my husband, Mike, for listening to my convoluted plot and helping me find its essence, for offering suggestions, and for bringing some reality to the antics of my characters. Thank you to my amazing beta readers, Christine and Deb; I would be lost without your guidance, patience, and ability to see the bigger picture as well as the tiniest of details.

To the entire Swoon Reads team, thank you. As always, you are an amazing group to work with (with which to work?). Special thanks goes to my editor, Emily, whose clear thinking helped me iron out the wrinkles in my manuscript (figuratively) and add humor to a host of new chapter titles. (I really had fun with the stampede of goats.) Your enthusiasm is contagious and invigorating, and it spurs my creativity. Thank you, Rich, for the gorgeous cover—I can't think of enough superlatives to describe your hard work. The parasol is a perfect touch! Thank you again, Swoon Reads authors, for your encouragement and fervor, especially Danika, Kate, and Kelly. I would also like to thank all the readers who have contacted me through Facebook, Twitter, and the Swoon Reads website.

Last, but *never* least, I would like to thank the rest of my family and friends near and far, particularly Dan, Mom, Ginny, Susan, and Paul. I really appreciate your excitement and support!

Check out more books chosen for publication by readers like you.

DID YOU KNOW...

this book was picked
by readers like you?

Join our book-obsessed community
and help us discover awesome new
writing talent.

1 Write it.

Share your original YA manuscript.

2 Read it.

Discover bright new bookish talent.

3 Share it.

Discuss, rate, and share your faves.

4 Love it.

Help us publish the books you love.

Share your own manuscript or dive between the
pages at **swoonreads.com**